RENEGADE GUARDIAN

STAR BANDITS: UPRISING BOOK 5

JENNIFER M. EATON

CHAPTER 1
CAL

**Welcome aboard Renegade Guardian,
Book Five in the six-book epic space opera
Star Bandits: Uprising**

CAL'S PULSE drummed in his ears as the Kever prince he'd been running from for years walked up the *Star Renegade*'s cargo ramp flanked by more enforcers than Cal wanted to meet in a lifetime, let alone see entering his ship. The high prince's Commander, Orion, and his lower-level enforcer buddy, Fallon, stood facing the prince, both with obnoxious smirks Cal would have punched off their faces if he were able.

Dania's former subordinate, Commander Kile DuBane, stood scowling at Cal and his crew like a massive wall of attitude, his pearly white hair drifting about him while nearly pulsing with the star-forsaken primordial energy that turned normal human beings into unstoppable automatons.

Behind him, blocky, tall Michel and even taller, broader, Shivana stood at attention on either side of the *Star*

Renegade's entrance while two more enforcers entered the ship, followed by the Kever prince Geron Bane.

The enforcers' pearly-white uniforms gleamed with each step as their heavy footfalls echoed on the metal grating below them.

Less than an hour ago, the *Star Renegade* had been incapacitated and pulled into the prince's cargo hold. Cal had managed to stay one step ahead of Prince Geron for years, but now they'd been swallowed whole with no chance of escape.

The overhead lights glinted off the prince's green-and-blue skin as he ducked into the doorway, his gaze sliding over the crew with no discernible change of expression.

A chill ran over Cal's skin, and the stale, recycled air seemed to grow thinner as the unwanted guests filled Cal's small world.

The walls of the familiar, normally cozy cargo bay seemed to close in. This was supposed to be his home, one of the few places in the galaxy where he could feel safe. Now, he was anything but safe, and there was nothing he could do about it.

Dania's grip on Cal's hand tightened. She took short, staggered breaths as her attention remained latched on to the Kever like he was the only other person in the room. On Cal's other side, Alexander still held Rachel back after she'd tried to run to Kile. She'd finally stopped fighting and was now also gaping at the prince.

The Kever's odd, nearly reptilian eyes scanned the floor and the walls. His voice hummed and several warbled syllables left his lips before a voice in Cal's head deciphered the words. "So, this is the ship that has been causing so many problems." His gaze carried over the crew again. "I expected it to be far more formidable."

Cal shivered as the last word mixed over the Kever's actual voice. He'd heard reports that the king had the ability to send his translated words right into people's heads. He'd never thought he'd experience the sensation himself. Although judging by the way the long, silver-haired enforcer on Geron's right narrowed his eyes, concentrating on the prince, it was more than possible the enforcer was the one doing the translating.

The Kever blinked his iridescent, multicolored eyes before they latched on to Dania.

He lifted his palm. "There you are."

Dania's feet left the ground. Her hand slipped out of Cal's grip as she floated toward the prince. Her limbs fell to her sides and her legs hung lax, as if she were sleeping, but the horror in her eyes showed she was more than awake and knew exactly who, and what, she was floating toward.

Heat flooded Cal's veins. The Kevers had taken Dania from her family as a child, turned her into a monster, and then wielded her like a weapon. They'd stolen her humanity and her life. He'd be damned before he'd let them get their hands on her again.

Cal reached into his boot and grabbed the small handgun Doc had given him. He wouldn't survive this, but if he got in one lucky shot, maybe he could free Dania forever.

He raised the weapon, and Alexander's hand shot out, grabbing the firearm from his hand. Cal winced as Alexander threw the small handgun to the floor, where it skidded across the tile and slammed into the wall behind Doc and Alanna.

"Hold her!" Alexander flung Rachel into Ethan's arms before he grabbed Cal's shoulder.

Sizzling, burning energy seared through Cal's shirt, scorching his muscles from his shoulder all the way to his toes.

Cal gasped, unable to move. He glared at Alexander, but he should have expected no less. Dania's best friend was still an enforcer, and he couldn't allow anyone to hurt his sponsor.

The air seemed to hum around the prince, like every molecule of hydrogen and oxygen pulsed in reaction to his power. He must have been over a hundred times stronger than any enforcer Cal had ever come up against. Even if Alex hadn't been holding Cal, there would have been nothing any of them could do.

Behind Doc and Alanna, the gun slid across the floor of its own accord…most likely Max, their invisible, fox-like new crew member, stashing it away with other trinkets the animal had taken a liking to. Cal was probably better off that way. The blasted gun most likely would have melted before he'd even been able to shoot it.

Dania hovered inches from the prince's face, tears streaming from her eyes as the Kever's hand combed through her hair, petting her like a dog. Cal wanted to pummel the star-forsaken prince. He wanted to make him pay for every horrible thing he'd ever done to her.

Alexander's grip on him tightened as he leaned close to Cal's ear. "Dying here won't do her any good."

Maybe not, but Cal was dying inside already. Why was that blasted prince just staring at her, studying her like an expensive cut of meat?

The prince cocked his head before a slight smile played on his lips. "Hello, Dania."

She whimpered, tears staining her cheeks.

"Shh," he cooed. "It's all right. I'm here."

It damn well wasn't all right! Cal tried to break free from Alexander's hold, but he barely got his body to twitch. Either Alexander was that strong, or he was wielding the primordial energy that all enforcers held—the power of the very prince standing before them, a power that turned normal human beings into monstrous puppets, ready to do his will.

Alexander's grip tightened. "Stay here and don't move. Don't make me hurt you."

Star-blasted traitor! Cal knew he should have thrown Alexander out an airlock the first chance he'd gotten.

Dania continued to dangle in the air in front of the prince as Alexander approached.

"Ada." Alexander inclined his head. "I've kept her safe, as you requested."

"She does not look safe. She's near death." The Kever's gaze left Dania and fell on Alexander. "You look horrible as well. I will take care of you shortly."

Dammit! Cal had thought Alexander would be an ally. But all this time, all he'd wanted was to get back to that blasted prince and get jacked up on whatever alien drugs the Kevers had been feeding him. Maybe Doc's experiments had been a failure. Maybe there really was no chance of saving either Alexander *or* Dania.

Ty moved closer to Cal. "Boss, you need to calm down. You're turning purple and red."

Calm down? That was easy for him to say. The woman he loved wasn't about to be turned into a totalitarian death machine.

Chris Columbus whispered from somewhere behind Cal. "The time's not right, my friend."

That might have been true, but when *would* the time be

right? Doing nothing sliced into his soul far deeper than any weapon possibly could.

Alexander bowed his head as the prince held out both his hands. Dania started to whimper as she hovered closer to the man who'd stolen everything from her.

"Shh." The Kever smiled at her in an almost fatherly way, but Cal knew nothing was further from the truth.

Alexander looked in Kile's direction, then Orion's. Kile seemed to ignore him, but Orion's nose flared, and Fallon shifted uneasily beside his commander. Were they plotting? Coming up with ways to execute them all? Or worse, having Dania do it for them?

Cal cringed. That had always been her worst nightmare since gaining her freedom. She'd always known the possibility was there—that she could be made to execute her friends. Her *family*. Now that the prince had finally caught up with them, Cal couldn't believe that her nightmare might actually come true.

The Kever wrapped his arms around Dania. Cal didn't know how the feeding process worked, but he knew it had something to do with contact. Just how much contact, he didn't know. Cal's heart wedged in his chest as Dania cried out, her back arching and her head falling back. A deep ache settled in his chest. Not fear for himself or his crew, but for Dania. She'd come so far, tasted freedom, only to be dragged back into the oblivion she'd worked so hard to escape from.

What was she feeling? Pain? Fear? Would she really forget everything she'd learned living on the *Star Renegade*? Was she worried about the crew? About him? The love they'd shared? Losing the friendships she'd gained?

Her hair took flight, the brown strands lightening as a tear dripped down her cheek and splashed to the floor.

They'd come so far, and now the day they'd been running from was here, and he was powerless to do anything but watch.

"Prince Geron." Orion stepped forward with his hands folded behind his back.

The Kever leaned away from Dania, his eyes pulsing with green and blue hues. Dania twisted and moaned as her hair swirled about her.

Orion stopped a few feet from the prince. "As much as I'd prefer your general were returned to her full strength, there are others in more dire need of your care."

The Kever furrowed his brow. "What do you mean?"

Orion lowered his head. "I regret to inform you that I have failed my mission. Zindiria is dead."

"What?"

Dania fell to the floor in a crumpled mess. Cal took a step toward her and gasped, realizing he could move.

Ty grabbed him. "Alex was right about that not-dying thing. Hold on."

Since when had Ty been the voice of wisdom on the crew? He was right, though. For now, she wasn't in direct contact with the prince, and that had to be better than nothing.

Orion's feet left the ground as he flew across the room and slammed against the storage containers where they kept the spare weapons. Fallon raised his hands as if he were about to help his commander, then glanced at Geron and stepped back, closing his eyes and looking down.

"What do you mean my sister is dead?" Geron stormed toward Orion.

Kile stepped into his path. "Ada, you may want to consider the wisdom in killing your brother's commander. The high prince would be most perturbed."

"Since when have I cared about what my brother thought?" He shoved Kile out of the way. "He was tasked with finding Zindiria."

Dania lifted her head, moaning.

Doc sighed from behind Cal and cursed under his breath.

"Is she in pain?" Cal asked.

"You could call it that," Doc whispered. "She's in withdrawal. The damn prince just undid all our hard work."

Dania crawled on the floor toward her sponsor. Cal took a step to help her, but Ty pulled him back, whispering, "Steady, boss."

Rachel rubbed Cal's other shoulder and leaned close to his ear. "I get it, Cally. We all want to help her. But I don't want you dead, either. I kinda like you."

Didn't they all understand that death was the eventual outcome of any scenario concerning enforcers, let alone a full-blooded prince?

Dania whimpered, pulling herself along the floor like her legs didn't work, not trying to get back to Cal, but crawling toward the prince who'd stolen everything from her.

"What is she doing?" Cal asked.

"That's what addicts do," Doc whispered. "They know whatever they're addicted to will kill them, but they can't help wanting more. She's not in control anymore."

Alexander walked around Dania as if she were no more important than a pile of laundry. "Ada, I have to agree with Kile. Killing the commander would be unwise. Orion had a good reason to relay the news to you with such a lack of empathy."

The Kever audibly hissed as he spun toward Alexander. "And what reason would that be?"

Alexander lowered his eyes. "Several of Zindiria's

enforcers survived. As you can imagine, they are all severely depleted and close to death."

The Kever stared at him, seething.

Alexander took a deep breath. "You share the royal bloodline, Ada. You may be the only one who can save them."

"Why would I care about her enforcers?"

Alexander raised his eyes. "Forgive me, Ada. I thought all life was important to you."

The prince growled, and Alexander gulped.

Smart-mouthing a prince, even so innocuously, was a huge risk on Alexander's part. Cal held his breath, waiting for the rebuke, but the prince's eyes continued to bore through the enforcer.

Cal glanced between them, still holding his breath. The statement had to have been true, or Alexander wouldn't have been able to say it. Enforcers couldn't lie. It was part of their programming. Maybe that was the only reason the prince hadn't lashed out.

The silence on the deck was deafening, though. Dania now lay with her cheek pressed against the floor, only a few feet from the being she'd been crawling toward. Even the machinery seemed to cower in the face of the Kever's anger.

Had Geron forced everything around him to stop? Did he have that kind of power?

Cal had no idea of the scope of what the Bane family could do, but the tales he'd heard were the stuff of nightmares. He'd just never thought he'd be living that nightmare himself.

Alex held steady under the scrutiny of a being who could tear him in two. Cal had gotten used to the enforcer's cockiness, but this bravado seemed foolish, even for an enforcer.

Alexander folded his hands and lowered his eyes again.

"Please forgive, Ada. You told me once your appreciation for life was why you made me such an efficient healer. Perhaps I was mistaken."

"You are not." The prince looked down as Dania began crawling toward him, again.

She grabbed his ankle. "Ada, please."

Please? Please what? Addiction or no addiction, she needed to remember what he'd done to her. Why was she moving toward him and not running for her life?

The Kever stepped away from Dania like she was now an inconvenience, rather than his reason for being there.

"My sister is dead." Geron looked at Kile. "You will find who did this and eviscerate them."

Kile bowed. "Yes, Ada." He headed for the cargo ramp.

"Stop." The Kever sighed. "Not right now, and not you personally. You have important knowledge of this smuggling ship. I require your services here."

Kile returned to his side, moving between him and Dania. "Of course, Ada."

Dania whimpered, trying to get around her commander, but Kile held her back with a boot on her shoulder.

A week ago, she would have punched him in the face, even without her powers. But now she lay on the floor, sobbing, crying for the being she feared most in the world. Cal's heart clenched. Was she already beyond saving?

Orion got up from the floor, shaking slightly. Cal was half-horrified, half-pleased to see the guy get a taste of his own penchant for throwing people around.

The high prince's commander frowned at Dania rolling on the floor before inclining his head slightly to the prince. "Forgive, sir. It was not my intention to make light of Zindiria's death or any familial attachment to her. But I have witnessed more enforcers die in the past few weeks than I have in my lifetime, and I think it would be prudent in the current climate to save as many soldiers as we can."

Geron glared at him. "Fine. Where are they?"

Orion pointed at the crew, and a swath of blurry air encircled the smartest member of Cal's team.

Doc cried out as his feet left the ground and he drifted above their heads waving his arms like he was falling before his feet set on the ground in front of the prince. Doc looked over his shoulder at the crew, and Cal tried to give an encouraging smile, but that was all any of them could do at this point.

Orion held his hand out. "This human has been treating the enforcers with his limited knowledge of medicine. He will come with us in case you have questions."

The Kever nodded. "Very well."

Doc gulped, and Alexander stepped beside him, giving him a curt nod. Doc returned the gesture, but that slight show of possible solidarity didn't seem to give him much courage.

Dania reached up to the prince. Again. "Ada, please."

"I'll come back for you." The Kever turned away, following Orion and Kile up the cargo ramp on the far side of the wall.

Dania shrieked, rolling onto her back like she'd been lanced through the heart.

The enforcer who appeared to be translating smirked at Dania before he followed the prince up the ramp. Dania's cry reverberated off the walls as she clawed at the floor and pulled her hair.

Cal's throat closed, and his hands trembled. How was he supposed to stand there with her in so much pain?

Alexander took a step toward Dania like he might reach for her before he stopped and looked at Alanna. Sorrow flashed across his face before he inclined his head to Cal, took Peter's arm, and led their doctor to follow the prince. Hopefully, that was a show of unity and not a goodbye, because if Alexander had truly returned to Geron, there was little Cal could do to save his crew.

THE COLD TILES chilled Dania's hands as she lay on the floor. The room spun, and her stomach churned, pressing and flexing. She pulled herself along the tiles, following Geron as Orion led him away from the small, human ladder to the wider cargo ramp leading to the upper decks.

"Ada!" She reached for Geron and he paused, his green-and-blue eyes finding her. Her heart quickened, and her breathing grew shallow. How had she been able to live so long without him?

Alexander dragged the human doctor up the ramp and stopped behind their sponsor. He whispered something to Geron before their prince nodded, looking away from her and continuing up the stairs.

Her heart clenched. Her blood ran cold in her veins.

"Ada!" Dania reached for him again. How could he leave her? She was lost...powerless...*nothing*. He needed to make her whole again. She could barely breathe. Barely move.

Alexander frowned at her before lowering his eyes and following.

Why had Geron chosen Alexander over her? Was this a punishment for being gone so long?

When her sponsor reached the next level and ducked under the doorway, Dania rolled onto her back and screamed, her cries echoing off the walls. One of the enforcers guarding the exit glanced at her. His face went from fuzzy to clear.

Miguel—one of her lieutenants. Miguel's eyes narrowed before he continued his surveillance of the cargo deck. How could he stand there, seeing her in pain? Why didn't he drag her to Geron so their sponsor could fix this? She screamed again, grabbing her head. Nothing was worth this pain. She would never leave him again.

"Dania!" a dark-haired human man pulled her into his arms.

Was he here to save her? Bring her to her sponsor?

The man shook her. "Dania, it's me, Cal. Snap out of it. Please."

She reached past him toward the ramp. "Ada! Ada, please don't leave me!"

The ice in her blood turned to a fire only Geron could quench. Her sponsor knew this, yet he had left her. Her vision blurred with tears. Had she been replaced? Didn't he want her anymore?

A shrill, oddly-accented woman's voice filled the room. "I've got this!"

Cold water splashed over Dania's face. She choked, her clothes drenched and clinging to her flesh.

"Rachel, have you lost your mind?" a man yelled.

A chill swept over Dania.

Why was she wet?

The space around her spun, faces and walls blending together. The iridescent uniform of one of Dania's enforcers blurred as they grabbed on to an auburn-haired human woman.

Dania's stomach churned and she bent over, vomiting.

Geron. She needed Geron.

"I ain't hurt'n her!" the human woman screamed. "Can't you see she's messed up? I'm trying to snap her out of it!"

Dania closed her eyes and searched beyond the noise and voices chattering and arguing. Finding the pull that always brought her home, Dania crawled across the wet and frigid floor.

"Proceed." The voice of Dania's lieutenant, Shivana, sounded like it was in the distance.

Whatever the problem was, Shivana was more than capable of handling it.

Now, if Dania just followed the draw to her sponsor, she'd find him. He could end this torture and bring Dania back to life.

The shrill voice came back. "Where ya going, Dani? Get her, Chris."

A booted foot pushed her onto her back again. An unpleasant-looking man with a cropped beard and cargo pants leered at her. Lights above whirled before another splash of chilled water covered her. Dania blinked, spluttering.

The auburn-haired woman loomed over her, holding a bucket. "Are ya gonna stay put? 'Cause I can do this all day."

The man who'd held Dania earlier—had they said his name was Cal?—stood beside the odd woman. He held his head, his red, puffy eyes focused on Dania. A woman with pink-tipped hair tapped keys on a screen in the wall, looking over her shoulder at Dania with concern in her eyes before returning to her work.

Another man with bright, copper curls held another bucket, while the unpleasant-looking man in cargo pants hung back, his eyes shooting from the two with the buckets to Shivana and Miguel standing guard at the doorway in their opalescent uniforms.

Why all these people were here seemed vaguely familiar, like a dream or a memory long forgotten.

The man holding his head lowered his hands. "Dania?"

How did he know her name? She sat up and her stomach twitched. She looked over her shoulder. Geron… Geron had been there. She needed to get back to him.

The woman grabbed the bucket from the copper-haired man. "Get that look off your face, Dani, or I swear I'll hit you again."

Dani? Why had the woman shortened Dania's name?

The woman with pink hair clapped her hands and ran toward the back of the ship.

Shivana stepped away from the exit, her muscular bulk easily blocking the woman's path. "Hold!"

The human stepped back. "Oh, I'm just going to the rear area where the other enforcers are. They have some medical supplies that may be able to help your general."

Fallon stepped away from the wall. "She is correct. There are more depleted enforcers in the rear. I will escort her to make sure she does nothing nefarious."

Shivana glanced at Dania and stepped back. "Proceed."

The pink-haired woman gave Fallon a concerned look before they both walked toward the rear of the compartment.

The woman had been startled by the enforcer, but she hadn't lied. She truly was going to get medical supplies. But why were there other enforcers in the rear of the ship? Dania rubbed her temples. She knew, or she *had known*, why there were other enforcers, but the memory seemed shrouded and hard to find.

And why was Fallon here?

Not that any of this mattered at the moment.

Dania looked back to the ramp. If she could just get up to the next level of this ship, Geron could help her. Everything would be clear. She tried to push herself up.

The auburn-haired woman held up the bucket. "Ya need another one?"

Why this woman thought Dania needed to be drenched with cold water was beyond her. These people had lost their minds.

The pink-haired woman returned and showed a vial to Shivana. "This is an electrolyte solution. Our doctor gives it to weak enforcers to help them get a little stronger. It will help Dania." She held up a needle. "This is a syringe. It helps administer medication."

Shivana looked at the vial and then nodded. "Proceed."

Fallon strode in behind them and scowled at Dania before heading up the ramp following Geron.

Dania reached for him. "Fallon, wait! Take me with you!"

The unpleasant man in cargo pants—Chris, they'd said his name was—shoved her back to the floor with his foot. "Get over it, princess."

Dania clenched her teeth. She *was not* a princess. This man would be the first she'd eviscerate.

The woman with the bucket placed it down and crouched beside Dania as the other human woman walked over and handed her the vial she'd shown Shivana, and another one concealed in her hand.

The worried-looking human man squatted on Dania's other side. "Rachel, do you know what you're doing?"

The woman who'd drenched Dania with the bucket—Rachel, apparently—nodded, taking both vials. "Alanna asked Doc what to give Dani." She held up the vial that read *Serum Eight*. "He told me about these *electrolytes*. They work wonders when the enforcers get all messy like this." She poured that bottle into the actual electrolyte vial.

Dania eased away. "Those are not electrolytes."

"Hold!" Shivana approached and grabbed the vial.

"See?" Rachel slid the empty one into her pocket. "There are electrolytes in there. Our girl is just a little delirious."

Dania tried to back up, but the man with the beard knelt and shoved her back to the floor.

The one they'd called 'Alanna' hugged her shoulders. "See? It's the same bottle I showed you already."

"It's not," Dania screamed.

Rachel shook her head. "She's seriously messed up. All she can think about is that prince. I don't think we should be bothering his royal-ness with something we can fix ourselves though, right?"

Shivana handed the vial back to Rachel. "Proceed."

"You fool! They switched the medications."

Chris held Dania as they injected the serum into her arm.

The room spun faster, and she closed her eyes. How could Shivana have been so easily fooled? Hadn't she detected the lie? Then again, none of them had lied. Alanna had shown her a vial of harmless electrolytes, then told her it was the same bottle as before. They'd just been systematic about how to lie without actually lying. Dania breathed slowly as her blood warmed from her arm down to her heart and then spread through her body. Whatever they'd done, it was too late.

Shivana narrowed her eyes at the copper-haired man. "You seem familiar."

Miguel stormed over, leaving his post. "You're the one who shot me. You were executed for your crime."

The redhead held up his hands. "Yeah, I was executed, but your commander got me un-executed."

Miguel balked. "One doesn't *un-execute* someone."

Dania eased up. "He's correct. Kile deemed his life essential to the mission." Her temples started to throb, and she massaged them. Why did she know that one fact, when so many other things seemed hazy?

Both Miguel and Shivana stared at her before Miguel sneered at the human. "We will corroborate this man's story with the commander."

Dania's vision cleared, and the man who'd been holding his head came back into view.

He combed his fingers through her hair. "Are you okay?"

The lines of his jaw seemed so familiar, as if she'd been this close to him before. His smile was genuine and caring, and a new warmth spread through her.

But why?

The woman, Alanna, grabbed Dania's hand and placed her other palm on her forehead. "Stay with me, Dania. You're almost there."

Almost there? Almost where? The woman's hand chilled, or maybe Dania's skin heated. It was an odd, tingling sensation. Dania blinked twice as the rest of the room started to brighten and clear.

Her gaze fell on Miguel, then Shivana. She choked, struggling to get her next breath.

"Ya gotta breathe," Rachel said. "Slow and steady or you're gonna pass out."

Alanna squeezed Dania's hand. "Come on, girl. You got this."

Alanna… Yes, that was Alanna. Dania's friend.

She took another slow breath as Cal smiled at her. Cal… Not a random man with agreeable features.

But these people were smugglers. Criminals.

Dania's stomach clenched, a deep dread settling over her as the small ship began to come into focus around them.

Geron had returned.

The *Star Renegade* had been captured.

They were inside Geron's cargo hold.

Her heart clenched. There would be no escape for any of them.

Dania closed her eyes. Geron had been warm, strong, and ready to take her back. His energy had scorched through her, returning life to her cells.

But no…it hadn't been life. At least not the life she'd wanted to live.

Miguel and Shivana glared at her from their positions beside the exit. Dania understood their disdain. She'd done the worst possible thing an enforcer could do…forsake her sponsor. However, they'd seen Geron begin to feed her. They should have thought she was back under Geron's control—a mindless puppet, just like them.

Dania took a settling breath. Thank the stars he'd only *started* feeding her…given Dania just enough of a taste to gladly give up everything she'd accomplished. If she hadn't had friends who'd refused to give up on her, things would have ended much differently.

But Shivana and Miguel didn't know that. They may not even have been able to comprehend that Dania would want or be able to avoid a feeding. For now, it was best if they both thought she'd turned back into the monster she'd been.

She grabbed Alanna's hand, squeezing twice as hard as she could, trying to evoke a non-verbal communication. The woman furrowed her brow, and Dania squeezed twice again, flicked a glance at Shivana and Miguel, and then tilted her head slightly.

Alanna had to understand what a precarious situation they were in, and the very real threat that she and the crew could be executed for interfering in what Geron had started. It was imperative that all of the enforcers believed Dania had been reverted back to the monster she had been.

Alanna gave a curt nod and released her hand. Hopefully, she understood that Dania was okay and needed them all to play along.

Dania pulled herself up and took a deep breath, lifting her chin as she addressed her subordinates. "Why was I left with these smugglers?"

Miguel sneered, though that had been his default expression for as long as Dania could remember.

His eyes traveled over her, possibly gauging if she had returned to the formidable threat he was accustomed to. "It seems our sponsor had more important issues to deal with."

Dania shivered. That had been true. Geron had been quick to entertain Orion's plea to help the enforcers, although that may have been more of a reaction to concerns about how his brother may perceive the incident, rather than her sponsor actually caring about the dying enforcers.

Geron's first reaction on seeing her, though, had been to feed her. To him, she must have looked close to death. No amount of time and no distraction would stop him from taking her back now. What that meant for her, for her future, or for the crew, she didn't know.

She lowered her eyes. The draw to him…the need for him to continue the feeding, had been more intense than she'd remembered. She wasn't sure what the crew had given her to break the stupor, but one thing was certain: Once Geron had touched her, nothing else in the galaxy had mattered. She'd wanted him. *Needed* him. And the moment she came near him again, she'd *still* need him.

No matter how badly she wanted to stay away, she knew she couldn't. As soon as Geron returned, he would restore her to her former self, and there was nothing she or the crew could do to change that.

DANIA HAD LOOKED into Cal's eyes, and she'd recognized him. He was sure of it. Yet now she stood in front of the two enforcers who'd been with Kile before the attack on Rachel's home planet of Ephershia with her head held high. Dania's voice was sure, strong, and very much like the voice of the woman they'd dragged onto the *Star Renegade* in handcuffs the day they'd first met.

She lifted her chin toward the enforcers. "Why did Geron leave the smugglers alive?"

"The plan was to execute them in time," Shivana said. "His priority was re-attaining you."

Cal shivered. He'd almost succeeded. Maybe he *had* succeeded. He wasn't sure.

Dania seemed to contemplate Shivana's answer. Cal wished he knew if the woman he loved was still inside there, or if she'd been erased…stolen from him by a prince with no concept of humanity or human rights.

She looked up again. "It is unwise to leave the smugglers near the exit unsupervised."

Miguel sneered again. "That is why we are here."

Dania's eyes narrowed. "Weren't you recently incapacitated by a member of this crew? They are resourceful, and I don't want any chance of them making it onto Geron's ship without escort. I will bring them back to the crew area for later sentencing."

Miguel's lips thinned. "It is unwise to have them free in their own ship."

"There is nowhere to go. Their ship's weapons are disabled, and we no doubt have control over propulsion." Dania walked over to the lockers and opened the doors, revealing the weapons stored inside. "It's more dangerous to leave them down where their supplies are."

Had she just sold them out? Was she really gone?

Miguel's eyes widened, then he inclined his head. "Agreed, General."

Dania spun toward the crew. "Up the ramp, all of you. Stay together where I can see you."

Alanna grabbed Cal's arm. "Come on."

They all moved up the ramp single file, Dania in the rear. Once again, Cal felt like he was being walked to the executioner's block, even though they were all probably safe until the prince ordered their deaths. Which, of course, could happen at any time.

They all filed into the lounge, and when the door closed, Dania ran into his arms. The tension ran out of his shoulders as her warmth engulfed him.

She kissed him. "I'm sorry. I'm so sorry."

"You didn't do anything wrong."

She stepped away, swiping back her hair. "But I almost did. I almost went to him."

"But you didn't."

"You don't understand. I wanted to." She rubbed her

chest, then her stomach. "I think I *still* want to."

Alanna stepped forward. "Doc said the new formula might fight off the withdrawal symptoms."

Rachel folded her arms. "Hopefully, it will tamp down the whining and *crawling on the floor* thing, too. Because I ain't gonna lie—that wasn't a good look for you, Dani."

Dania looked down. "I think it's helping, but I still feel like I need to go to him." She met Cal's gaze. "It's so much stronger than I'd remembered. It's like I can't breathe without touching him."

Cal tensed. He didn't like her thinking about touching another man. Ever. But especially not the one who could so easily steal her soul. Geron had only touched her for a few moments, and she'd been reduced to nothing. She hadn't even seemed to remember any of them.

He held her shoulders. "You need to fight him."

"I can't."

He pointed at the door. "Did you see those other enforcers? Half of them were automatons. They did nothing but walk where they were supposed to walk, do what they were supposed to do. Hell, even Kile was about to leave the ship on an order your prince accidentally gave him. Do you want to go back to that existence?"

Dania rubbed her face with her palms before her hands fisted. "No, but I don't know how I can avoid it. You can't understand what it's like to crave something that you know might kill you. I don't want this, but I'm not sure I'm strong enough to stop it."

Then Cal was sure as hell going to figure out a way to *make her* strong enough.

He turned to Rachel. "What did you give her?"

The med tech held up the vial. "Serum Eight. Dr. Pete

made this with part synthetic pathogens and part of good old princey-poo himself."

Dania cocked her head. "How is that possible?"

"He used the elixir that was in the trap Mr. Big, Blue Highness set for you back on Kirato. Once Doc had the real thing, he worked on figuring out how you got addicted in the first place."

Cal placed his arm around Dania's shoulder. "Does that mean she's healed?"

Rachel shook her head. "Not if she still wants to get all touchy-feely with him. But it looks like the dose was enough to bring her back from oblivion."

The door opened, and the small weapon Doc had crafted to bring down an enforcer floated into the room.

Cal reached down and grabbed it. "Thanks, Max." He tucked the small gun back into his boot. He'd probably speed up his execution if any of their new guests found out he had a gun that could take down an enforcer, but he still felt safer knowing he had a bit of power in the situation.

The space above the floor where the gun had been smeared out of focus as Max shook out his fur. His gray head appeared first, followed by his back, legs, and long, fluffy tail. He growled a few syllables that sounded like words before he jumped into Rachel's arms.

She patted his head. "Good job, buddy."

Alanna walked away from the comm pad on the wall. "I let Doc know Dania stopped screaming and is herself again, but that she's still not feeling great. I don't expect him to be able to answer, though."

Of course not. He was showing around a man who wanted them all dead the second he decided they were no longer useful.

Alanna dragged her fingers through her hair. "I'm worried about Alexander. If Dania couldn't resist, how is he going to stand being with the prince that long?"

Dania shivered like she'd shaken off a chill. "He's stronger than me, and he didn't need feeding as badly."

"You didn't need one, either," Cal pointed out.

She lowered her eyes. "No, I suppose I didn't."

But she still wanted one. Just as Doc had predicted.

Stars! The enforcers really were all junkies. "Well, the good news is we didn't all get executed on the spot, and I'd like to keep it that way. We need to come up with some sort of a plan."

Chris pointed his thumb over his shoulder. "Maybe I should get our guests across the hall?"

Cal rubbed his face. With everything going on, he'd forgotten they had more passengers. "Yeah, go ahead."

Alanna sniffed, rubbing her shoulders. "I just can't stop thinking about it. That prince has the power to take away the people we care about. He didn't even look like he broke a sweat." She rubbed her face and spoke under her breath, "Hang in there, Alex."

Curious that she was more worried about Alexander than she was about herself. Then again, Cal had pulled a gun on the prince, knowing full well he'd be dead the second it went off. That hadn't mattered, though; he'd been willing to take the risk for the chance of saving Dania.

The door opened, and Chris returned, followed by the other seven pirates who'd been hiding in storage.

Victor entered last and folded his arms over his considerable girth. "Glad to see you're all still alive." He looked around. "Did you have to sacrifice the doctor?"

"No. They wanted him to show the prince what he's doing in the infirmary to treat the enforcers."

Victor frowned. "Wait a minute...*treat* enforcers? You're helping the enemy? I mean, I knew you had a few with you, but your doctor treating them is a whole new level of stupidity."

Cal glared at him. "If you're not happy here, feel free to walk off the cargo deck. I'm sure the enforcers standing outside would love to walk you into their brig."

"Outside? What?"

Ethan leaned against the far wall. "We're stuck inside one of the massive Kever cruisers."

Victor's nose flared. "We'd never make it to their brig. We'd be dead the moment our boots hit the deck."

"Then I suggest you show a little respect to the people who saved your lives." Cal turned to the others. "Okay, we're quite literally stuck in the belly of the beast." His gaze lanced each of them. "Suggestions?"

Their silence sliced through him like a knife. The truth was, they needed the smartest member of their crew, and at the moment, he was showing the enemy around their med bay.

CHAPTER 4
ALEXANDER

ALEXANDER FOCUSED on Geron's back as he pulled the doctor through the hall toward the med bay. The very air around them pulsed with Geron's primordial power. The swirling energy seemed to reach out and caress Alexander's cheeks, promising insurmountable strength and the sweet ease of oblivion.

He centered his thoughts on Doc, using the man as an anchor to reality—to Alanna. This crew had shown him there was far more in the galaxy worth experiencing than being an enforcer. He'd hoped the small trickles of pathogens Alanna had accidentally been feeding him would be enough to quell his need for Geron. Each moment he spent in his sponsor's presence, though, made him realize it wasn't.

Seeing Dania on the floor, writhing...

He shuddered. She'd seemed fine when their sponsor had first entered the ship. Upset and frightened, but she'd still had her wits about her, as had he. It wasn't until Geron had started to feed her when the *need* had taken over again.

He took a deep breath and released it slowly. His own skin had started to tingle with anticipation when Geron had sent her strength and her hair had started to lift, reigniting the latent primordial energy inside her. The memory of the power coursing through him, the nearly limitless possibilities and strength, made his body yearn to walk faster, to stand beside his sponsor to gain any energy he could. Alexander took another deep breath and concentrated on the sound of Doc's breathing. Being with Alanna had sustained him, but it was nothing like what Geron would do for him.

He closed his eyes and tried to shake away the certainty in that thought. He'd decided not to go back, but now that Geron was here, he wasn't sure freedom had ever been a possibility. The draw to his sponsor was still far too strong, and he knew, even now, he'd do anything Geron asked without question. It would take all his strength not to crawl on the floor and beg as Dania had.

The doctor started to stumble the closer they got to the med bay, and Alexander tightened his grip so the man didn't fall.

Peter looked up at him. "Please tell me the last several months haven't been a lie. Please tell me you're still with us."

Alexander took another settling breath. The humans seemed to think that speaking softly protected them. If anything, it piqued enforcer senses, allowing them to hear more.

He squeezed the doctor's arm. "You will speak when spoken to."

Peter paled, his jaw falling open. Alexander tried to push a calming sensation, a mental healing through their contact, but the man still lowered his eyes. Alexander needed to find another way to get through to him without placing either one of them in danger.

Only a day ago, this crew had been vibrant and alive. Sometimes annoyingly so. The lack of courage in Peter's eyes made Alexander want to shake the doctor to make him remember who he was. Who they *all* were.

Peter's head hung low. Alexander dug his fingers into the doctor's arm until the man raised his eyes.

"You will keep up." Alexander smiled, loosening his grip.

The doctor's eyes widened, and Alexander flicked his chin to the three enforcers walking ahead with Geron, then Alexander quickly pointed to his ear.

Color returned to the doctor's face. He smiled, then masked it, turning forward and taking deep, steady breaths. Hopefully, if Alexander could save the doctor, he'd be able to get news to Alanna that Alexander was still okay. Of course, that would only be true until Geron decided it was time for Alexander to be fed.

When they reached the infirmary, Alexander shoved Peter ahead to open the door. The doctor complied without hesitation, and his gaze met Alexander's as Geron ducked to keep from hitting his head on the archway. Alexander wished he could give the man some sort of consolation, but he couldn't lie, and he had no idea what they would face once inside.

Alexander looked over his shoulder and down the hall toward the stairway leading to the cargo bay. Geron hadn't ordered the crew's execution, so they'd be safe for now. But he dearly hoped none of them openly broke a law over the next few hours, because Miguel and Shivana would be more than ready to pass judgment if they deemed it warranted.

Geron stopped just past the entrance, barring Alexander and the doctor entry as he seemed to take in lines of beds filled with enforcers. "There are so many."

He stepped inside, and Alexander and Peter followed.

Hendry moved from a patient's bed and inclined his head to Geron. "Sir, I'm so incredibly happy to see you."

Geron's gaze carried over him. "You belonged to my sister."

"I did."

"Yet you are standing."

Hendry closed his eyes. "It's been hard, sir. But since I was one of the few able to walk, I focused what energy I had to assist. The doctor has been quite agreeable in saving as many as possible."

Geron turned to Peter. "Why would you do this? Their deaths gave you a tactical advantage."

Peter shrugged. "All life is important. It doesn't matter if I disagree with their politics or that they don't particularly like me."

Geron frowned. "You're a smuggler. Any one of these enforcers would execute you in a moment."

The doctor managed to keep his expression placid. Alexander supposed the man had been threatened so many times in the past few months that the idea of being executed had become commonplace. "Just because I want to live doesn't mean that I should let them die if there's something I could do to save them."

Geron continued to stare at the man. "Interesting."

Fallon stormed into the med bay and shoved past the doctor, taking his place at Orion's side, just behind Geron. Alexander would have preferred fewer fully-charged enforcers in the room, but he supposed that four was really no worse than three.

"Sir." Hendry motioned to the enforcer who'd arrived at the med bay the same day he had. They'd both been close to death after Orion had drained all their energy searching for the princess. "If you are thinking of taking any of Zindiria's enforcers as your own, Bleven would make an agreeable addition to your team. He is an accomplished tactician."

It wasn't long ago that Hendry had asked Cal to drop himself and Bleven off at a waystation in an attempt to avoid being sent back to certain death if forced to serve Orion again. And now he was offering up his friend to Geron? Although, Hendry's goal had never been to escape the Banes...only to hide from Orion until his princess came for them. Now, with Zindiria gone, that was impossible.

Geron looked at Alexander. "Do I need to recode these enforcers to keep them alive?"

An interesting question. "No, but if you do recode them to you, the first feeding will be harder, but every feeding after that would be as easy as maintaining your own enforcers." Recoding an enforcer to a new sponsor wasn't common because Banes rarely died. However, Alexander had read accounts in the histories where enforcers had been bequeathed to kin like physical assets and then recoded after their original sponsor had died or no longer had use for them.

Alexander's stomach turned. At the time, he'd found the idea fascinating and necessary. Now, though, recoding felt far too similar to the larcenous dealings of the slave traders that they'd been trying to abolish from the galaxy. If the enforcers hadn't been so dependent on their sponsors, they could have retired and lived out their lives in peace, but their choices were few: death from pathogen depletion or being assigned a new sponsor. They'd have no choice in whom they'd be assigned to. They'd be forced to serve whoever had absorbed them. Of course, once they'd been recoded, their choice wouldn't matter. For an enforcer, their sponsor was everything.

Orion looked down at Bleven. "There are others in more need of assistance. This one has been stable for some time. The doctor has been treating him."

"But he's never woken up," Alexander pointed out. "He may be the strongest, and the easiest candidate to start with." And, if Geron got involved in absorbing new enforcers, that might buy him and Dania more time.

The doctor inched to the comm station and typed a few keys, no doubt checking on the rest of the crew in the cargo bay. Hopefully, he had some ideas on how to help Dania—and maybe even Alexander, for the eventuality of his own impending feeding.

"Very well." Geron raised his palm in the direction of the incapacitated enforcer.

Alexander took a step back as the power in the room swirled and licked at his skin. He closed his eyes, breathing deeply. The primordial energy warmed him from the inside, and his cells screamed, reaching for Geron.

Alexander took a steadying breath as Bleven's unconscious body rose, the sheets slipping off him as he drifted to Geron. The prince's arms wrapped around him and the primordial energy in the air hummed. Alexander took another deep breath, relishing in the essence, before Bleven's eyes widened and he screamed, pushing against Geron's chest like he was fighting for his life. A flash of white light engulfed him. His arms fell lax at his sides and his head lolled against Geron's chest. Bleven sobbed as his hair lifted a few strands at a time, and the sickly, pink tinge in his cheeks whisked back to a perfect enforcer porcelain.

Geron released his grip and Bleven slipped to the floor on

his knees. Bleven's breaths were shallow. His eyes didn't blink.

Hendry shifted his weight uneasily, possibly wondering if he was still happy Geron was here. He glanced at Alexander, then back to his friend on the floor. A tingle of fear hung in the air as Hendry took a tentative step back. He'd seemed to enjoy having his own thoughts, even though he'd made it clear he'd wanted to return to Zindiria. Possibly seeing the blank expression on Bleven's face made him remember the sense of oblivion. The feeling of…*nothing*.

Peter crouched beside Bleven and ran a scanner over him. "Physically, he seems fine, but all brain activity seems erratic and barely functioning."

Geron looked at Alexander. "I am in need of your opinion, as a doctor and as an enforcer."

Alexander bowed his head. "Of course, Ada."

"Would it be best to erase his memory and start him fresh and unencumbered, or leave his faculties intact?"

Alexander flinched. He had no memory of his past life. His childhood before waking on Keveron was non-existent. Was this the reason?

Hendry stepped forward. "If I may, sir… As I said, his expertise may be valuable. If you choose to take his memories, is there a way to keep his skills intact?"

Geron considered the shell of a man at his feet. "Not that I'm aware of."

Hendry frowned. He and Bleven had obviously been friends. He was probably worried about more than his skills being erased.

Alexander crouched beside Bleven. The man was breathing but motionless—most likely awaiting orders.

A newly hatched enforcer.

So full of potential.

So full of horror.

Alexander gulped. "Is his mind still intact, Ada?"

"Yes."

"Then I suggest leaving him that way. He will probably mourn Zindiria for a moment, but once he senses his draw to you, his feelings for her will be inconsequential. He will be the soldier he was, but in your fold."

Geron nodded. "Very well." He held up his palm. "Stand."

Bleven complied, keeping his head low. "Your orders, sir."

Geron cradled the enforcer's face in his palms and kissed the man's forehead. Primordial energy pulsed in the air about them.

"You're mine now," Geron told him. "You may call me 'Ada.' 'Sir' is unnecessary."

Peter ran another scanner over Bleven. "Brain function is back to normal. Cellular decay has improved, and his hair is floating, which is probably good. That's fascinating." He looked at Geron. "I'd love it if I could put some sensors on the next person you—um—*feed* or whatever you call it. I'm fascinated by the whole process. I mean, I was barely keeping him alive. But he's healthy now."

Geron walked to the next bed. "Fine."

Peter pulled down the sheets from another patient and began placing silver adhesive circles on her chest.

Orion stormed to Geron's side. "I must object. This human is resourceful. He may do something that could hurt you."

Kile pulled him back. "Their doctor is a charlatan, but he's not lying. He's genuinely interested. And despite his lack of training, he's proven to be competent. Any information he may glean could be useful in the future."

"I agree," Alexander said.

Geron nodded, leaned close to Bleven, and whispered in his ear. Oddly enough, Alexander couldn't hear.

Kile appeared at Alexander's side. "It's good that you are still intact. I had concerns about leaving you with the humans. They can be…" He looked down. "Persuasive."

An interesting choice of words, but accurate. "True, but not persuasive enough to detach me from my sponsor."

Which was, unfortunately, the truth. Alexander wasn't sure he'd ever be free, despite sharing Alanna's strength.

Kile nodded as Geron began feeding the next enforcer. "When this is done, we'll bring Dania to him. We'll have our general back."

Alexander nodded, but more as an affirmation that feeding Dania would bring her back to the fold than that this was something he *wanted* to do. But after seeing her reaction to a small burst of primordial energy, he knew she'd throw herself at Geron the next chance she got, begging to be fed. The Dania he'd known over the past few months may have already been gone.

The next enforcer woke, screaming in Geron's thrall. What would it be like, to forcibly be taken by a new sponsor? Alexander had been taken by Alanna slowly, over time, with no intention on her part. Would Geron realize this when he tried to feed Alexander? Would Alexander fight him as well? And if he did, would Geron start searching for the person who'd tried to steal a piece of his property?

Alexander's stomach soured. When Dania had started calling for Geron and crawling on the floor to get to him, Alanna's eyes had widened. She'd looked from Dania to Alexander, agape. Was she in the cargo deck now, holding on to Dania, begging her not to go back to Geron? Was she worried that Alexander may already be gone?

He closed his eyes and took another steadying breath. He'd tried not to get attached to her, but he'd enjoyed their time together far too much. Maybe if he'd kept away, refused to do repairs with her, he would never have started absorbing her extra strength. Still, he couldn't regret any of it, other than the pain she would eventually feel when Geron erased her from Alexander's mind.

Geron moved to the next patient.

Peter backed away and started typing into a data pad and then moved to his desk. He scanned the patients in the med bay, then returned his attention to his screen. All normal actions for a doctor; however his slight elevation in temperature suggested deception. His brow furrowed and his lips thinned.

Alexander moved beside him and pretended to look into another screen. He typed on a data pad. *'What's wrong?'* Hopefully, the doctor remembered his earlier caution about not speaking.

Peter typed, *'Need 2 talk 2 Cal. And need 2 check on Dania.'*

Alexander nodded. He was interested in what the doctor needed to speak to the captain about, but he knew Dania needed help, although he doubted Peter could do anything for her now that she'd tasted real primordial energy rather than the synthetic pathogens they'd used to help her survive.

The doctor frowned. *'Are you okay?'*

Alexander glanced at his sponsor as the next enforcer hit the floor. Should he admit to being afraid? That he didn't want to spend his last moments of freedom alone?

Peter gripped his shoulder and nodded, before turning away and walking back to the prince. "Your Highness?"

Geron's eyes were a paler green than before, and the blue hues were nearly gone. "You may address me as Prince Geron, or simply Geron. I'm barely in line for the throne."

Orion glared. "These humans should respect you, sir."

Peter held up his hands. "Oh, I respect him, all right." He pointed to the beds. "I mean, all of this is amazing, and I can't wait to get more data." He looked over his shoulder at Alexander. "And I wanted to remind you that there are more enforcers downstairs, all in similar shape. These are just the worst."

Geron grimaced. "More?"

Doc nodded. "Yeah, and in my professional opinion, you are looking a little weaker than you did when you first came in, so I suggest you pace yourself."

Orion growled. "No Bane is *weak*."

Peter held up his hands again. "I'm not saying he's weak. I'm just suggesting caution." He turned back to Geron. "I'd only work on the worst of them now, and not help any more of them before you get a good night's sleep."

Alexander had to hold back a grin. The doctor had just bought him some time.

Peter grabbed several vials and a syringe, placing them in a small bag.

"What are those for?" Orion asked.

Peter held up a bottle. "It's an emergency pack for Dania. She didn't look so good. No reason for her to suffer until our illustrious prince can do his thing."

Orion narrowed his eyes. "Deception. You have synthetic methods of treatment."

Doc shrugged, turning to Geron. "All medicine is synthetic, if you think of it. I mean, nothing I have works as good as what you're doing. The truth is, all the enforcers in these beds are in actual danger of dying. All I've been able to do is keep them comfortable." He held up a vial and shook it. "It's the same thing I'm doing for Dania."

Kile grabbed the vial and looked it over before handing it back to Peter. "The doctor's medicines are an abomination; however, I have seen their efficacy. Now that Geron is here, they are of no concern."

Backing toward the door, Peter pointed his thumb over his shoulder. "Do I have your permission to go check on her, Your Highness?"

Ada rubbed his eyes. "It's Geron, and yes, I don't want her to suffer."

The doctor glanced at Alexander before he slipped from the room. The man had indeed bought Alexander some time. However, deep down, Alexander knew that time would quickly run out.

CAL SAT at the end of the large table in the lounge, rubbing the bridge of his nose as the pirates continued to argue. How any of them could possibly think they would have been better off staying on the tank ship that had exploded was beyond him.

Rachel, Ty, and Ethan leaned against the windows with smug smiles on their faces. What the joke was, Cal had no idea. Dania sat at the table beside Alanna, drinking a mug of electrolyte water. Cal rubbed his temples, hoping to ward off the oncoming headache before it exploded like the tanker had. He had to bring these people together to act as a cohesive unit, or they were all going to die.

The door opened and Doc burst into the room. He skidded to a stop, his gaze landing on the pirates, and then on Dania. He let out a breath in a *whoosh*. "I see the little gift I sent worked?"

Dania nodded, rubbing her chest. "Yes, but it still hurts."

"That's to be expected. I nearly had you weaned off natural pathogens, and he just went and re-infected you.

Quite rude, if you ask me." He puffed out a breath. "And now the detox process starts all over again."

But unfortunately, the cause of her addiction was now onboard the ship. Cal didn't know a lot about addiction, but one thing he had heard was that the patient should avoid whatever they were addicted to. That was a little hard when it was a walking, talking person who thought he owned her.

Alanna inched closer. "What's going on in the med bay?"

Doc started rooting around in his bag. "Well, our boy Bleven is finally awake, completely healed, and he's playing for team Geron now."

"That fast?" Cal asked.

Doc nodded. "It was a little scary, if I'm being honest. His Highness had already fed two and was moving on to the third when I left."

Dania shivered. "He's recoding all of them?"

Doc nodded. "Looks like it."

"What does 'recoding' mean?" Ethan asked.

"It means he owns them now." Dania rubbed her shoulders. "Just like he owns me and Alexander."

Cal placed his arm around her. "He doesn't own you anymore." But from the way she lowered her eyes, she apparently didn't agree.

"About that." Doc pulled a syringe out of his bag. "Let's try to avoid any more real pathogen contact as long as possible." He tapped on the syringe, holding it up to the light before walking to Dania. "Here's some more synthetics. I don't want to give you any more magic serum because frankly, I'm not sure what it will do to you."

Dania nodded and winced as he gave her an injection.

Cal rubbed her back. "No more IVs?"

Doc placed the needle and empty vial in the recycler. "I'd

rather do an IV, but right now, we're going to have to improvise. I have different grades of solution hidden all over the ship. I had a slew of stuff in the cargo bay in case I needed it for the enforcers. I had no idea I'd need it to save Dania." He felt her forehead. "How do you feel?"

"Shaky. Like I need something."

Doc patted her hand. "Hang in there."

Alanna moved beside him. "Is Alexander okay?"

"Yes. He's still Team *Star Renegade*, but right now, he's doing a good job of making the enforcers think he's on their side."

Victor folded his arms. "Because he is. He's an enforcer."

"You don't know him like we do," Alanna said.

"Then he's pegged you for a fool. Don't let his pretty face blind you to reality. He's a monster like the rest of them."

Tingles of purple energy sparkled around Alanna's hand as she bore down on him. "You have no idea."

Victor sneered, walking toward her with the slow, deliberate gait of a predator. "I've got tons of ideas. I've seen those enforcers do things that would curl your toes, sweet thing."

Rachel pushed away from the wall and shoved the pirate away from Alanna. "Back off, you jerk. And if you call her a *sweet thing* again, I'm going to *sweet thing* you right out an airlock!"

Cal pulled Rachel back. "We don't have time for bickering, people. If what you have to say isn't constructive, I don't want to hear it." He pointed at Victor. "Remember, you're guests. We're not in the greatest position at the moment, but this is still my ship."

Victor pointed back at Cal. "Let me tell *you* something…"

Chris came up from behind, caught the pirate's neck in

his elbow, and drew him to the other side of the room. "You'll do nothing until you calm down."

Doc waved Cal to the food storage cubbies. Ethan, Rachel, and Ty followed while Alanna and Dania huddled together in a whispered conversation.

Across the room, Freddy and George exchanged a few words under their breath before Freddy took a swing at his compatriot.

Chris grabbed the pirate's fist mid-swing. "Calm the hell down."

Chris flicked a glance at Cal from across the room and stayed with the pirates. With any luck, he'd be able to keep them from wrecking the place.

Cal appreciated the help. Chris had screwed the pirates back on the tank when Cal and his team had been trying to save the princess, but pirates were strange that way. Chris was still one of their own, and they'd trust him over a smuggler no matter what.

Dania looked over her shoulder as Chris held Freddy and George apart, and then she gave Alanna a hug. Alexander being basically alone with the prince had to be hard on them both.

Dania leaned on Alanna's shoulder and kept her eyes down as they walked over to the cubbies to join the rest of the crew. Cal wanted to be the one to comfort Dania, but Alanna probably needed the reassurance that if Dania was still with them after being completely lost an hour ago, then maybe Alexander had a chance, too.

Cal understood the need for hope. When Geron had grabbed Dania, Cal had thought he'd lost everything. It had been like being ripped apart from the inside. He wouldn't have been all too happy if it had been Dania alone with the prince.

Doc leaned against the glass protein bar case. "I tapped into long-distance feeds while I was in the med bay."

"Right in front of the prince?" Ty laughed. "Your balls are even bigger than mine, my friend."

"What's going on?" Cal asked.

"The war isn't going well. The princess isn't the only Bane to fall. The military princes and princesses and all the royal forces from Keveron are scattered, fighting off an enormous influx of Carteks."

"Why now?" Ethan said.

"It's been brewing for years," Ty said. "And we've been in the thick of it. It's been getting worse and worse."

That was certainly an understatement. "How far into Earth's space have they gotten?"

Doc shrugged. "It doesn't appear they've gotten much closer to Earth, but if the fighting stays as intense and the Banes keep suffering losses, that might not be the case for long."

Cal rubbed his face. "We need to dump this prince and get back to the outer rims. I don't want any of you near a war. You've given up far too much already."

"And how, exactly, do you recommend dumping the prince?" Rachel asked. "Remember, we're in his cargo hold."

Doc sighed. "Not to mention, His Royal Highness is the only chance most of those enforcers have. It was a little unnerving watching the feeding, but also fascinating."

Cal's skin heated. The prince may be giving the enforcers a second chance at life, but he'd be doing the opposite for Cal's newest crew members. "Keep that prince busy and keep him away from Dania and Alexander."

Doc held up his hands. "That's a little hard to do when Alex is in the med bay, but I made a point of telling His Royal Highness-ness he'd need to rest once he was done doing his *creepy thing* to my patients."

Cal didn't even want to think about what their mad scientist doctor would consider creepy. He turned to Alanna. "Is there any possible way you can jump us out of here?"

She shook her head. "No way. I can't jump the ship through metal. It's the same thing as how I have to be careful not to hit anything when we jump out in space. That's how the Carteks caught us in a net the last time."

"But you jumped us out of that," Ty said.

Alanna shrugged. "We weren't inside a big, closed metal box. I jumped out of the net like jumping over a wall."

Cal deflated. Alanna had always been their very own *deus ex machina*. She'd been able to jump them out of almost anything. Maybe they'd grown too reliant on her.

Alanna's eyes lit up. "I just had a crazy idea. Maybe with Alexander's knowledge of ships, he may know if this cruiser we're stuck inside has any weaknesses, and if we can get him away from Geron, maybe he could help Ethan and me do some modifications that will help us get back helm and propulsion control, and maybe even blast out of here because seriously, we've just scratched the surface of what our alien tech can do."

Rachel narrowed her eyes at Alanna. "How did you just say all of that in one breath?"

Ty huffed a laugh.

Rachel glanced at him. "No, I'm serious! That's some amazing lung capacity."

"Focus, people." Cal rubbed his chin. Lung power aside, it was interesting how Alanna had stressed the idea of getting *Alex* away from the prince, when *Hendry* was the one with intimate knowledge of the alien tech. But Cal supposed if it were Dania down there in that med bay, he'd also be grasping at straws, looking for excuses to get her out.

Alanna's idea had merit, though, if it were even possible. "Wouldn't modifying the ship for the sole purpose of escaping arrest be considered illegal?" He turned to Dania. "Would Alex be physically able to help?"

She took in a deep breath and released it slowly. "He looked just as frightened to see Geron as I was. As long as we aren't talking about hurting Geron, and he hasn't been fed, I think he'd help." She grasped Alanna's hand and squeezed. "He's learned there are things here worth fighting for. We'd just have to word things carefully so he could rightfully believe what he was doing wasn't illegal."

Cal had to fight from shaking his head. The enforcer work-arounds to thwart their own programming dumb-founded him the more he learned about them.

The truth was, though, that they were trapped in what appeared to be a no-win situation. The Banes had proven themselves to be arrogant enough to believe that the *Star Renegade* being trapped in their hold gave them the upper hand. Which it did, of course…until a few resourceful smug-glers figured out how to stir things up a bit.

Alanna and Alex had worked wonders before, and with the *Star Renegade*'s systems down, and no need for a pilot, Ty could help, too.

Cal rubbed his palms against his thighs. "It's not a bad idea. Let's all put our heads together and do everything we can. And as soon as we're out of this monstrosity and in clear space, Alanna will be able to jump us away."

"What can I do?" Rachel asked. "I'm not much help if the med bay's not full of patients anymore."

The air about her ankles wavered, and the solid floor blurred into a brownish-tan mass of fluffy fur. Max pushed up on his hindlegs and waved his arms, making a chittering noise.

Rachel reached down and stroked his fur. "He wants to help, too." The animal cuddled his face in her palm, then faded from view again. No matter how many times Cal saw the little guy fade in and out, he still had trouble fathoming his ability to disappear.

Ethan shifted his weight. "Well, the big problem no one is mentioning is Kile. He knows way too much about the ship. Maybe Rachel could distract him?"

"That will be dangerous," Dania said. "He's fed, and it looks like any emotional attachments he may have had are gone."

Rachel stood from petting Max. "I can try. I mean, the Big Guy couldn't have completely forgotten about me, could he?"

Cal lowered his eyes. It had been less than a day since Kile had instructed Cal to herd the crew—including Rachel—into the cargo bay. He had to have known that the chances were they'd all be executed.

Rachel pointed at Cal. "I see that look on your face, Cally, and I don't care. He loved me once. He'll love me again."

Doc held up his hands. "I get you, girlfriend, and I have every confidence in your persuasiveness. Hell, you got him into bed the first time, but this time, he's got a fresh charge of pathogens running through his system. He might not be as easy a target."

Rachel shook her head. "I refuse to believe he doesn't

remember anything about me. If he's still inside there, I'll find him."

"What about the pirates?" Alanna asked. "They look like they're going to be a problem."

On the other side of the room, Chris was now holding Iggy and Urvin apart. There was a lot of pent-up anger over there, mostly aimed at the enforcers. Maybe they could use that to their advantage. Cal just wasn't sure how, yet.

Cal puffed out a breath. "We'll keep them in storage as long as we can. The longer the enforcers don't know about them, the better for everyone."

"But they do know about them," Doc pointed out. "Orion and Fallon must have told the prince that a bunch of pirates escaped the tank with us."

"It is kinda weird," Ethan said. "It's like they don't care that they're here."

Cal rubbed his chin. "I doubt they don't care. They're just not a priority. We can't get out of this hangar either way. The Kevers probably couldn't care less that they have a few extra human prisoners confined to this ship."

A chair moved, and a soft growl filled the air.

Cal looked at the floor, and, of course, saw nothing. Not even their fox-like friend's bushy tail. "It's all good, Max. I still don't think anyone but us knows you're here." He turned back to his crew, scanning the concerned faces of his friends. His family. "I don't think any of us are a priority because they probably figure we're all too terrified to leave."

"Speak for yourself," Ethan said. "I'd sure love to get a look at this big baby's engine room. The propulsion systems must be monstrous."

"Our own systems are our one and only focus. We need

engines. We need weapons. And then we need a way out of here."

Ty rubbed the back of his neck. "So, I guess we have a half-cocked plan, as usual. We do our best to get our engines back online... We hope Alex can find a weakness in one of the most powerful military cruisers in the galaxy... And while we're figuring out how to act on that weakness, Rachel will use her feminine wiles on the Big Guy to keep the rest of the enforcers from noticing." He snorted a laugh. "What could possibly go wrong?"

"There's a lot of unsaid maybes in that plan," Doc pointed out.

Cal nodded. "There always are, but it *is* a plan. They made a mistake giving us time to regroup. We need to take advantage of it."

The comm beside them went off.

Ethan's brow furrowed. "It's the med bay."

The med bay? Rachel and Doc were already with them in the lounge.

Cal tapped the panel. "Yeah?"

"Cal," Alexander's voice called. "Prince Geron wants to speak with you."

An icy, detached chill settled over Cal. "Only me?"

"Yes. He asked for the one who killed Filluck Palogivan."

Dania gasped, covering her mouth.

A shudder eddied up through Cal's soul as he closed his eyes and took a deep breath in, then out. This was probably the end of the journey for him, but maybe, if he was smart enough, he could buy his people some time. "Tell him I'll be there in a few minutes."

Dania shook her head. "Cal, no."

He held her cheeks and kissed her. "I have to. Maybe if I can get him to listen…"

"He won't listen, Cally." Rachel wrapped her arms around her midriff. "Did you see how he threw Orion around? He don't have to listen to no one."

"Maybe not, but if I can get him to listen to me, even for a minute, maybe I can lobby for all your lives."

"This is…" Ty shook his head. "This is not a good idea."

"Probably not, but it's not like I can say *no*."

Dania held her throat, like it hurt, before taking a deep breath. "If you're going, I'm going with you."

Heat flashed over Cal's skin. "Like hell you are."

She lowered her hands. "You're hoping to lobby for the crew. Well, I'm going to lobby for *you*."

Doc placed his hand on her shoulder. "Sweetie, I don't think you should go anywhere near that prince if you can help it."

"I don't care. I'm not letting Cal face Geron alone."

CHAPTER 6
DANIA

DANIA TOOK STEADYING breaths as she, Cal, and Peter made their way down the hallway to the med bay. The air in the lounge had seemed lighter and easier to breathe, but each step she took, her awareness of her sponsor's presence grew. Part of her wanted to run back to her room, jump into her bed, and pull the blankets over her head, although a thick layer of cloth would provide little protection when Geron came for her.

Cal stopped at the hub in the middle of the ship and turned her toward him. "Are you sure you want to come? I don't want to tell you what to do, but Doc's right. After what happened downstairs, I don't want you anywhere near that prince."

She understood. Her memory was a partial fog, but the pain, the *need* she'd felt when her sponsor had dropped her to the floor were ingrained in her soul. She didn't want to be near Geron, either, but she might be the only one able to stand between Cal and a swift execution. She needed to remind Geron of his promise to review the evidence that exonerated Cal.

Dania wove her fingers through Cal's and squeezed, mostly for her own comfort, although she hoped she could offer the same for him. She still might not be able to save him, but it was a small glimmer of hope in an otherwise hopeless situation.

His eyes pleaded with her, despite his silence. He obviously wanted her to stay behind, but Peter had bolstered her with a synthetic treatment. Right now, she had the best chance of facing her sponsor without begging him to bring her back to full strength.

To Geron, hopefully, she'd look somewhat better than she had earlier. There was a chance he wouldn't be as worried and he may not seek her out as quickly, giving the team more time to free the ship.

At least, that was what she was *telling herself*. Hopefully, she wouldn't fall at his feet the second she saw him, begging to be fed—again.

Peter ran a scanner over her forehead. "You do look pretty good, sweetie, but I'm not going to lie—I have no idea what's going to happen when you walk into that room."

Dania didn't, either, but she *needed* to know. If she had no chance of freedom, then even Doc's treatments wouldn't be enough to help her, no matter what she wanted. In many ways, Geron calling for her was inevitable. All she could do now was hedge as much time as possible to help the crew. She hoped...in fact, she was *relying* on Doc's observation that Geron was already tiring. If he had continued feeding the weakened enforcers, he'd be far too exhausted to feed her as well.

She bit her bottom lip. If Alexander were there, he'd tell her this was foolish, that she was letting pride get in her way, and that she would be jeopardizing everyone by walking into that room. But she still needed to go. Not only to protect Cal, but to prove that she could face her sponsor again, no matter the outcome. If she felt the urge to feed, even remotely, she'd back out of the room.

She gulped, hoping she'd be able to resist.

Cal placed his hands on either side of her face and kissed her again. "Do you really think you're up to this?"

"I said I'd stand at your side, and I will." She grabbed his hands and lowered them. "Geron is probably angry with me, but hopefully, my opinion will still hold weight."

The words sounded better in her mind than when she'd verbalized them. She dearly wanted to think of Geron as a reasonable, thoughtful being. But she knew the truth was far different. For some time, the crew had been trying to convince both her and Alexander that they were only pieces of property to Geron. She'd wanted to deny it with all her heart, but she knew it was true. She didn't doubt that Geron loved and cared for her, but no differently than his favorite shoes or a cherished toy. She was something that was to be at his side, at his disposal, ready to do anything he needed or wanted at a moment's notice.

At one time, she'd yearned to please him almost as much as she'd yearned for the primordial energy he offered her. Her own life had meant nothing to her.

Then this crew had shown her what life could be for a person who didn't live under the absolute control of another. That was the life she wanted, and she needed to see for herself just how free she was—or if being a part of the *Star Renegade* crew was simply a nice dream destined to fail at the onset.

Cal pulled her close. "I just want you safe. Can you understand that?"

Interesting that he was still worried about her, while he was about to meet his judge, jury, and executioner all at the same time. Some parts of humanity were easy to understand, while others were hugely foreign.

"I know you want me safe, but that's not possible anymore. Please understand that I need to know how much power he still has over me. He barely even fed me earlier, but my body remembered and wanted more. I need to know if what he's already done to me is irreparable. I need to know if I still have control."

"And what if you don't?"

Dania lowered her eyes. The answer was the unthinkable. And if that was the case, this would lessen their chance of escape, and she knew it.

She took a deep breath. "Right now, I feel like Geron has command again, and it's killing me. I need to know that I still have a chance. I need to know that if we get away, I can live my life without him."

Cal sighed. "I can't even pretend to understand what you're going through, but I support your decision."

She smiled. Cal would never try to control her, no matter how much he wanted to protect her. That was what *real* love was, and she needed to remember that. No matter what happened in that room, Cal was the one she wanted to be with.

Doc stepped away. "I'm going to head downstairs and get a reading on how our passengers in the cargo bay are doing. We might need them to help buy us some time. I'll meet you in the med bay in a few minutes."

Cal nodded. "Make it fast. I like strength in numbers, and I'd much rather have three of us in there."

Had he forgotten that Doc wasn't the only one on their side? "Alexander will be in the med bay, too. He'll help us."

Cal nodded, but that news didn't seem to give him comfort. He hovered at the door, staring at the pocked metal as if reading words that weren't there.

He took a deep breath and turned to her. "Are you sure? No one will think differently of you if you decide to stay away."

For months, she'd been living in Geron's shadow. She'd yearned for the power that had once coursed through her veins. She'd felt weak and inept without her powers, in some cases not even willing to try to figure out how to live and be important as a person in her own right. Part of finding out who she really was, or who she *could be*, was facing the being who'd kept her captive for so long.

She lifted her chin. "I know walking into that room is dangerous. But I need to prove to myself that I can. If I don't do this, I'll be running from him like a child for the rest of my life. I need to prove to myself that I'm still strong."

She gulped as Cal's eyes fell on her shaking hands. He wove his fingers through hers and squeezed. "You are the strongest, most amazing person I know. You've already beaten him despite the odds, and I want you to know that I've got your back."

An interesting thing to say, since *she* was the one who'd come to stand at *his* side when he faced Geron.

Still, she nodded. What he thought he'd be able to do up against a being with nearly insurmountable power, she wasn't sure, but she appreciated his courage.

They entered the infirmary and Dania gaped. All but two beds were empty. Several enforcers whom she'd only seen unconscious surrounded the room lining the walls like security or—more likely—awaiting orders from their new sponsor.

Geron's existence pulsed through the room, and Dania did her best to look anywhere but in his direction. She considered each risen soldier, trying to recall if she'd met them before but not finding a familiar face among Zindiria's former guards.

Alexander glanced at her and paled before he ran a medical instrument over the forehead of one of the newly awakened enforcers. His voice exploded in her mind. *You shouldn't be here.*

Dania took a slow, steady breath. Alexander would always be her protector, even if that meant trying to protect her from Geron while he still could. Each of them were far too aware that they were one feeding away from not caring about the life they'd lived and the friends they'd made over the past few months.

The pull to the center of the room continued as Dania turned to her sponsor. Geron stood beside a bed, his arms gripped around one of Peter's former patients. The enforcer's hair floated about him and his head lolled back. The air in the room tingled—a warm, pleasing sensation. Dania took a step forward before retreating, pressing against Cal. He placed his hand on her arm and rubbed gently with his thumb...a tender reminder that he was with her, and there was more to life than the pulsing energy surging through the room that offered solace, power, and complete erasure of who she'd become.

The enforcer moaned as Geron placed him on the floor and whispered into his ear. When Geron released him, the enforcer walked toward the wall and stood alongside the others despite being completely naked. Alexander handed him a pile of white cloth and instructed him to dress.

Geron grunted, grabbing the side of the mattress with one hand and his head with the other. Alexander and Kile bolted to his side, Orion and Theon following, standing in standard shield formation.

Dania twitched with the need to join them but managed to hold steady. She was in no condition to guard her sponsor, anyway.

Geron looked past the commanders and smiled at her. "That was exhausting. I wasn't sure I'd ever finish." She could sense Theon's translation filtering through the room, but Geron's own rich, distinct words surrounded her. How she'd missed his voice!

She blinked, cringing. It was just a voice, like any other. There was nothing special about him. Still, she gritted her teeth to keep from reaching out and embracing the being she'd been avoiding for so long.

"You should rest, Ada," Alexander said. "Recoding all of them has taken too much of your strength."

Recoding *all of them*? Dania glanced at the last two occupied beds. One man and one woman were on their sides rather than their backs, and their hair floated about them in constant motion, like all enforcers. They were no longer patients, only sleeping. Geron had managed to heal them all.

Cal moved closer, and she took solace in his warmth. Hopefully, it wasn't for the last time.

Geron pushed Orion aside, and his gaze fixed on Cal. "You are the one who killed my friend."

Cal folded his arms, just as defiant as always. "That wasn't how it happened."

Dania tensed and her skin grew cold. This was why she'd

come, and she needed to keep calm and in control. Steadying herself, she stepped forward. "Ada, we spoke about this on the long-distance communications channels. I sent you the tapes proving Mr. Espinoza's innocence. Did you watch them?" She dearly hoped he had. He'd promised her. Her sponsor had never broken a promise.

He stared at her for a moment before he nodded. "Of course." His attention returned to Cal. "Was Filluck involved in anything nefarious?"

Cal unfolded his arms. "It doesn't matter anymore. He's dead. Your enforcers may not have doled out the punishment, but fate gave him what he deserved."

Filluck's death had come by accident at the hands of a small child. Filluck had used the boy as a shield, and when the child had struggled for the gun, it had gone off. Cal had told the boy to run and had been shouldering the blame for Filluck Palogivan's murder for years.

The tapes that had proven Cal's innocence had been sealed by someone in House Bane, and they'd never found out by whom. Part of Dania wished she were still close enough to Geron to discern if he knew how that could have happened. The other part of her never wanted to be that close to him again.

Geron rubbed his eyes. "I find myself angry. All evidence implies multiple illegal acts and countless victims of crime. I had no idea."

Dania's heart fluttered. Of course he'd had no idea! Geron would never allow anyone to break the sacred law—even his friend. Cal glanced at her and she tried to settle herself. She shouldn't have been so thrilled by this. But she was, like her faith in the galaxy had been restored. Maybe because Geron *was* the galaxy to her.

She blinked, shaking her head. He *had been* the galaxy to her. Past tense. She needed to keep that straight.

Geron turned to Kile. "Inform our people that Calvin Espinoza has been exonerated of the crime of murder."

Dania's breath hitched. Had she heard that right?

Orion's hair took flight. "Sir, that is highly irregular and unnecessary. He is guilty of countless other crimes."

"That's true, but I do appreciate you removing *that one*." Cal closed his eyes and took a deep breath.

Did being accused of murder bother him, even though he hadn't been guilty? Was there someone, somewhere whom Cal cared about who maybe didn't know the truth?

Geron blinked tired eyes, holding up his hand until Orion stepped back. "My brother's commander is correct. You do have a significant number of crimes to answer for, Captain Espinoza, as does the rest of your crew."

Dania inched closer. Geron's power pulsed, warming her even from several feet away. "Ada, there is no value in punishing the crew now. There are more important things to deal with, and they are already at your mercy."

Geron nodded. "Good counsel, as always, Dania. They will all have value until the remainder of the enforcers on the lower deck have been dealt with. After, they will pay for their crimes."

Dania gulped. With the speed with which he'd healed those in the med bay, that maybe gave them another day or two. That was probably the best they could ask for.

Geron smiled at her. "I've missed you." He held out his hand and she bolted to him, skidding across the floor and landing on her knees at his feet.

Her heart fluttered, her breaths fast and shallow. His heat surrounded her, warmed her from within. Yet his essence was off. Tired. She wanted to wrap herself around him and give him comfort. She held up her hand to him.

"Dania!" Cal reached for her, but Kile grabbed him, drawing him back. "Dania, don't!"

She blinked, ignoring the voice as it faded into the distance. Her sponsor was so beautiful, so perfect...

So *alien*.

She lowered her hand. *Stars!* How had she ended up at Geron's feet?

She cleared her throat and choked on her next breath. "Ada, you've overtired yourself. You should rest."

Geron nodded. "It's true, but I always have time for you." He ran his fingers through her hair. She leaned into the touch. Her body ached for more.

Her sponsor frowned. "Seeing you this way is disagreeable. I'm not feeling well myself, but if you are in pain, I'll give you a full feeding."

Dania closed her eyes, a moan escaping her lips. There was nothing she wanted more.

Cal's voice broke through the haze. "Your Highness, I mean no disrespect, but you look like you're going to fall over."

Kile shoved Cal aside and moved beside Dania. "As much as I loathe siding with the criminal, I have to agree, Ada. She's survived this long—she will make it through to tomorrow morning when you are well."

Geron reached out and cupped her cheek. "What do you want, my Dania?"

Dania trembled. Behind her, Cal's breaths came slow and staggered. He'd been exonerated of his crimes. He'd received a temporary reprieve. His heart rate wasn't spiking for himself, but for her.

She drew in a deep breath, concentrating on the erratic rhythm of his breathing.

Cal. She wanted Cal!

Dania blinked, easing back until the intensity of Geron's thrall subsided a little. What had almost happened?

She forced a smile. "I'm fine, Ada. Kile is right. I will survive. It's more important that you rest. Your health always takes precedence over my own. I will be waiting for you in the morning."

Dania cringed, realizing she'd meant it. She would *always* be waiting for him.

Geron nodded. "I will return to my ship." He stood, and Kile moved to his side, helping him balance. Her heart clenched. She should be the one to help him.

But no. She didn't want that. She stood, her muscles aching.

Cal appeared at her side, taking her arm. "I've got you."

She nodded. Cal would always be there for her, and he expected nothing in return. She didn't need Geron anymore. So why was it so hard to watch Kile lead him from the room?

One thing was perfectly clear. When Geron called for her, she'd have to go. It had nothing to do with what she wanted. He still owned her. She had no choice.

She turned and looked at Cal. The pain in his eyes told her what she already knew. They had precious little time before Geron took her away forever.

CAL PULLED Dania away from the star-blasted prince as His Royally-Arrogant Highness and Kile walked toward the door. There was no way Cal was going to let him anywhere near Dania now, in the morning, or ever. The *how* part of the statement was what he needed to figure out, though. He'd been in hard places before but never sealed inside a ship with no way to escape. What Cal needed was to keep this prince occupied until his brilliant crew figured out a way to blast the hell out of this no-win situation, and he only had one possible way to do that.

"About tomorrow morning." Cal did his best to keep himself between Dania and the prince. "Orion has several more enforcers downstairs who need just as much help as these people."

The prince's odd, reptilian eyes looked almost bored. "How many?"

Cal had no clue. "A lot."

The doorway opened, and Doc entered. "More patients, unfortunately."

Fallon stepped in behind him, floating two unconscious enforcers, followed by Miguel and a third lax enforcer.

The prince gaped, backing away and leaning on the edge of a bed. The sheen to his scale-like skin turned a lighter shade of blue.

"Whoa there." Doc approached the prince, pulling out a penlight.

Both Orion and the guy Cal was fairly certain was doing the translation trick in Cal's head jumped in front of Geron.

Alexander appeared at Doc's side before Cal had even noticed he'd moved. "This is a doctor. He means no harm. Stop being fools and stand aside."

Kile lifted his chin to Alexander. "This criminal is not a doctor. I'd prefer if you heal our sponsor."

Alex lowered his head. "Of course." Alex eased the prince down to sit on the bed. It lowered the Kever's face to a more human level. Alex moved his hands around the prince, not touching him. Probably a good move after what had happened to Dania. "You're exhausted, Ada."

The prince sighed. "This, I already know."

Doc held up both his palms. "I'm just a lowly human, but in my useless opinion, I think you need to rest and do whatever it is you need to do to increase your pathogen count before you try to heal anyone else."

Geron furrowed his brow. "*Pathogen count?*"

Alexander took a step back. "He means primordial energy, Ada."

Geron looked at the two enforcers Fallon hovered onto gurneys on the other side of the room. "Will they live?"

Doc shrugged. "I'll do my best. I've been running at about a seventy-five percent survival rate since the loss of their sponsor." Doc bowed slightly. "My condolences, by the way, for the loss of your sister."

Geron nodded. Doc was a master of this kind of diplomatic conversation. Cal couldn't care less that the guy's sister was dead, and he was fairly certain his poker face would only bring him so far.

The prince stood, wavering.

Kile grabbed him. "Ada, they just said you need to rest."

Geron shoved him away. "I'm not letting enforcers die just because I'm tired, even if they don't belong to me."

Which was kind of an interesting development, since the guy hadn't given a shooting star the first time he'd heard about the sick enforcers. Maybe hearing about them and seeing them in person were two very different things.

Orion folded his arms. "Your brother would not approve. They are not your responsibility."

"Not yet, they're not. Hasn't he been pestering me to increase my guard?"

Orion's lips thinned. "Not at the expense of your health."

The prince continued to the first bed and sat on the edge. "Alexander?"

Alex glanced at Cal and Dania before taking a tentative step toward the prince. "Ada?"

"You will tend to me if I falter."

Alex nodded. "Always, Ada."

Geron placed his hands beneath the unconscious enforcer and lifted him to his chest. He held the man, cheek to cheek like an embrace, until the enforcer's eyes sprang open and the man let out a scream that echoed through the chamber. Dania bit her lower lip, tears glistening in her lashes as the enforcer clawed at the prince like he was trying to push him off. A wave of heat swept through the room, and Dania closed her eyes and took a deep breath, like she was breathing clean air for the first time in years.

"What the hell?" Cal whispered.

Doc held up his hand like it was okay, but all this insanity seemed far from fine. The enforcer shrieked again, punching the prince like he was trying to beat the Kever off him.

The enforcer stopped screaming, and Geron eased him back onto the bed. The room cooled before the prince grabbed the man's temples and leaned against the mattress.

Alexander whispered something to him, and the prince nodded.

The air continued to cool. Was it possible that the prince's powers were so strong, they could affect the temperature on the ship? And if Cal could feel it, what was this doing to Dania and Alexander?

Dania twitched as Geron reached for the enforcer on the second gurney.

Cal kept himself between her and the prince as the room started to heat again. He wasn't sure if his body provided any protection, but he needed to do something to shield her from the one thing that could destroy their future together.

He leaned closer to her ear. "I need to get you out of here."

She shook her head. "I can't leave him. He looks so tired."

The second enforcer started to scream. The sound reverberated off the walls, like Geron was ripping the man's soul out and tearing it to pieces.

Cal cringed. Couldn't Dania see what her sponsor was doing to these other enforcers? They were fighting him, trying to get away.

The screaming dulled to a pitiful whimper, like the last

sobs of a person dying, and finally giving up, before the room fell silent. The enforcer's head swayed before it lulled, like he'd fallen asleep—probably out of exhaustion from fighting for his life.

Cal understood Dania still felt like she needed whatever the prince did to them, but deep down, couldn't she see this for the horror show it really was? Doc had said this was like an addiction. Cal understood that. But after all the prince had done to her, how could Dania still allow herself to still be so drawn to him?

The second enforcer fell to the ground, crumpled at Geron's feet like a discarded toy. The prince groaned, grabbing his head and stumbling back three steps before he, too, collapsed.

In one sweeping motion, Orion's, Kile's, and Alexander's hands stretched toward the prince, and Geron's fall stopped, like he'd been wrapped in a blanket of air.

Which one of the enforcers caught him, Cal had no idea, but none of them lowered their hands until Geron had floated seamlessly onto a gurney and settled onto the sheets. The tall Kever's lower legs hung off the bed, and Doc wheeled another gurney over.

"Here you go." Doc helped Alexander lift the Kever's legs onto the other gurney. "I don't know anything about Kever physiology, but I'm thinking we should try to keep him warm." He frowned. "If keeping a Kever warm is even a thing. Do his people like to be warm?"

"This is ridiculous." Kile shoved Doc away from Geron and faced Alexander. "Heal him."

Alex's nose flared. "From exhaustion? He's not a soldier on a battlefield. He needs sleep."

Doc walked toward the storage shelves in the back of the

room. "I agree with the diagnosis that he needs rest, but not here. He's going to fall off these small beds. We need to get him back to his own Kever-sized ship."

Getting His Royal Ridiculously-Tallness off the *Star Renegade* was the best idea Cal had heard all day.

Doc grabbed a bottle off the shelf and handed it to Alexander. "If you could please confirm this is water, I'd like to throw it on your lord's face to wake him up."

"He's not a lord. He's a prince." Alexander popped off the cap and threw it in Geron's face himself.

The Kever sputtered and sat up, holding his head.

Orion folded his arms. "Will you listen now, or do I need to contact your brother and tell him you are being unnecessarily reckless again?"

Geron rubbed his eyes. "What I do with my time is none of my brother's business."

Cal suppressed a grin. Trouble in royal paradise? How interesting.

The doorway opened and all the enforcers turned as Ethan entered.

Orion advanced on him. "What are you doing here?"

Ethan held up his palms. "Whoa, this is the med bay. I need a bandage."

"You look unharmed."

Ethan raised his middle finger. "Hangnail. Super painful."

Orion's face twisted into a sneer as his hair took flight. Was Ethan out of his mind?

Kile held his arm between them. "This little one isn't a threat."

"Hey! I'm not *that* little." Ethan grinned. "I'm the most competent one, though, right?"

The commander scowled at him and walked away.

Cal grabbed Ethan's arm and pulled him from the enforcers. "What are you doing here?"

"Alanna is freaking out. I promised to message her if there was anything wrong."

Odd, that she would send Ethan and not come herself. There was no love lost between Alexander and the engineer, and Alanna knew that.

Ethan leaned past Cal to Dania. "How you doing, Dani?"

Dania simply nodded, her eyes trained on that blasted prince. Cal needed to find a reason to steer her out of there.

Orion still stood near the door, frowning at Ethan. No doubt he'd heard the entire conversation and knew Ethan was just doing recon. Cal grabbed an adhesive bandage and handed it to Ethan, just in case.

The commander shook his head and returned to Geron. "I agree that the small one is of no concern. The only threat to Prince Geron, at the moment, is his own stubbornness."

This guy seemed to get away with a lot. That must have been a fringe benefit of working for the person who was next in line for the throne.

Kile folded his arms. "While I do not agree that you are stubborn, Ada, I do agree that you should rest."

Geron nodded, still rubbing his eyes. "I *am* tired. I will go back to my rooms and retire for the day." He gave a slight, weak smile as he held out his hand to Alex. "You will join me for the night, Alexander."

Alex's eyes widened as his jaw fell open. His lower lip trembled as it slowly closed.

Cal's throat went dry. Not long ago, Alanna had come to him, furious, after finding out that the prince had not only slept with Dania, but Alexander as well. They'd both been reluctant to admit to what had happened behind closed doors, but the big problem was that neither Dania nor Alexander had the ability to say *no*. Dania had denied some of Cal's assumptions, but the dread in Alexander's eyes told Cal that his worst nightmares were probably true.

Alex looked down and gulped, taking a tentative step forward. "Of course, Ada. I am honored, as always."

Like hell he was. Alex had spent the last month sharing a room—consensually—with Alanna. Cal wasn't crazy about the enforcer getting involved with a member of his crew, but it had happened, so that made the guy a de facto member of the *Star Renegade* family, whether Cal liked it or not.

And now Alex was walking—against his free will—back to his sponsor.

Cal couldn't let that happen, but what in the name of Jupiter's moons was he supposed to do about it?

Ethan pushed past Cal. "Oh! I almost forgot. I came down here because I have an emergency. I need Alex's help in the engine room."

Orion narrowed his eyes. "You are lying. And you just told us you were here because you had pain in your finger."

Ethan held up his middle finger again. This time, on the other hand. "Yeah, I do. Because I burned it on an over-heating engine."

"You said you had a hangnail."

Ethan shrugged. "Those hurt too." He spun back toward Alexander. "But seriously, if you check, you'll see the computers say we're having a big engine overload."

Sweat broke out on Cal's forehead. Had Ethan lost his mind? Why was he telling them to check the computers? That would just confirm he was lying!

"Fix it yourself," Orion said. "You don't need an enforcer for that."

"Oh, yes I do." He turned back to Alexander. "It's all those weird modifications that you did that I could never understand. I told you I wouldn't be able to fix it without you if anything went wrong, remember?"

Orion stared like he was doing that weird temperature-checking thing to try to ferret out a lie. Judging by his expression, he wasn't quite sure. "If there is a problem, then fix it in the morning."

Ethan shrugged. "Well, I would, If I had time. Unfortunately, according to the computers, those engines are going to explode within the next half hour."

"*Explode?*" Orion and Kile said at the same time.

Ethan held up both his hands. "You enforcers always tell us how incompetent we all are."

Kile pointed at him. "*You* are not incompetent."

"Yeah, well, maybe the rest of them are rubbing off on me. I can't fix it without Alexander's help."

Orion puffed out his chest. "I sense a lie, but also truth. However, my instincts encourage me to *not* believe him."

Geron rubbed his face. "Will someone *please* take the initiative to check the computer systems and see if there actually is a problem?"

Ethan fiddled with something behind his back while the translator-guy walked over to the wall and started tapping on a screen.

The translator turned back to Geron. "He's telling the truth. The computers are registering a critical abnormality in the engine room. The temperature in the rear of the ship is rising."

Wait. *What?* There really *was* a problem?

Orion folded his arms and scowled at Ethan. "One would think you would have mentioned that sooner."

Ethan shrugged. "Well, you know, hangnails hurt."

"I thought it was a burn?"

"Yup, that's what I said." Ethan turned to Geron. "I may be a lowly human, but I'm kinda thinking it would be a really bad idea to let a ship blow up in your cargo hold. I mean, we had a small box of parts ignite and explode in our cargo hold once, and we were finding nuts and bolts lodged in nooks and crannies for months, and that box was nowhere near as big as the *Star Renegade*."

The prince growled from between his teeth. "Fine. Go."

Ethan grabbed Alexander's wrist and dragged him from the room. Cal had never seen Alex move so fast without someone shooting at him. But that left someone in the room that Cal cared about even more.

He stepped in front of Dania and looked over his shoulder. "Inch toward the door. Now." They'd gotten Alexander out of a bad situation. The last thing Cal needed was for Dania to be Alexander's replacement.

Orion helped the prince to stand. "I'm going to personally bring you to your chambers and lock you in to make sure you sleep."

Kile straightened. "You won't be locking our sponsor anywhere."

That sounded like a fight that Cal didn't want to be anywhere near. He tapped his hand on the door control and pushed Dania through and into the hall.

Dania pulled him into a hug as the doors closed behind them. She murmured words into his shoulder that he couldn't make out, clinging to him like her life depended on it. Maybe she thought it did.

He wanted to hold her and console her, but it was more

important to get her away from the med bay. They moved down the hall past the ladder before they stopped.

Cal placed his hands on either side of her face and kissed her. "Are you okay? How did you do in there?"

She took a deep breath, like maybe she hadn't breathed since leaving the med bay. "I felt drawn to him, but it wasn't the all-consuming hunger like earlier. As long as Peter keeps giving me artificial pathogens, I might be able to fight this."

Cal frowned. "I'm not all that comfortable that you used the word *might*." Nor that she'd lunged for him and sat at his feet the second he'd called her name.

She lowered her eyes. "I'd be lying if I didn't admit that I wanted to go to him in there. I lost myself for a moment, but I was able to bring myself back. Without Peter's help, I know that wouldn't have been the case. It was hard, though." She looked up. "Harder than I'd hoped it would be."

He brushed his lips over hers again, a gentle movement, soaking her in. "Then I'll just have to figure out how to keep you away from that blasted prince." He gave her a gentle tug toward the lounge. "Come on. Let's get out of the open."

He tapped the door control and was only partially surprised to find Alexander within, hugging Alanna. Ethan leaned against the wall, talking to Ty.

"I see the phantom emergency has been dealt with."

Ethan's eyes widened. "Oh!" He ran to the control panel on the wall and typed something in. The red light flashing overhead swirled once and then faded. "Sorry, I almost forgot."

Cal closed the door behind him. "How were you able to trigger a fake alarm that quickly?"

Ethan reached into his pocket and pulled out a small, silver cylinder. "Remote control. It's an old trick that I adopted from my previous captain as a way of getting rid of boarding parties. Works like a charm."

Alexander gave Alanna a kiss and turned to Ethan. "Why would you do that for me?"

"Well, I'm not gonna lie. I'm not all that fond of you, but I *am* fond of Alanna." Ethan shrugged. "If anything happened to you, she'd be upset, and that would break my heart."

Alanna burst into tears and hugged him. Ethan nodded to Alexander over her shoulder.

"Thank you," Alex said. "I'm in your debt."

"Nah, I got a hug out of it. That's worth gold."

Alanna gave him a playful tap on the shoulder. "You're a good guy, you know that?"

"I've been telling you all that for years."

Cal huffed out a breath. "I hate to break up all this happiness, but we're still in the middle of a very big problem. We ducked a punch with getting Alexander out of there, but the prince point blank said he was going to feed Dania tomorrow. And we all know that everyone on this ship has a one-way ticket to a death sentence as soon as he decides we're not needed anymore."

"Which could be any minute." Alexander pursed his lips. "Our sponsor does tend to be..."

"Moody," Dania finished. "He could suddenly remember he wanted someone executed and an enforcer will be knocking on our door."

"Then we need to get moving on our plan to get out of here."

A yellow light started flashing from the corner of the room.

Cal braced for the worst. "What's that?"

Ty glanced at the light as it flashed three times. "Proximity alarm."

"Like the broken light on the bridge?"

"Well, yeah, but no. The one on the bridge flashes when it wants to. This one only flashes when there actually is a proximity alarm."

"How is that possible when we're inside another ship?"

"It's only possible if what's coming at us is even bigger than what we're inside."

"What's bigger than a cruiser?" Ty asked.

Cal wasn't sure he wanted to know.

The door opened, and Kile walked in. He glowered at Alexander and Ethan. "What happened to the engine trouble?"

Ethan held up his hands. "Our boy Alex fixed it already. He's a guru in the repairs department. He's great with his hands. Just ask Alanna."

Alanna swatted his shoulder.

Kile turned to Alexander. "Did you fix the ship?"

Dania stepped forward. "I'm sure you didn't come here to argue about repairs."

"True." Kile inclined his head to her. "You are needed on the command deck."

"Needed by who?" Cal asked.

"Needed by me." Kile turned back to Dania. "You are my general. It's time to take your place. Now."

CHAPTER 8

DANIA

DANIA STEPPED onto the command deck of Geron's cruiser amid a swirl of enforcers and common Kever military personnel scampering between navigation, security, scanners, and operations reconnaissance. A wide expanse of computer stations lined the deck in even rows in front of a massive collage of screens relaying camera footage from space around them, looking much like massive windows showing all outer angles of the ship.

Orion leaned away from a console and glared at her, then Kile. "She does not need to be here."

Kile lifted his chin. "She is disabled, but she is still my general."

Orion's eyes narrowed. "That remains to be seen."

Dania tensed as a tingle of primordial energy filled the air, but she couldn't tell if it was general agitation sparking between them or a true threat. Orion was making a play for power, trying to take control of the ship—a ship Kile had probably been in charge of since Dania had left.

Kile and Orion were both commanders, but Orion's sponsor ranked higher than Geron. By rule of law, Kile and

Orion were equals, but the weight of the high prince still loomed over them just as much as if Orion spoke for the king.

The room heated with power tingling beneath Kile's skin as Orion's hair started to float about him. They were posturing, seeing who would back down first.

This was why Kile had brought her here, and why he'd said she needed to take her place. Whether or not she could remained to be seen—but she was more than willing to play the part.

"Enough!" She walked between them, wishing she could make her hair take flight and increase her height, but she'd have to depend on the attitude that had given her a reputation of being a general not to be toyed with.

Orion gritted his teeth and seethed at Kile. "She is not capable of handling this situation."

Dania shoved Orion away from her commander. "I refuse to be ignored. Step back and wait to be addressed."

Orion's eyes met hers and the temperature about him warmed 0.002 degrees. "I will not be pushed aside like a common enforcer."

Dania took a step toward him, channeling the defiant, powerful general inside her. "You are no better than any other enforcer while you're on this ship, and you'll do what you're told."

Orion glared at her again, and she held his gaze—unflinching—until he stepped back.

She turned from him and walked toward the screens, keeping her breathing steady to hide the very human adrenaline surging through her veins. Any show of weakness would be acted on. If she didn't keep control now, she may never get it back.

Kile moved behind her, stepped up to a console, and tapped on the screen.

"That was wildly satisfying." He grinned. "Welcome back."

Dania's gaze carried over the room until she found the lighter-blue complexion of the Sisten family from Kever's largest moon. Captain Quaren had been in secondary command of this cruiser for Dania's entire life. He'd taught her the positions on the command deck before she'd been named general and officially outranked him. "Report."

The captain stood and tugged on the edge of his dark-blue uniform, straightening his appearance. "We have seventy-one ships incoming, General. Different classes, different sizes. At least two class-two cruisers. The lead cruiser is asking to speak to our commanding officer."

Orion shifted uncomfortably against the wall. He'd probably tried to take the transmission, but the captain had refused. A wise but dangerous decision on Quaren's part.

Dania nodded to him. "Good work. Put it through."

A female enforcer with silver hair draped across her shoulders appeared on the screen. Dark circles marred her eyes, and her hair barely drifted as she looked through the screen. Her lips parted and she tilted her head, probably confused by Dania's civilian clothing and dark hair.

Dania held her hands behind her, keeping her back straight and feet slightly apart. "I am General Dania DuBane. Explain your situation."

A console behind the woman on the screen shot out sparks. She barely flinched. "We are transporting two hundred and twenty-seven enforcers. Most have fallen grievously ill."

Dania frowned. "Ill?"

The woman took a steadying breath. "It is our belief that their sponsors are dead. We've identified most as belonging to lower-level Banes and some nobility or noble relations. Most of them were stationed in and around section R-9."

R-9? Dania had never heard that reference before. Then again, Geron was not a military prince. She'd never needed to know numerical systems designations.

The enforcer continued. "The ships under my protection also house over a thousand common personnel, many with combat injuries."

Dania rolled over the information. "I understand your situation, but why are you here? Shouldn't you be seeking a medical port to treat your wounded?"

"The commoners we can handle with our own medical teams, but the enforcers…" She looked down. "They're getting worse. A few of them have died." She met Dania's gaze. "Prince Geron is the only Bane outside the war zone. We can't get them to anyone else."

Dania gaped, glancing at Kile. His expression was equally shocked. Geron had just passed out from treating a handful of enforcers, and there were more in the cargo bay. How could he help hundreds?

Kile's lips thinned as ships continued to fill the screen. He motioned to the communications officer to disengage the transmission's audio signal. "There are too many to help."

Dania nodded. Too many, indeed. "My larger concern is that if they found us so easily, our enemies might be able to do the same." And now, with so many ships clustered around them, they were an even bigger target.

"We should skip space," the captain said.

Dania nodded. That would be a valid move, but the only one capable of skipping space, especially with this many ships, was Geron—and even then, he was only capable of skipping short distances. At one time, Dania had been able to conjure black holes for travel, but that was before she'd given up her powers.

Alanna could possibly help them, but that would put a target on the navigator's head. The last thing Dania wanted was a bunch of overzealous enforcers dissecting her friend to try to figure out why she was able to skip space.

"Your orders, General?" the captain asked.

Orion smirked, folding his arms as he leaned against the wall. "Yes, General, I'm very interested in hearing your orders."

Dania turned back to the screen, concentrating on trying not to sweat. She was disabled. Geron was disabled. And now Orion was drooling, waiting for her to ask for his counsel, if not for him to take over completely. She'd do neither.

She'd been getting by on her smarts for months. It hadn't always been easy, but one thing the *Star Renegade* crew had taught her was that intellect could be just as powerful as primordial energy.

She just needed to take this one step at a time. The first problem was how traceable they all were.

"Give me a line to all ships."

The captain tapped a few keys on his console. "At your mark, General."

A myriad of ships hung in space from every vantage point around Geron's cruiser, and more appeared by the second. It was possible some were not as fast as others, or maybe even disabled. She'd need to study those statistics once they were safe.

"This is General Dania DuBane. Every ship will immediately stop sending out signatures. We're going dark."

"That will make it impossible for our own ships to find us," Orion said.

"That's the point." Dania tapped a series of keys on the panel to her right, changing the view screens above. From every angle, ships gathered around them three to five hulls deep. With the comm center sending out their signature, they may as well have been flashing a beacon saying: *Here we are, come annihilate us.*

She took a settling breath. "Keeping our signatures visible is not an option. If our own people can find us, so can the Carteks."

"Our technology is too advanced for the Carteks. That's why we drove them off so easily when the Banes took the Earthan systems under their protection."

Dania didn't give Orion the satisfaction of turning toward him. "Judging by the condition of these ships and our enforcers, it appears this is no longer the case."

"So you expect us to hide like smugglers?"

"No. We will be going dark, regrouping, and treating our wounded."

Orion stormed toward her. "The Dania DuBane of the past would be tracking down the ships that did this and annihilating them."

"The general you speak of didn't have to worry about casualties and thousands of civilians. We treat our wounded, and then we strike. That is my final decision." She turned to Kile. "The next time Commander Orion speaks out of turn, throw him in the brig."

Orion looked down at her. "You wouldn't dare."

Dania smiled but didn't answer. Her former self would have already had him on his knees, begging for mercy, and would have dealt with the high prince's consequences later.

She still may have to deal with the high prince, but she stood by her decision.

She turned to Captain Quaren. "Do a short-range communications link and make sure every one of those ships complies. Then I want you to move this entire fleet twenty-seven desdens from here."

"Do you have a preference on direction?" Quaren asked.

"In the opposite direction of the fighting. Once the slower ships catch up, see to it that all the enforcers closest to death are transported to Geron's cruiser."

Orion would probably think this an unnecessary risk. He may even think Geron weak if he chose to help the dying instead of worrying about himself first—but there were hundreds of enforcers on those ships. She couldn't abandon them.

The only problem was, she wasn't sure anyone on this cruiser would be able to save them, either.

CHAPTER 9
DANIA

DANIA SAUNTERED across the floor of the command deck, soaking in the power of the royal cruiser as they reached their planned meeting point twenty-seven desdens from their last location. The massive walls of Geron's cruiser hummed around her. She loved the *Star Renegade*. It was small and fast and very maneuverable, but this was real strength...and it felt like home.

A chill settled over her skin and she stopped, considering the screens and the cold, hard titanium walls. This couldn't be her home anymore. This was someone else's life now, and she needed to find a way to get back to Cal. Of course, her being on the *Star Renegade* just made things worse for them all. She hated to be yet another reason the crew always had to be running, keeping one step ahead of the law, but deep down, they all seemed to like it.

A smile played across her lips. Always being on the run—staying one step ahead of people hunting you—did evoke a spark of a thrill. There was some excitement in not knowing what the next day would bring.

She could have lived her life like that, adoring her new

family, enjoying time with Cal. Unfortunately, though, the *Star Renegade* had only been a dream.

The screens around her changed, showing more ships gathering around the cruiser, huddling for safety close to the thick titanium-composite walls and gun turrets designed to rip through ships far larger than the cruiser itself. This was a prime example of the weak clinging to the strong, as they always had since the beginning of time. She was part of that puzzle, part of the machine that protected those below them.

This world…this *power* was her reality, and she was far beyond escape.

Captain Quaren appeared at her side. "Thirty-two incapacitated enforcers are en route to our hangars."

Dania took a deep breath and released it slowly. It wasn't as many as she'd expected, but that wasn't a small number, either. And these were just the worst. There would probably be more tomorrow, if not by the end of the day.

"Geron is going to be angry," Orion said. "You should have asked him what his wishes were."

Dania gave him a slow glance over her shoulder. "Does your prince think so little of you that he needs to hold your hand with every decision? How sad for you." She turned back to the screens. She tried not to allow a sense of satisfaction to seep into her soul as the commander's blood pressure accelerated and his temperature spiked 0.014 degrees, but she had to press her lips together, keeping her back to him.

Captain Quaren barely held back his own grin. "Shall I have the wounded brought to our infirmaries?"

Dania nodded. Luckily enough, the cruiser had several infirmaries. Each had a specialty, most doing research in times of peace, but they each had a staff capable of tending to wounded.

"Contact the medical personnel and give them the number of patients. Not just those arriving now, but how many we could expect in the coming days. Have them decide the best way to divide the incoming so none of the stations are overloaded."

Orion shook his head. "You give too much power to your people. They'll think you're weak."

Kile folded his arms. "General, may I have permission to consider Commander Orion's interruptions officially out of turn?"

Dania tapped on a control panel, reviewing stats on ships as they arrived. "Permission granted." Which meant, of course, Kile could now throw him in the brig.

Orion's hair took flight. "If you take a *single* step toward me, I'll—"

Dania continued looking into the screen. "Then I suggest you remember you are a guest here, Commander. You will not be warned again."

Captain Quaren moved closer to her. "General, Prince Geron is awake. He's asking for you."

Dania nodded. "Inform him I'm on my way." She turned to Kile. "The command deck is yours. If Orion gives you any trouble, you have my permission to shoot him."

Orion folded his arms. "You'd never get a shot off."

Thirty-six side arms appeared in the crew's hands, all pointed at the high prince's commander.

Dania smiled. "Care to see if you can disarm them all before you feel the sting of a laser?"

Orion sighed, his face stony, but his eyes seething. "I will comply."

Dania smiled as she headed for the door. "I figured as much."

She breathed deeply as she walked through the halls. The ship was large, airy, and pristine, with shiny, silver walls devoid of shadows, even in the most remote corners and eaves. There was an ease about being on a cruiser—a sense of safety and security. Although she missed the charm of the scorch marks inside the *Star Renegade*, parts of her could hardly believe she'd been comfortable there. Then again, her attraction had never been about the ship. It had been about the crew. The family. The sense of belonging. She did still have a sense of belonging on Geron's cruiser, but the feelings were worlds different.

Adrena and Snibel stood at attention outside Geron's door. Their silver hair flowed with primordial energy, shimmering against their white-opal uniforms.

Adrena smiled as Dania approached. "Welcome home." She looked her up and down. "You look even worse than everyone said."

Snibel folded his arms. "Our sponsor will attend to her. It's good to have you back, General."

A chill ran over Dania. She'd come, as called, not even questioning why she'd been summoned. She'd followed orders just as she always had. But there was one huge difference this time. She was free, and the one person who could take away her freedom was behind that door.

"Is there a problem, General?" Adrena asked.

Dania gulped. Other than being trapped, there was no problem at all. A calm settled over her. Part of her wanted to fight, but she knew it would be useless. Geron had called for her. If she didn't come as ordered, any one of her people was strong enough to drag her back to him. It was best to comply.

She took a deep breath, then released it. She only wished

she'd had a chance to say goodbye to Cal properly. Hopefully, the next time they met wouldn't be for her to pass judgment.

The door opened, and Miguel stepped out. Dania balked, but she shouldn't have been surprised. Geron had asked Alexander to join him while he'd slept. If Alexander wasn't available, he would have chosen another.

Part of her twitched, as it always did…a pang of jealousy? Was that real, or something Geron had placed inside each of them, making sure they were more than amicable when he asked for company while he slept?

A smile played on Miguel's lips. "You stink of humanity. Hopefully, today will see the end of that."

Dania simply inclined her head in a curt nod and walked past him.

Geron's room was only partially illuminated. Kever eyes were sensitive and didn't require as much light. It never occurred to her that the brightness of the ship might bother him.

"Dania." Geron sat on the end of his bed: a barely padded, stone-like surface.

She lowered her eyes. "I'm here, Ada."

He held out a hand to her. "And I'm well rested. Come, let me feed you."

Sweat beaded her brow, and her hands shook. Her body screamed to throw itself into his arms, while her mind rebelled, holding on to her last moments of autonomy.

Geron lowered his hand. "What's wrong?"

Her lips formed words, but no sound came out. Her feet remained glued in place.

"Has it really been so bad for you? I should have sent out more people to find you. I never meant for you to be so far gone." He lifted his fingers, and she floated toward him. She shivered as his lips traced the edges of her cheek. "Don't worry. I'm here."

The room pulsed with primordial energy. She took a deep breath, drinking in the sweetness. The comfort, the sense of rightness, swirled around her, decadent power waiting to be allowed in.

He dragged his fingers down her cheek. Her skin tingled, and a moan escaped her lips. She closed her eyes. How could she have allowed herself to be away from this for so long? What did that tiny smuggling ship have that wasn't here? It was small, beaten, decrepit...

Her eyes shot open. "No!" She shoved Geron away.

He frowned. "What's wrong?"

Nothing. And everything.

She loved her sponsor, and she craved the power he promised.

But she loved Cal more. She loved her new family. And her new, wonderfully decrepit, dented, and battle-worn home, even if it was only a smuggling ship.

But how could she explain that?

She couldn't. Geron would simply think she'd lost her mind. And then he'd give it back to her, whether she wanted him to or not.

But maybe there was a way to hold on to her humanity for just a little while longer. "There are more enforcers for you to heal. They are in far worse shape than I am."

"I don't care about them. I care about you. You are my priority. Always."

Dania's heart twisted, knowing he meant every word. Geron would never lie to her. This was one thing that Cal had been wrong about. Geron *did* care for her. He cared for all of them.

She took a steadying breath and stepped back. "There is news that I need to make you aware of."

"Your report can wait until you are healed."

"No, Ada. I insist." She took another breath. "While you were sleeping, I took a small fleet of ships under our protection."

"*What?*"

"They are carrying a large number of wounded from the sectors where the Banes have engaged the Carteks."

His gaze remained centered on her, his expression blank. "I'm not qualified to protect them."

"This ship is battle-ready, Ada."

"That it is, but I've never had a battle-proven crew."

"No one has, Ada. We've been at peace for years."

He nodded. While his brothers and sisters had been trained in the military, not even they had seen battle until recent months, when the Carteks had returned to Bane space.

"Apparently, several low-ranking nobles have fallen. There are dozens of enforcers on those ships dealing with the pain of losing their sponsors."

Geron stood. "How is this possible?"

It was very possible. Geron's sister Zindiria had been the first Dania had known to fall, and she had been a power to be reckoned with. Everyone expected minor nobles to fall if war returned to Bane space. Lower-ranking nobles were like pawns in Earth's ancient game of chess. Their use was to be a first line of defense, and to be sacrificed if necessary. To lose this many, though, was unexpected—at least by Dania, and, judging by the deep crease in his brow, by Geron as well.

He rubbed his face. "Many of my friends are lower-ranking nobles."

Dania nodded. Geron had always been inclined to spend his time with what his father considered *commoners*. It had caused some strife in the royal family, and good fodder for sensationalists. Geron had never been one to care what anyone thought of him. Which, of course, always angered his father even more.

Geron lowered his hands. "Do you know which nobles are gone?"

"I have no idea."

He stood and walked across the room. "I don't understand. I haven't been away from home that long. How could things have changed so drastically?"

Dania bit her lower lip to keep herself from responding. Geron's idea of not being gone for long could mean he'd been out of touch for a month or more. In general, he cared more about enjoying himself than politics. And if he'd also been looking for her on top of that, he may have been out of touch longer than he realized.

He turned to her. "Is the rest of my family in good order?"

Interesting that he'd even care. He rarely talked to any of them. "As far as I know, the only casualty is your sister."

However, the enforcer on the comm had mentioned that they'd only identified a portion of the enforcers who'd fallen ill. Those remaining, and those who'd died, could have belonged to anyone. After his reaction to the news of Zindiria's death, it was probably best to stick with facts until they knew more.

He lowered his eyes, rubbing the tips of his thumbs together. Zindiria was not a small loss by any means, but her death must have sparked a rage in Geron's father like this galaxy had never known. If the king discovered who'd been involved, they were probably already dead. Or, more likely, in the process of dying a very long, very painful death.

Geron continued to stare at the floor. "How many enforcers need my help?"

"Thirty-two from the newly arrived ships need immediate care. I don't know if any on the *Star Renegade* have degraded enough to need an emergency feeding this morning."

Yesterday, he'd healed eleven enforcers and he'd nearly passed out from exhaustion. How could he possibly handle so many now?

Geron's brow furrowed as he reached for her and stroked her cheek. "Are you sure you're all right? I can give you some power to keep you going."

She placed her own palm on his hand and smiled. "I'm fine, Ada. I'm not going to die. They will." Luckily, this was the truth, and in this instance, the truth was in her favor.

Her skin pricked as Geron kissed her forehead. "You are always the voice of reason, looking out for your people, even at the cost of your own health." He smiled. "That's why I assigned Alexander to you, to save you from yourself."

That was an interesting admission. She'd known Alexander was her protector, like a bodyguard among her own people. She'd never considered why Geron had thought that had even been needed.

She lowered her hand. "Come. Let's go to the infirmary and see how bad the new arrivals are."

The Deck One Infirmary was normally the quietest. Being the closest to Geron's suite, they did mostly research, while also being prepped for any of Geron's personal needs. Today, all their beds were full. It was oddly quiet, though, as the physicians moved from bed to bed taking readings of their new patients.

One of the physicians approached.

Geron kept his eyes on the beds. "Which is the worst?"

The physician pointed to one of the beds. "This one. She's very weak and dehydrated. Her chart says she'd been vomiting for five days."

Dania cringed. Several of Zindiria's enforcers had been vomiting as well. Peter had managed to help them keep fluids down, but that had been about all he could do, other than the few he'd given artificial pathogens to.

Geron walked to the enforcer's bed. "I suppose we'll need to get started, then."

He pulled the unconscious enforcer from the bed and into his arms. As he held her, the room heated, and Dania's skin tingled, her cells screaming to reach out and touch just a trickle of the power being infused into that woman. After a moment, the enforcer screamed, clawing at Geron, trying to push him away, just as the others had.

Would she do the same, if another Bane tried to recode her? She was certainly loyal to Geron and wanted no other sponsor, but if faced with death, would her loyalty still cause her to fight, or was it something more deeply seated inside them that felt violated? That would mean this was a reflex action, like an animal fighting for their life in the jaws of a larger predator.

After what seemed like hours, six enforcers stood around the room with blank expressions. They reminded Dania far too much of the synthetic workers used in the mines on Effitis waiting to be programmed for their daily duties.

Did she look so blank after feeding? She didn't think so.

Then again, if Geron reprogrammed her each time she was fed, she would have no idea.

The physician insisted Geron drink a light-blue liquid before he continued. Her sponsor's eyes appeared puffy, as if he hadn't slept.

Dania inched toward him. "Ada, maybe you should rest."

He smiled at her and took another sip of his drink, before an enforcer on the other side of the room vomited. Sighing, Geron placed down his cup and walked over to their bed.

"This one keeps getting worse," the physician said. "I'm not sure why."

Geron gathered the enforcer into his arms, resting the man's head on his shoulder. The room heated, just as the enforcer in the next bed also started vomiting. Geron glanced at the puking woman and closed his eyes, no doubt concentrating on the one in his arms.

Dania wanted to join him, hold him up and share what little power she had. But she, of course, had nothing to give. And if she got any closer, she may get enough of a taste of primordial energy that she wouldn't be able to resist tapping into some of that power her sponsor was giving away so freely.

The enforcer in Geron's arms screamed, then vomited down Geron's back. The energy in the room skewed and twisted erratically.

A sense of *wrongness* set in, and Dania stepped back, shivering. A deep dread settled over her, but why? What Geron was sharing was a gift—something pure and wonderful. Why was the energy circling the room suddenly dark and tainted?

The shriek of the enforcer gained in pitch, and he started to gurgle. Geron grimaced and grunted, dropping the man.

His lips twisted like the enforcer was a piece of spoiled food he'd accidentally tasted.

Two physicians tried to help the flailing, screaming enforcer while the woman in the next bed wretched over and over again, green bile dripping from her lips.

"What happened?" Geron asked.

One of the Kever physicians prepared a syringe. "We don't know."

Geron turned and stumbled to the heaving woman in the bed. He gathered her in his arms, the puke from the previous man still slick across his back as the room started to heat again. But the wrongness returned just before the woman started to scream. Geron dropped her as well and sidled back toward the wall.

"Ada?" Dania reached for him but stopped herself.

Geron breathed heavily as the first enforcer stopped screaming.

"He's gone," one of the physicians announced before moving to help with the writhing woman on the floor. Her screams stopped soon after, and the physicians stood around her, their expressions lost.

"What's going on?" Geron rubbed his chest. "I feel ill."

One of the physicians approached, running a scanner over him. "What do you feel, sir?"

"My chest is heavy, and the room is spinning."

Dania's own chest clenched. Ada was ill? She needed to save him. But how?

She moved closer, then forced herself to move back. The physicians were what he needed right now. It was best for him, and best for her, to not make any contact.

Another enforcer in the back of the room vomited.

"This is unacceptable," Geron said. "What's happening?"

He held his head and shut his eyes tightly. Was he in pain?

One of the physicians working on the dead man frowned, looking into a handheld computer. "Sir, I believe I've found the problem."

Geron blinked several times. "And?"

The physician took a step away from him, like he was possibly worried about Geron's reaction to the news. "This enforcer was not a Bane. His sponsor was Kever, obviously, but not from your family's bloodline. There's no possible way you could have saved him."

A doctor working on the dead woman also stood beside her former patient. "This one, as well. There are no Bane blood signatures."

Geron growled, and they all stood back. "None of you thought to check?"

One of the Kever technicians gaped. "They'd just arrived. We barely had time to get them into beds before you came."

The technician's feet left the ground, and he slammed into the wall. Dania gasped, stepping between the technician and her sponsor. "Ada, we need all our medical practitioners. I understand you are angry, and possibly ill due to their negligence, but they're doing their best."

Geron's heated gaze switched to her, and Dania did her best to hold that gaze. Her hands trembled, but she tried to channel the energy she'd had in her previous life, where she'd been unafraid of the power coursing through his veins.

He growled, and the technician slid to the floor.

The room remained still.

"My general, as usual, gives good counsel. Be clear that I am still angry none of you realized this, but I understand."

He walked in and out of the rows of beds. "How many of the rest of them are Bane?"

The technician he'd thrown across the room dusted himself off and grabbed the handheld computer he'd dropped. "From the initial scans, it appears only three of those remaining in this room are Bane."

Only three? That left twenty-one more that Geron wouldn't be able to help.

Geron eased onto the edge of a mattress. "If I try to help those who aren't Bane, will I see similar results?"

The technician sighed. "I'd say *yes*. And I would imagine it would have an increasingly negative effect on you, sir, so I would caution against trying."

The retching enforcer in the back went silent, and the attending physician pulled a covering over her face.

Geron closed his eyes. "Are you telling me they are all going to die?"

The technician handed him another mug of blue liquid. Interesting that he seemed to have no hard feelings about being thrown across the room. "They've lost their sponsors. In the general order of things, they are no longer needed. Once an enforcer runs out of energy, they die. It's simply the way it is."

Geron seemed to contemplate that, before he turned to Dania. "You look close to death, but you're fine. How have you lived so long without being fed?"

Dania gulped. The answer was simple, but she wasn't sure he'd want to hear it. "You met the *Star Renegade*'s doctor. Kile and Orion were correct that he is not legally a doctor, but he's brilliant. He developed some sort of artificial primordial energy. It doesn't give me any power, but it counteracts any degradation to my internal organs caused by the lack of feeding."

He stared at her, as if not quite comprehending.

Maybe she needed to cut to the base truth. "He found a way to artificially feed me just enough to keep me alive."

His lips twisted into a sneer. "It disgusts me that you had to resort to something unnatural. I'm sorry I didn't get to you sooner."

Another enforcer started to retch.

Geron sighed. "Is that one Bane?"

The physician shook his head. "No, sir."

Dania's heart sank. Did that mean all they could do was watch him die?

Geron's lips thinned as the physicians tried to help the dying enforcer. They all looked lost. Hopeless.

Geron took a drink of the blue liquid, then held the mug a few inches from his lips, studying the contents as if it held a world of answers.

He took another sip, then placed the mug down beside him. "Bring me the ones I *can* save."

The physician raised a brow. "I highly suggest you rest, sir. At least let us examine you to see why you are feeling ill."

Geron stood. "I gave you an order. I will not stand here and watch enforcers die if I can help them." He turned to Dania, his lips still twisted in disgust. "Bring me the smuggler's doctor. Now."

CHAPTER 10
CAL

CAL PAUSED outside Dania's door. She wasn't inside and hadn't been since they'd been captured. Knowing that crushed him, but he also felt a little warmer standing near that door, like he could feel her presence.

Which was absolutely ridiculous. He knew that, but he'd hold on to any bit of hope he could that she'd return to them with her humanity intact.

Doc walked toward him from the opposite end of the hall. "Taking a few deep breaths before dealing with our pirate brethren?"

Cal glanced at the entrance to Engineering across the hall. "Yeah, maybe. Every time we get together, they pick a fight."

"Most of the time, it's with each other."

"True. I'm a little nervous to look into the storage area they're living in."

Doc nodded. "At this point, you may want to offer an olive branch and give them some better living arrangements."

"We only have one more living space available."

"Yeah, but the unfinished rooms on the other end of the ladder are more than big enough to house a few people each.

I can't spare any cots from the med bay, but we can probably find more blankets and stuff in the emergency supplies to make them more comfortable."

Cal nodded. "Yeah, that's probably a good idea, and it might keep them from killing each other." He headed for the entrance to upper Engineering. "Let's get this over with."

Ethan let out a big breath and clapped his hands once when they'd entered. "The boss is here. Thank goodness." He waved them down to the lower level. "We've been discussing our progress."

Cal took the stairs down and scanned the room. Ethan and Alanna stood close to the aft intake manifold while the pirates scattered around the rest of Engineering. Ty had stayed on the bridge to keep an eye out for unwanted visitors and Cal supposed Rachel was keeping tabs on their guests in the med bay.

Chris Columbus pushed away from the wall. "We've been pulling all the panels out and reversing the wiring to run power back to Engineering. It's been tedious, but we're making progress."

"They're doing great," Ethan said. "We're pretty close to schedule."

Victor folded his arms. "We'd go faster if we didn't have to slink round and hide. I feel like a rat in a cage."

Cal folded his own arms, taking on a stance similar to the pirate. "I only have a temporary reprieve for my own crew—not for the rest of you. I highly doubt that those new enforcers would have any trouble with striking down a known pirate—so you all need to keep a low profile. That's not negotiable."

"You say that because you're not the one crawling around in walls and sleeping on beds made out of cans."

"Hey!" Chris poked Victor with his index finger. "For the first time in your life, someone cares whether or not you live or die, so I'd show some respect if I were you."

The pirate blushed, looking down and nodding.

Chris turned to Cal. "As you were, Captain."

Good. It seemed like Chris had managed to gain the pirates' respect. As long as that stayed true, things had at least a chance of running smoothly.

"Doc and I were just discussing your living arrangements. We have a few more storage spaces. We can try to split you all up a little to give you some more privacy."

Victor sucked on the inside of his cheek. "I guess that's better than the closet. We certainly won't say *no* to more space."

The other pirates shifted their weight. Under other circumstances, Cal might have been afraid they'd try to mutiny. Things being as they were, though...where would they go if they even tried?

Alanna pointed to the cables overhead. "We've only been able to connect one of the relays, so I've started some testing on the overall weapons realignment. I think it's going to work."

"You *think* it's going to work?" Iggy, Victor's former pilot, scratched his thick beard. "You got us all doing this rewiring and you're not sure?"

Cal stepped between them. "Nothing like this has ever been tried before. I think it's pretty safe to say that no one has ever had the opportunity to blast out of a royal cruiser, so we're writing the book here, people."

"So, you're telling me this big master plan for escape is based off a weapons modification that may have no chance of working?"

Ethan laughed. "Welcome to life on the *Star Renegade*."

Cal shook his head. There really wasn't much more to say about that. "Let's keep at it." He turned to Alanna. "If you even get a *spark* of a feeling this won't work, I want to know. If we need to pivot, I want to pivot fast."

She saluted. "Aye-aye, Captain."

Cal headed up the stairs and through the door.

Doc followed into the hall. "That could have gone worse."

"It sure could have gone better, too." Cal rubbed the back of his neck. "I don't trust our guests. I'm not used to all that negativity."

"I guess the crew hasn't started to rub off on them yet." Doc pointed his thumb over his shoulder. "I'm heading back to the med bay. Are you okay?"

Cal nodded, glancing at Dania's door. "Yeah, I want to get back to the bridge."

"Worrying about her isn't going to bring her home faster."

Maybe not, but that didn't mean he was going to stop doing it.

———

Cal stood beside his console on the *Star Renegade*'s bridge, leaning toward the main screen overlooking the cruiser's cargo hold. Technicians walked past, most barely even noticing—or pretending not to notice—the enforcers standing guard around the *Star Renegade*.

It seemed like Dania had been gone forever already.

He dragged his fingers through his hair and paced the small area between Alanna's station and the wall. Dania hadn't even tried to argue when Kile had come for her. Had she given up on freedom? Given up on *Cal*?

He rubbed his eyes. The not knowing was driving him crazy. They'd been so close to making a life together. It seemed like a nightmare that everything they'd built could be taken away so easily.

Ty reached out and grabbed his arm. "Boss, you're going to wear a hole in the deck. Pacing is not going to bring her back any sooner."

A blue-skinned technician stopped and spoke to an enforcer before continuing past the ship. This was their everyday…their jobs. They just went through the motions again and again, like people's lives weren't on the line.

Cal puffed out a breath. "The waiting is driving me insane."

"No, really? I hadn't noticed."

Cal flopped into his chair. "Aren't you worried?"

"Hell yeah. Not just for Dania, but for all of us. But getting yourself sick over it isn't going to help you, and it certainly isn't going to help Dani. You need to get a hold of yourself."

Cal rubbed his eyes. "I know you're right. It's just hard."

"I get it." He pursed his lips, looking out the window. "Looks like we've got incoming."

Outside, Kile stormed toward the ship until he disappeared beneath them. "What does he want?"

Ty tapped on his panel, and the screen in front of them changed three times before finding Kile in the hallway a few steps from the ladder leading to the cargo area. "Looks like he's headed to the med bay."

"Let's see if I can beat him there."

Cal raced down the hall and turned the corner just as the

door to the med bay closed. Cal slapped his hand on the access pad and squeezed through the doors before they'd even opened.

Kile glared at him. "You do not need to be here."

"Yeah? Well, my ship, my rules. What do you want?"

Doc wiped the edge of a flask with a cloth…like having a fully-fed enforcer in his medical bay was no big deal. "Apparently, Big Bad wants me to go with him. I was about to explain that I have a med bay filled with patients."

Which was true. Once again, all the beds were full.

Kile grimaced. Or kept the same expression. It was hard to tell sometimes. "Prince Geron has requested your presence. Your compliance is not optional."

Doc put down the flask. "Well, then, that wouldn't be a request, then, would it? That sounds more like a demand."

Kile narrowed his eyes. "A request from a Bane is one and the same. You will stop what you are doing and come with me now."

Rachel appeared from the back of the room. "You know, you didn't used to be such a jerk."

Kile's gaze remained on Doc. "Now."

Cal shifted his weight. It wasn't too long ago that Rachel had had this massive death machine at her beck and call. Now, he acted like she wasn't even there.

Cal gulped. Was this why Dania hadn't returned? Had her memory of Cal also been completely erased?

Doc held up his hands. "Fine. Rachel, I trust you can take care of things while I'm gone?"

She shrugged. "Sure, as long as they don't start dying."

Cal grabbed Doc's arm. "You're not leaving the ship."

"He doesn't have a choice," Kile said.

"Cal…" Doc pulled his arm from Cal's grip. "We're

already screwed. There's no reason to make it worse on any of us."

"Then I'm coming with you."

Kile unfolded his arms. "Your presence is not required."

"I get that. Your prince said to bring the doctor, but did he say *not* to bring me? How can you be sure he didn't want me, too?"

Kile sighed. "Very well. But you will be watched."

Doc walked to the door. "Of course we'll be watched. Because one little human is going to do so much damage to your giant, impenetrable cruiser."

Doc was going a little heavy on the snark today. He was starting to sound a little more like Ethan. Then again, they'd all been living on zero sleep since being swallowed by the prince's ship. He was bound to snap sooner or later.

Cal followed Doc out and shouted over his shoulder. "Rachel, let everyone know where we're going."

She nodded, but her eyes were on Kile's back as he passed through the door. Cal couldn't even imagine what she was going through. She was living the nightmare that Cal and Alanna feared most...losing the person they loved but still having to gaze into the eyes of a stranger who looked just like them. Cal knew he might be walking right into his own nightmare, but he was tired of waiting. He needed to know what was going on.

The Kever ship had high ceilings...which made sense, with Kevers being so tall. The walls were starkly metallic and buffed to a shine. This ship had obviously never been boarded and had probably not seen battle of any kind. If everything they'd heard about what was going on in the galaxy was true, Cal wondered how long that would last.

The hallways seemed to go on forever, and the group

barely passed another person. Was the cruiser short staffed, or was the ship so big that the crew was simply scattered? He'd hoped to possibly run into Dania, but with a ship this size, she could be anywhere.

He sped up so he was closer to Kile. "We haven't heard from Dania."

"Of course not."

Cal's chest clenched. Did that mean she was already gone? "Do you know where she is?"

"On the command deck, doing her duty. I assure you, she will no longer have time to play useless games with smugglers."

Useless games? Heat coursed through Cal's veins.

Doc grabbed Cal's arm and shook his head. "Not worth it, boss."

Dania was definitely worth it.

Picking a fight with a walking death machine, though, wasn't the best plan. Doc was right about that.

A door opened as Kile approached, and they stepped inside.

"The smuggler's doctor, as requested, Ada." He grabbed Cal by the back of the neck and shoved him forward. "And the smuggler as well, who apparently is looking forward to a speedy execution."

The Kever glanced at Doc, and then Cal. His coloring seemed lighter, but Cal wasn't sure if that meant he was pale, or something completely different. The room was lined with beds, just like their own med bay, and they were all filled with silver-haired enforcers attached to medical equipment. A few were awake, but most of them seemed unconscious.

What was going on?

The prince returned his attention to Doc. "You've polluted Dania's blood."

Doc shrugged. "That's one way of thinking about it."

"She should be dead, but whatever you did to her allows her to live."

Doc nodded. "Yeah. I pretty much had her cured until you gave her another taste of whatever it is that you do to juice them up with power."

The Kever's eyes widened, narrowed, and then widened again. It was possible that words like 'juice' and 'taste' weren't translating well. Which was probably good, because pissing off a guy who could melt the skin off your bones wasn't the best idea.

Geron's gaze carried over the beds. "I cannot save these enforcers. Our bloodlines are not compatible."

Not compatible? How was that even possible? The Banes stole kids…human kids, and changed them at a cellular level, turning them into mindless killing machines wrapped up in sparkly-white enforcer uniforms.

"Where'd they even come from?" Cal asked.

"Inconsequential," Kile said.

Doc walked over to one of the beds. "Not really. These aren't the ones from our ship." He frowned. "Are your enforcers dying, too?"

Kile stepped between him and Geron. "Of course not, you fool." He turned toward the prince. "Ada, this man continues to prove he's not worth your time. This is a mistake."

The prince held up his hand, silencing the commander before turning back to Doc. "These are not my enforcers. They belonged to other Kevers who died in battle."

Doc cocked his head. "And you can't fix them like the ones on our ship?"

"No. The enforcers on your ship belonged to my sister. We share the same bloodline. We are similar enough that I could recode her enforcers to me. These, I cannot save."

Cal shifted his weight. He had a bad feeling there was a reason the prince had asked for the smartest person from Cal's crew. He eyed the door, but he wasn't sure where they'd go, even if he could get Doc out of there.

Geron stood, looming over Doc. "You will do whatever you did to Dania to these enforcers."

Doc's eyes widened. "What?" He scanned the room. "I'm just one person, and I have nowhere near enough supplies to treat all these people."

Two of the enforcers who were awake looked at Doc. One of them closed their eyes and flopped their head back on the bed. They seemed oddly lost and defeated for enforcers.

Geron shoved Doc toward the exit. "Remove yourself. Now."

Doc stumbled, then started floating above the floor as the prince followed him out.

Kile grabbed Cal's arm and dragged him through the door with them. The translator-guy slipped into the hallway just before the door closed and then stood by the wall.

Geron flicked his wrist and Doc's feet met the ground again. "How dare you deny treatment directly in front of dying soldiers? If you are a doctor, like you claim, you should understand they need hope."

Doc huffed a mirthless laugh, shaking his head. "It's the truth. I don't have the supplies for that many people."

"There are more patients than those in that room," Kile said.

Doc gaped. "You have to be kidding me."

"We're told there are hundreds. We only had them bring in the sickest."

Doc dragged his fingers through his hair. "I may be able to save one. Possibly two. But no more."

Kile stormed toward him, heat irradiating the air around him. "You will not tell the prince what you cannot do. You will comply."

"Without supplies? Do you want me to pump them full of placebos and hope for a miracle?"

Geron started walking. "Come."

Kile grabbed both Cal and Doc and dragged them through the hall to keep up with Geron's considerably longer gait.

The prince walked through a door and the lights came on. A long, glossy table seemed to hover on its own accord in the center of the room. As each of them entered, a chair slid from the wall to a place around the table. Cal couldn't tell if that was some sort of automation, or if the prince had done it. The translator entered last and leaned against the wall, once again becoming part of the scenery.

"Sit." Geron took one of the chairs and rubbed his eyes. "You say you don't have enough supplies. What do you need?"

Doc rattled off all the supplies, and how they were used. The prince made a good show of nodding and pretending he understood what Doc was saying, but he suspected the Kever was just as lost as Cal was.

When Doc finished, Geron drew a few invisible symbols on the tabletop with his fingertips, and a computer-like screen rose out of the glossy surface. Kever characters scrolled on the screen, and after a few more swirls on the table, the characters changed to English.

"The computer just searched my ship and all the ships surrounding us. It appears we have most of what you need."

Cal glanced at Doc. *All the ships surrounding them?* Cal had only been worried about the ship that had swallowed them. He had no idea there were more out there.

Doc read the inventory of supplies. "This is quite an eclectic list, and it looks like there are a lot of ships out there. Do you always travel with an entourage?"

"Before today? Never. They are here out of necessity. For protection."

Interesting. Why would they all flock to a prince known for partying or otherwise lounging about the galaxy? There had to be someone—hell, *anyone*—better to protect them than this guy.

Geron's thick jawline flexed in what may have been a grimace. "I watched two enforcers die today and there was nothing I or my medical staff could do to save them. These people need my help."

This guy sounded almost like a thinking, caring being, not a Kever monster. What game was he playing, and if this were a trap, how could he make sure not to fall right into it?

Doc sat back and puffed out a breath. "If there really are hundreds more sick enforcers out there, this still won't be enough, and there are a few things missing."

"I've already asked for the bloodlines of the sick to be checked so we will know which I can save naturally. The rest, I need you to keep alive until we can find them a suitable sponsor willing to take them on."

Willing to take them on? That meant that most Kevers would probably be liable to stand there and let them die, which sounded about right. Geron had nearly passed out after recoding just a few of them. The high and mighty

Kevers were probably too lazy to do the work. Which wasn't really a surprise to Cal. Their entire race wasn't exactly known for humanitarianism.

Doc bit his lip as he scrolled through the available supplies. "The big thing I'm missing on this list is a conductive liquid polymer, but we should be able to get that almost anywhere. It's cheap and accessible."

Geron glanced at Kile, who tapped a few times on the invisible keys on the tabletop. The screen changed, showing a standard planetary star map, but with a jagged red line running across it, and the upper part shaded in pink. "Can you get this polymer anywhere outside the shaded area?"

Cal frowned. Most of the star map was in the shaded area.

Doc rubbed his chin. "Sure. Themyscira is one of the main production sites. But I'm not all that sure they'd be happy to see a convoy of Kever ships near their border."

An interesting problem. One that might just benefit them both.

Cal leaned on the edge of the table. "The *Star Renegade* trades on Themyscira all the time. They'd welcome us—if we weren't currently locked in a cargo hold."

Kile folded his arms. "When the *Star Renegade* leaves our possession, the crew will not be on board."

Geron continued to look at Doc. "Can you get the other supplies you need on Themyscira?"

"Yeah, normally. They have a robust scientific community and make their own goods. Everyone's been tight with supplies lately, though, so I can't be sure. But they're our best bet."

Geron tapped the table a few times, and the screen glowed orange. "Change course for Themyscira."

A voice answered in the Kever tongue, but the translation

didn't manifest in Cal's head. Was the translator keeping them in the dark on purpose, or did he figure it wasn't important enough to waste the energy?

The prince tapped more keys, and the screen turned orange again. "Get me a list of all scientists or researchers not directly needed in the infirmaries. Prepare them for reassignment."

Another un-translated voice answered before the prince returned his attention to Doc. "You also mentioned being 'only one person.' I will give you all the staff I can spare, and more as the infirmaries clear. They will be at your disposal, and you will utilize them to make your synthetic life-prolonging amalgamation."

Kile eased closer. "Ada, I think this is a mistake. All records of this man's work should be eradicated."

"Possibly." The prince perused his fingernails. "But at the moment, the amalgamation works to my benefit."

Which meant that Doc's death sentence was on hold at least until his services were no longer needed. "My crew can help as well. They've been helping treat Dania, so they're the most qualified to assist." They'd been helping treat Alexander as well, but it might be best if he didn't mention that yet.

Kile glared at him. "You are searching for reasons to stay your executions."

"Of course I am. But that doesn't change the fact that it's the truth. You spent time on my ship. You know my crew values life. Even yours, despite you betraying us. They'll help."

"Does he speak the truth?" Geron asked.

Kile closed his eyes. It looked like he didn't want to

answer, but it seemed none of them could deny a request from their sponsor.

"Yes," Kile admitted. "I have seen callous disregard for their own safety in hopes to save others. They can be trusted on this task. However, they cannot be trusted not to take advantage of any chance they discover if they think it will help them escape."

Geron held his gaze. "Fine. Since you are familiar with the smuggler crew, it will be your responsibility to monitor them."

Kile's eyes widened slightly before he inclined his head "Yes, Ada."

The prince returned his attention to Doc. "I will officially place you in charge of this project. All personnel will report to you, and you will report to me through the commander." Geron turned to Cal. "Is this agreeable with you, Mr. Espinoza?"

Cal gaped. "Are you *asking me* if this is okay?"

"This man is part of your crew. I am assigning him a task that will take every waking moment of his time. It is customary to check with a soldier's superiors before re-assigning them." He looked at his fingernails again. "There is no reason to act uncivilized, even when you are dealing with criminals."

Interesting, that this self-righteous prince had any moral code at all, but Cal would play since it suited him. This would make Doc and the crew even more valuable to the Kevers, and if this bought them a little more time, then that was a win-win for everyone.

Cal nodded. "Yeah, I agree. But I won't have you running him into the ground. He needs sleep, and he needs some down time. If I think Doc or anyone in my crew is working too hard, I reserve the right to call them back."

"Agreed."

Kile clenched his fists. "Ada, you are giving them too many concessions. They will use those to their advantage."

Geron's icy, reptilian eyes lanced the commander. "Is your fear that they are more intelligent than you, Kile? Are you concerned they will best you and do something to my ship?"

Kile gulped. "Of course not."

"Then I order you to be okay with this decision."

Kile lowered his head. "Yes, Ada."

Cal kept his breathing steady, despite the rising heat in the room—this time, coming from the prince. For now, they had a reprieve. Cal needed to make sure they kept finding ways to be indispensable so they had more time to do exactly what Kile had said they'd do...take advantage of the prince's hospitality and blast out of his star-forsaken cargo hold the first chance they got.

CHAPTER 11

DANIA

DANIA MOVED THROUGH THE CLEAN, stark halls. The wide corridors were a welcome reprieve from the stifling closeness of the *Star Renegade*. The cool, slightly humid air wrapped her like a hug from home. But, if Peter was telling the truth, Keveron had never been her home. She'd been stolen from her parents—or paid for, depending on how one read the records. Either way, she'd been taken to Keveron and changed…made into an enforcer.

She should have hated the Kevers for many reasons. Everything about this ship should have appalled her. But it didn't. It all felt so completely right.

She choked down the thought and continued down the hall. Geron's cruiser had a perfectly functioning communication system. She didn't need to deliver this message to him on her own, but security had informed her that Kile had not only brought Peter on board the cruiser, but Cal as well. Cal, of course, would have a double reason for risking himself. He'd want to protect Peter in any way he could, but he no doubt wanted to find out about Dania's condition. Chances were, Kile would be abstract at best and would probably refuse to answer any of the crew's questions concerning her status.

Cal must have been going insane, wondering if she'd been made whole again. She needed to let him know she was okay, at least for the time being.

The door to the secondary deck meeting room opened as she approached, and she stepped inside. Her gaze immediately locked with Cal's. His eyes were wide as they carried over her opalescent enforcer uniform. The last time she'd worn this attire, she'd threatened to kill him. That seemed like so long ago, but at the same time, it seemed like yesterday.

A few tendrils of her hair still danced about her face, the remnants of the power Geron had started to give her, but her hair hadn't completely lightened into the enforcer's shimmering silvery-white yet, and despite changing back into an opalescent-white uniform, she probably appeared remarkably human still, especially among her enforcer brethren. Still, he paled, maybe wondering how much of Geron's power she'd absorbed.

Kile frowned at her. "Why are you here? Who is in charge of the command deck?"

Did he think her incompetent? "The captain, of course."

"And Orion?" Kile asked.

"Observing only." And she'd keep it that way. This was her ship, and she refused to allow him to manipulate himself into a position of power simply on the merits of who his sponsor was. She turned to Geron. "There is a priority call for you, Ada. Royal signatures."

Geron looked bored, as usual. Calls from home rarely went well. His father was low on praise and high on condemnation. He'd never even called Geron by name, normally referring to him as *Number Eight*. Although after Zindiria's unexpected demise, she supposed that designation was now *Number Seven*.

Geron moved to the panel on the far wall and scrawled his finger over the touchpad. The temperature about him spiked, as it normally did any time he received a communication from home.

Cal stepped beside her. "Are you okay?"

Kile folded his arms. "Of course she's okay, you fool. She's back where she belongs."

Cal scowled at him. "How about you let her answer?"

"I'm fine. Geron has been too busy with the wounded to feed me." Dania filled Cal and Doc in on the arrival of the new ships, and how they'd changed location. As she had assumed, Kile had been purposely vague with them on the full details of their situation.

Kile shifted his weight. "They are prisoners. They don't need this information."

She glared at him. "According to the communications, the doctor has been given a temporary pardon in exchange for his help in treating the enforcers. That makes them allies, not prisoners."

"There is a very fine distinction between the two."

"But a distinction, it is."

Geron closed the communication. Instead of returning to the group, he stared at the blank screen. Communications from his father always infuriated him. It was usually best to keep out of Geron's way in times like these, rather than risk his anger.

The air in the room warmed with glorious, sweet primordial heat. However, Geron didn't throw balls of fire at the wall. He didn't spew defamatory rhetoric against his father.

He simply stood, facing the blank screen. What could possibly have been in that communication?

She approached slowly, staying in his periphery, waiting to be addressed, rather than risking unwanted attention landing on her.

His expression seemed vacant. Lost. "Dania?"

"Yes, Ada."

His gaze remained on the screen, as if he could see something other than blank pixels. An icy swirl ghosted over the power emanating from him—an odd mix of emotions she'd never experienced from her sponsor.

She inched closer. "Ada?"

He turned to her, his eyes oddly pensive, or possibly concerned. "My father and brother have called me home. Colima and Olom are dead."

The air about Dania grew thick. Colima and Olom were Geron's older sister and brother. They were Prime Five and Prime Seven. Or, they had been before Zindiria had died. But if they were now gone...

Geron's breaths were shallow. "They want me to take Olom's place in the ranks."

First Zindiria, and now Colima and Olom? How was this possible? "What happened?"

"Colima has been gone for weeks already." He shook his head. "I had no idea."

He hadn't known about Zindiria's death, either. Did that bother him?

"Olom's ship was destroyed yesterday while protecting Reglia. The planet was saved, but..."

But at too high a cost.

Reglia was on the outskirts of the Earthan Cradle. It was

the closest planet to Bane space, well out of the reach of the Carteks. "How is that possible?"

"It's not. None of this is." He rubbed his face. "What's going on? This isn't how things are supposed to be."

No, it certainly wasn't. Dania and her enforcers were his private guard, but they were also meant to be an army for the king to pull from as needed. The most she'd been called to do, though, was track down and execute criminals on occasion. But they were always small interplanetary matters. Deaths among the Banes were unheard of. Which, she supposed, was normal since her entire life had been lived in relative peace.

"What are you going to do?" she asked.

Geron took a deep breath and hissed on the exhale. "I'm certainly not taking Olom's place. Even before our sisters' deaths, he had...*responsibilities*."

Something Geron had avoided his entire life. But with both Zindiria, Colima, and now Olom gone, this may no longer be an option for him. What this meant for her, or even worse, for the *Star Renegade* crew, she didn't know.

The stars in the window began to shift.

"Are we moving?" Geron asked.

"It appears so." Dania tapped the panel, calling the command deck. "Captain Quaren, who authorized the course change?"

"We received a direct communication from the High Prince. He ordered Commander Orion to bring the ship home."

Dania gaped at the speaker. "We did not allow that order."

"I understand, General, but the high prince gave the order himself. I couldn't refuse."

No, he couldn't. The high prince would have ordered Orion to execute the captain and face the consequences with Geron after the fact. "I understand."

"I do not." Geron stormed toward the door.

Cal grabbed Dania's arm, stopping her from following. "I don't want to go anywhere near the Kever home world."

Dania didn't, either, but it was a little hard to refuse when the only ship on which she could escape was locked tightly in Geron's cargo hold.

CHAPTER 12

ALEXANDER

ALEXANDER MOVED QUICKLY through the halls of Geron's cruiser, ignoring the intense feeling of familiarity…of home. This ship was no longer his home, though. He belonged where Alanna was, and Alanna was on the *Star Renegade*. And she'd stay there, if he had any say in it.

Still, the sudden change of course was disconcerting. As much as he wanted to stay away from Geron, and even Kile, he needed to know what was going on.

A surge of primordial energy swirled around him, and Alexander skidded to a stop as the doorway to the secondary deck meeting room opened and Geron stomped out, Kile following close behind.

Geron called over his shoulder. "Get me ten of our strongest enforcers and meet me on the command deck."

"Of course, Ada." Kile glanced at Alexander before turning down the opposite hall.

Alexander fell in step beside the prince. He was one of Geron's strongest enforcers. At least he had been, before being away for so long. If Geron needed his strongest, Alexander would remain at his side until ordered otherwise.

His chest tightened as he looked back down the hall that led to the cargo bay, and the *Star Renegade*, though. Belonging in two worlds was getting increasingly hard.

Heat rolled off Geron's scaly blue-and-green skin, the energy filling the hallway.

"Is everything all right, Ada?"

"I'm angry."

This, Alexander could tell on his own. Geron rarely effused power unintentionally. Then again, if he was angry enough, maybe having primordial energy primed at his fingertips was entirely intentional.

Alexander struggled to keep up with Geron's gait before the prince shoved a bolt of energy in front of them, forcibly opening the door of the command deck before they'd even reached it.

The deck crew jumped to attention as Geron entered. "Belay the order to return to Keveron. Resume the course I gave you."

Orion folded his arms. "The high prince called directly and gave us our new course."

Geron's eyes narrowed. "This is not my brother's ship."

"An order from the high prince is an order from your king."

"On this ship, orders come from me." Geron turned back to Captain Quaren. "Resume the original course. Now."

The captain bowed. "As you direct, sir."

Orion unfolded his arms. "You cannot disregard an order from the king."

"Why not? I've been doing so for years." Geron scrawled circular shapes on a control panel, probably more to annoy Orion with his lack of interest than actually doing anything.

Kile arrived with Shivana, Miguel, and several of the new

enforcers. They panned out, standing along the walls like an honor guard.

Orion glanced at them before he stormed toward the captain. "Send this ship home."

Geron continued to gaze into a screen that seemed to be scrolling too fast to read. "We'll go home eventually. But first I have an inordinately high number of enforcers who need medical care. We are stopping at Themyscira for supplies and then I'll consider my brother's request."

"*Consider?*" Orion spoke through clenched teeth. "A call from the king cannot be ignored."

"Really?" Geron turned from the screen. "Once, I raced home when my father called on a secure line at top priority. When I arrived at Keveron, two medical vessels were detained to allow my expedient arrival. When I got to him, he made me wait three hours, only to find out he wanted to ask me a simple question that could have been taken care of through an interplanetary communication."

Orion lowered his eyes, and then raised them. "The king does prefer to speak in person."

"And is that always necessary?"

Orion's expression became stony. This probably meant that he agreed that many of House Bane's requests were not emergencies, but he'd never speak out against the king. Geron shouldn't have, either, but it obviously had never stopped him before. The queen had mentioned in her journals...which Alexander had *borrowed* in one of his more foolish escapades as a child...that she'd felt Geron had been acting out for attention since his father had spent all his time grooming the three children he'd been priming for places of power.

Geron was more complicated than a simple child acting

out, though. It was less a call for attention, and more an act of spite. With a direct call to return home, Geron might purposely avoid Bane space. They might not get near Keveron for years. Which might not be a bad thing.

Geron perused his fingernails. "Is my father's impatience worth the chance of risking the lives of the severed enforcers?"

Orion looked down again before taking a steadying breath. "They aren't your concern."

"They became my concern when they showed up and asked for my help."

"Since when do you care about anyone but yourself?" The commander's cheeks flushed. "The galaxy is in danger. Stop playing the part of hero and do what you're told for once in your life."

Geron's lips thinned. Alexander expected a flush of power that didn't come.

But why? One thing Geron could be counted on for was losing his temper, and this occasion actually called for it.

Orion returned his attention to the captain. "Set a course for Keveron. Now."

"Do. Not." Dania's voice boomed through the command deck. She stood in the doorway, holding on to both sides of the frame, somehow appearing just as large and terrifying as if she'd grasped the power. She marched toward Orion. "This is my ship, and you will not give orders to my crew."

"You gave up your right to this ship the day you took up with smugglers. You no longer belong here." He gestured up and down at her. "Look at you. You are a withering shadow of who you once were."

"This. Is. My. Ship," she hissed through clenched teeth. "No one can take it from me, especially the likes of you."

"You're just a little girl. You never belonged here, anyway."

HEAT FLUSHED through Dania's veins. She itched to grasp her power, but none came. Orion's lips twitched slightly. He knew full well she didn't have the primordial energy to back up her bravado.

A trickle of heat ghosted over her skin and Dania flicked a glance at Shivana. Her lieutenant locked eyes with Dania and gave a quick nod. Shivana had been in one of the ships that had fired on Dania when she'd been defending the *Star Renegade* months ago, just before Dania had been accepted by her new family. Dania had thought there was no love lost between them, but Shivana obviously didn't like the comment about Dania being a *little girl*. Shivana flexed her hands slightly, primordial energy blurring the air about her fingertips. Dania took that as a show of solidarity.

Dania strode toward Orion with her head high. "I've *always* belonged here."

"You are nothing but a child pandering at the beck and call of a prince not worthy of his title."

Dania gaped before rage took over. She instinctively raised her hands and called on power that wasn't there. A burst of primordial energy came from her left, and another from her right, swirling through her hands and blasting against Orion's chest, tossing him against the wall. He coughed like the wind had been knocked out of him before he glared at her.

The absolutely stunned look on his face was fitting. Since her enforcers had channeled the energy into Dania's hands, he'd have no way to know the shove had not come directly from her—a *little girl* devoid of power.

Half that strength had come from Shivana. Dania didn't pause to see who else had helped, but it emboldened her to know her enforcers were back on her side.

She stormed toward Orion. "I have made grown men cower and beg for mercy. I will not be insulted on my own ship."

"Your sponsor is denying a direct order from your king. As a general, you answer to the king first. You know this."

Yes, this was true. Luckily, she was not fully fed, and she was able to bend the rules to her liking.

Geron moved behind her. "Stand down, Dania."

She turned to him. "I refuse to allow him to force himself on our command deck and—"

"Stand. Down." Geron's eyes were firm. Demanding.

Dania lowered her gaze. "Yes, Ada." He rarely admonished her, especially in front of her people. And never in front of another Bane's commander. Had Geron seen the bolt of power come from the others? Was that a reminder of how badly she needed to be fed?

Her hands clenched into fists. Any lack of primordial energy shouldn't have mattered. She was still the same general she'd always been. Geron had to have known that, or he wouldn't have placed her back in charge without feeding her.

Orion smirked at Geron. "I see you've finally come to your senses. Your father and brother will be pleased."

"Will they?" Geron twitched a finger on his left hand and Orion flew across the room, slamming against the wall, then the ceiling. He fell to the ground, coughed, and then flew back up to a standing position, hovering a few inches above the floor in front of Geron.

The commander grimaced, like he was trying to hide pain. "Your brother will hear of this."

"Will he?"

Flames exploded around the commander, and he fell to the ground, screaming.

Dania gasped, wide-eyed, before stepping between them. "Ada, I have to reiterate that killing your brother's commander would be unwise."

He glanced at her, and the fire went out.

Orion was on his hands and knees, parts of his uniform burned through and half his hair missing. He must have used his power to protect himself, or he'd already have been dead.

Geron crouched beside him. "Tell me, Commander. How many other commanders does my brother have?"

Orion groaned, then looked up. One of his eyes was blackened and closed. "Seven."

"Interesting. Do you really think he'll give you a second thought before assigning your duties to another? Do you really think you aren't replaceable?"

"I may be replaceable, but so are you."

Geron laughed, standing. Orion lifted off the ground and slammed into the floor again. The commander grunted like a thousand ships were piled on his back, pressing him to the hard, metal surface.

Dania opened her mouth to protest, but Geron held up a hand, silencing her.

Geron crouched again. "I ask one last time: Will my brother even miss you?"

Orion's one undamaged eye glared. "No. He wouldn't."

"Good." The temperature in the room cooled as Geron stood.

Orion took in a deep breath, pushing himself onto his hands and knees.

Geron perused his nails. "Now that we have an understanding, you *will not* give orders on my command deck. Ever. If you are here, it is as a guest, and for counsel only." Geron glanced at Dania before taking a step closer to Orion. "Be happy I don't make you kiss the *little girl*'s boots."

Orion kept his head down and nodded. "If I may counsel, then, it would be in your best interests to let your father know there will be a delay. Themyscira is in the opposite direction. It will add significant time to the voyage."

"I will take that into consideration." Geron turned from him. "Alexander, it appears Orion is having trouble with one of his eyes, and he's lost some hair. Please bring him to the infirmary and assist with his treatment."

Alexander inclined his head. "Of course, Ada."

Orion started to float, more gently this time, as Alexander guided him through the exit.

"Captain Quaren." Geron waited for the doors to close. "Erase all passcodes Orion has been using and restrict his use of the communications systems to those within this ship only. I won't have him running like a spoiled child and telling my brother I've treated him poorly."

"The high prince will eventually find out," Dania reminded him.

"Yes, but in my own time, when I want, and when I can have some control over the outcome."

Dania nodded, but she couldn't help but wonder if this one act of defiance might finally break his father's thinning patience. Geron's enforcers were strong, but they were few. There simply weren't enough of them if the entire might of House Bane were to fall on them.

CHAPTER 14
DANIA

DANIA STOOD on the command deck, centered between the massive screens showing the ships gathered around them. They'd become a small armada, although this armada was not meant for war. The ships around them were mostly people carriers, and the few warships appeared heavily damaged. She'd called for a survey of weapons and overall ship health and capability, but the information was still being compiled. She'd be surprised, though, if any of the ships out there had military value.

Orion shifted in her left peripheral vision, staying back against the wall...observing only, and giving counsel as needed. It had taken three days to heal his eye and the extensive tissue damage from nearly being burned alive, but Geron had made the necessary impression on the commander. Geron was a Bane, no matter the rank assigned to him at birth. He had a thousand times the power of Orion or any other enforcer. Orion had hidden behind the authority of the high prince for too long. He'd forgotten his place, and Geron had reminded him.

The commander had returned more complacent than

she'd ever seen him. Hopefully, he'd still have some use to her, other than cowering in the corner, inwardly judging those around him.

The communication's officer's station flashed once, and the Kever officer read the screen before standing, facing Dania. "General, Geron has requested your presence in the primary infirmary."

Dania flinched. There had been a time when her heart would have fluttered in anticipation when her sponsor called for her. But now her mild sense of panic dissolved into a deep dread. Any day now, Geron would decide to feed her. It was inevitable. Each breath of air she took out of her own free will could be one of her last, and nothing she'd done since returning to Geron's cruiser seemed worthy of her last free moments. She wished she'd had the opportunity to get away from the command deck and spend more time with the *Star Renegade* crew.

This cruiser was comfortable, maybe more comforting to her than the *Star Renegade*. But this place represented her previous life. If these were her final days, she wanted to spend them with friends.

However, she also knew the importance of keeping control. The best gift she could give the *Star Renegade* crew was to keep the enforcers occupied and steer their attention away from eliminating her new family.

Taking a steadying breath, she turned to Kile. "You have command until I return." She focused on Orion as she headed for the door. "Remember, you are here for counsel only."

Orion bowed slightly. "Of course."

Dania passed through the door, shaking her head. She wished she believed him. No doubt the simple show of

Geron's power had frightened the overbearing commander. But for how long? Eventually, the memory of the sting would dissipate, leaving only anger behind. If that should happen, she and her people needed to make sure Orion was dealt with before he could do any damage—either to the ship, or by following any previous directives from the high prince.

Dania headed toward the primary infirmary. She would have preferred to confine Orion in a cell, but Geron wanted to give him a chance. It was risky, and Geron normally wasn't the type to take risks. He possibly thought keeping Orion free would lessen the high prince's anger once he found out Geron had nearly burned one of his commanders alive. Dania doubted that would make a difference, though. His brother was just as temperamental as his father.

The infirmary door opened as she approached. Geron had kept her DNA signatures stored in the ship, despite her long absence. Her heart warmed each time the ship responded to her presence. That meant he'd never given up on her coming home.

She gritted her teeth and tried to push the warm feeling away. She needed to be calm and indifferent, especially now. Any break in decorum might take her one step closer to losing her freedom.

She stepped inside and instinctively scanned the room for her sponsor. She held her breath until their eyes met. Geron leaned against the edge of a bed. His eyes seemed slightly foggy, and his skin had paled.

He reached for her. "Dania."

She took two fast steps toward him before decreasing her pace. *Breathe in, breathe out. Slowly.* "You called for me, Ada?"

"Yes. I've helped all the enforcers in danger today. I'm tired, but I have enough energy to help you."

She stopped walking and managed a step back. "But, Ada, you look exhausted."

"Nothing sleep won't help. I've helped so many others. I need to take time for my own."

"The synthetic treatments are doing fine for me, Ada. There's no need for you to overexert yourself. There are far too many others in greater need." At least that was the truth, and he should already understand this argument.

He raised his hand, and her body slid along the floor to him. It was not an unkind or harsh gesture, but she shivered. It had been too long since she'd had no choices, and no control over her own life. His manipulation felt foreign and alien. Which was *exactly* what it was.

He dragged his fingers along her cheek. "Every time I see you, I'm reminded how much you need me. You're my responsibility, and I've neglected you for far too long."

Dania gritted her teeth as his energy skated across her skin. What he was incapable of understanding was that his neglect had allowed her to experience freedom for the first time. In this case, what he considered negligence was a priceless gift.

Still, the energy sparking across his fingers called to her, lulling her into a deep, warm, relaxed calm.

She leaned into his palm, and his hand heated, his touch offering so much more than comfort. Her skin started to tingle, and her head lolled back. A groan escaped her lips, followed by a soft whimper.

"It's okay." Geron pulled her tighter to him. "I'm here."

The door opened and Peter entered, pushing a gurney holding a male enforcer on it. "We got a new emergency, Your Highness-ness."

The heat on Dania's cheek winked out as Geron released her and stood.

The primordial energy ripped away from her skin, and she sucked in a deep breath. *Peter…Peter is here*. She clutched her chest. What had almost happened?

Her skin ached. Her muscles tingled as her cells cried out for the energy they'd been craving for far too long.

Geron sighed and took a step toward the doctor.

"No!" She reached for her sponsor. Why was he walking away? Didn't he know how badly she needed him?

He reached back and caressed her cheek again. "Just another moment. I promise."

She couldn't wait another moment. Her cells screamed, the ache exploding over every muscle in her body. She clung to the edge of the mattress as tears streamed from her eyes.

Peter locked the gurney he'd rolled into the room in place. "They brought this one in from one of the ships outside, but I'm already out of the synthetics I made last night. I can't do much for him."

Geron stood over the enforcer. "Is he Bane?"

"That's the catch. We don't know. There's no sign in the records that he passed out or had any of the bad reactions like the enforcers who lost their sponsors. The captain of his transport said Bob here was helping evacuate colonists when their ship was hit. He got knocked unconscious and didn't know who he was when he woke up."

Geron furrowed his brow. "Bob?"

"Yeah, that's what I've been calling him. He doesn't know who he is, but according to the captain, he still felt compelled to help the colonists, so his programming—or whatever you do to them—is still intact. He's just running out of the magic mojo that keeps these guys and gals alive."

"And his blood analysis?"

"Unfortunately, he's one of the few who's inconclusive. We have no idea if he's a Bane or not."

Dania moved beside them. "Ada, last time you accidentally tried to treat an enforcer who wasn't Bane, you killed them, and you got very ill." And that would waste pathogens meant for her! Dania's hands shook, her skin screaming to reach out and touch him.

"I don't need you to remind me of that, Dania." He looked at the patient. "How bad is he?"

"Very bad. He doesn't have long. Apparently, he was using his powers to try to help with repairs and just dropped."

"Can you wake him up?"

Peter nodded. "Yeah, but he won't be happy." He grabbed a small packet from a drawer, snapped it in two, and waved it under the patient's nose.

The enforcer's eyes sprang open. He coughed, then breathed heavily—nearly panting.

Of course he was panting. He craved primordial energy. Energy meant for Dania.

Peter turned to her and his brow furrowed.

He *should* have been concerned. She was dying!

Peter held up his hand and mouthed the word *'breathe.'*

Breathe? Of course she would breathe. What was that supposed to mean? Was the man as daft as Kile claimed?

The enforcer on the gurney glanced at each of them before entering his gaze on Geron. "What happened?"

"You're quite ill." Geron looked down at him. "Do you have any memory of who you are? Do you know if you're a DuBane?"

Dania took a deep breath and released it slowly. Oddly enough, the tingling in her skin began to subside.

Bob shook his head. "I have no recollection of my past. All I know is that I have this strong desire to help people and enforce the law." He closed his eyes and groaned. "I'm having trouble seeing."

Peter shook his head. Obviously, that wasn't good.

Geron continued to look at Bob. "There's a chance I can save you. But there is considerable risk to both of us. If you are not linked to a Bane, you might not survive."

The enforcer blinked and glanced to the side, as if contemplating the idea. "How long will I live if you don't try?"

"Maybe a few hours," Peter said.

Bob rubbed his hand across the edge of the bed before meeting Geron's gaze. "I feel compelled to survive. I understand I may die, but at least this gives me a chance."

Dania placed her hand on Geron's arm. "But, Ada, it will also hurt *you* if he's not Bane." And steal power he'd been about to offer to her!

Geron shook his head. "I can't just stand here and watch him die."

The doctor handed Dania a flask. "You should drink this, honey. It will make you feel better."

She flipped the bottle over in her hand. "What is it?"

His temperature flexed slightly. "Just electrolytes."

A lie, but she sensed no malice.

He gestured to the flask. "It's okay. It will give you a little boost." He leaned closer. "And I really think you need one."

The truth...interesting.

Geron held out his hand and Bob floated into his arms

and rested against his chest. The air about them heated, and Bob moaned.

So much for Dania getting her own feeding. She opened the bottle and took a sip. The draught chilled her throat, and she gulped it down until the bottle was gone.

The smuggler's doctor smiled. "That's my girl. Now just breathe through it. You'll be fine."

Bob's hair started to float as Peter ran an instrument over him.

"Looks like we have a winner. House Bane, it is. It's your lucky day, Bob."

Geron eased him back onto the bed. There was no screaming, no fighting. The enforcer simply lay back with his eyes closed, taking deep, long breaths.

"You didn't recode him," Dania said.

Geron shook his head. "He never showed symptoms of losing his sponsor. If there is a possibility his sponsor is alive, it would be wrong of me to recode him."

Not to mention exhausting. Geron rubbed his eyes. "Dania, I know I promised to take care of you, but once again, it seems I've put someone else's enforcer in front of your needs."

"Ada, I told you I'm fine. Saving him was the right thing to do." She frowned, holding up the empty bottle in her hand. A moment ago, she'd been ready to throw herself at Geron's feet again. What had Peter put in that bottle?

Peter winked at her and then ran an instrument over Bob. "He looks good. He's just asleep." He pointed the back end of the instrument at Geron. "Which, in my opinion, is what you need, too, Your Highness-ness."

Geron nodded. "On this, I can easily agree." He turned to Theon, who'd been standing by the wall, translating. "You may retire. Eat and get some rest yourself." He reached for Dania. "Will you walk me to my rooms?"

"Of course, Ada."

Peter gaped, looking from her, to Geron, and back. She wanted to assure him that everything would be fine, however she wasn't sure that was true.

Dania followed her sponsor out with her head low. Going to Geron's rooms normally meant staying the night for a full deep feeding…among other things. She'd given in so easily when he'd offered her a feeding earlier. How would she refuse if she were lying beside him?

As they approached his room, Geron glanced at her. "I need you to spend a considerable amount of time on the command deck. Constantly tending to the wounded is having more of an impact than I care to admit, and I'm afraid Orion will attempt to take advantage again."

"Kile is a capable commander."

"Yes, he is, but he's not Dania DuBane."

Unfortunately, neither was she at the moment.

The room opened as they approached, and Dania helped Geron to sit on the bed. She hated how frail he looked. Then again, even an exhausted Bane was deadly.

He rubbed his face with his hands. "What am I going to do? I can't hide from my father forever."

"When you do make it home, you'll simply listen to what he has to say."

"But he wants me to take a position of authority. I've never had authority. He's made a point of telling me my entire life how I wasn't as strong or as worthy as the others… How I was an embarrassment to the Bane name."

So, Geron had made a point of becoming a *genuine* embarrassment, taking advantage of his name and political standing to get whatever and whoever he'd wanted. Geron had learned to enjoy the finer things in life, while his brothers and sisters had prepared for politics and war. She could understand his trepidation. Nothing in his life had prepared him for this.

Dania folded her hands. "Well, you made two very authoritative decisions recently. You decided to go against your father's will to try to save lives. You also took a chance that you might hurt yourself when you decided to save Bob today. Someone *unworthy* wouldn't have done either of those things."

"That may be true, but I hope my brother's children come of age quickly so I can go back to being a useless embarrassment again." He tapped the bed beside him. "Come, lie with me. I don't have the strength to feed you, but I could still give you comfort."

Dania shook her head. "You just told me I needed to get back to the command deck. It's the right decision. I trust Kile. However, I don't trust Orion. I would feel better if I were up there."

He patted her knee. "Good counsel, as always, even though I don't like it."

She smiled and kissed his forehead. A slight tingle skated over her lips. "Goodnight, Ada."

Dania slipped off the bed before he could protest. Lying with him would have been the worst thing she could do. He was tired now, but he'd be fine in the morning. She needed to do everything in her power to keep away from him until he started expending energy saving the dying enforcers again. She'd gotten lucky three times, and Peter wasn't going to be there to save her forever.

WHEN CAL FOUND out Dania had gone back to the prince's room, he'd nearly blown a gasket. Alexander had been nice enough to show Cal where the prince's suite was and then he'd stayed with him to make sure he didn't do anything that would make the prince angry enough to kill him. It was probably a good call, because the longer Dania was behind that closed door with the man who'd stolen her life from her, the more he wanted to punch a hole through that wall and drag her out.

"There's no primordial energy in the air," Alexander said.

Cal kept staring at the door. "So?"

"So...he's not feeding her."

"Are you sure?"

Alex sighed. "As your doctor has pointed out, our dependency is very much like an addiction. Knowing, or *feeling* our sponsor feed another enforcer makes our bodies yearn for it, even if we're fully fed. Believe me, at this close range, I would know."

The door opened and Dania stepped out. She gaped, and her eyes widened as the door closed behind her.

"What are you doing here?" she whispered, looking over her shoulder at the door and the star-blasted prince on the other side.

Cal folded his arms. "The better question is, what are *you* doing here?"

She frowned at him, grabbing his arm and dragging him down the hall, away from the prince's room. Alexander stayed at the prince's door, tapping on a screen on the wall. Cal couldn't blame him. He probably didn't want to deal with an angry general, even if she was low on power.

Dania stopped, letting Cal go. "Geron needed me. It's not like I can tell him I'm busy."

Heat coursed through Cal's veins, probably hotter than any primordial energy they'd ever encountered. He grabbed her shoulders and searched her eyes. "Did he feed you?"

She still looked like Dania, sounded like Dania, but so had the monster who he'd dragged onto his slip in handcuffs so many months ago.

He slid one hand up to the base of her neck while stroking her hair back with the other. "Are you still...*you?*"

She grabbed his wrists, lowering his hands. "Of course I'm still me. I wouldn't be standing here talking to you if he'd brought me back."

That only made him feel slightly better. "Did you sleep with him?"

She let go of his hands, taking a step back. "What?"

"Did you *sleep with* him?"

She cocked her head to the left. "I'm not sure why that would matter anywhere near as much as a feeding."

Cal rubbed his face. "Look, I know you were raised in another culture, and you might find this ridiculous, but I'm only human, and it matters, okay? You and Alexander had a past with this guy, and human men are...well..."

She folded her arms. "Territorial? Suspicious? Unfoundedly jealous?"

Cal closed his eyes and took a deep breath. "Please tell me that it's unfounded."

Her eyes softened, and a smile played at her lips. She grabbed his shoulder and massaged it with her thumb. "It is. There wasn't even any sleeping. We talked."

"That's it?"

She closed her eyes and released him. "He did ask me to stay with him—for comfort, as he put it." She dragged her fingers through her hair. "But the reality is that he would be fully rested and strong in the morning, and the first thing he would have seen would be me, looking sickly in his eyes." She shook her head. "I know you think he's a monster, but he's concerned about me. He wants to save me."

"Saving is not what he'd be doing."

"I know that. You know that. Convincing Geron of that would be nearly impossible."

"So, we have to get off this blasted ship."

"Another thing that would be nearly impossible."

"Hey." He cupped her chin and lifted her eyes to his. "What happened to hope? What happened to beating this?"

Tears welled in her eyes. "I want to. You know I do. It's just..."

Two enforcers turned the corner and walked toward them. Dania stepped back and wiped her eyes before they neared.

The enforcers inclined their heads to Dania, ignored Cal, and headed down the hall toward Alexander.

Cal moved closer and whispered, "I care about you. I'm not willing to give up on you while I'm still breathing."

"I hope we're all still breathing when this is over."

She glanced back to the enforcers as they met Alexander in front of the prince's room. Her brow furrowed before she moved so that Cal's back was to them.

She eased closer and placed her hand on Cal's chest. "Please understand that I don't want Geron. I want you." Her voice was soft, barely audible. "I want the life you gave me. I want to live the rest of my life on your small, blast-stained ship."

Cal pointed to the walls around him. "And give up all this luxury?"

She licked her lips and smiled. "In a second."

The weight of the galaxy melted away. Cal leaned down to kiss her, but she held up her hand, shaking her head and looking past his shoulder.

Enforcers. Yeah.

Cal sighed and Dania stepped back as the two enforcers took places on either side of Geron's door, facing outward. Alexander said a few more words to them before he started down the hall toward Cal and Dania.

The enforcers standing guard were bad enough, but the biggest problem in the galaxy was on the other side of that door.

Cal leaned closer to her ear. "I feel like I can't protect you if you…" He swallowed the ball in his throat. "If you keep ending up alone with that prince."

She placed her hand over his heart again. "You can't protect me either way, Cal. You're just going to have to trust me." She gripped his shirt. "I *need you* to trust me."

Trust her? Cal's gut clenched. He wanted to trust her, but she had to realize what a precarious position she'd just put herself in by walking into that room alone with the one person they'd been trying to avoid.

Alexander reached them. "They'll guard our sponsor until he wakes." He waved for Cal and Dania to start walking. "I kept them busy while you were talking, but their interest was piqued. It's probably best that we relocate."

Behind them, the enforcers stared straight ahead, still on either side of the prince's door. Cal hadn't even considered they might have been able to hear from that distance.

Once they'd rounded a corner, Dania turned to Alexander. "Has Geron talked about feeding you at all?"

"No. I suppose I still look healthy enough. He seems very concerned about you, though."

"I've tried to explain that I'm fine."

"He knows you're stubborn, Dania. He probably doesn't believe you."

Which was exactly why Cal was so concerned. If this guy was a monster, or even if he really thought he was doing the right thing... Either way, he would be erasing the person Dania had become. It would be no better than killing her.

They moved farther down the hall, and Dania stopped at a communication pad. "I want to check on the command deck." Kile's face appeared on the screen. "Are you able to speak freely?"

"If you are asking if the high prince's commander is here, the answer is no. He is taking a meal, but I have no doubt he will return expediently."

"Has he been a problem?"

"Not as of yet, but as you directed, I have ten enforcers on the command deck at all times to make sure he stays that way."

"Excellent. You're handling him well, but Geron wants my presence on the command deck."

Kile frowned. "And you *are* present. Through me. If I may be mildly impertinent, General, you look worse with each passing day. At the moment, I think the best thing you can do is rest until you can be fed."

"You did hear that Geron wanted me, personally, did you not?"

The commander quirked a brow. "Did he say immediately, and without sleep?"

Cal smiled. Probably not. Enforcers, he'd found, were very good at manipulating orders when they saw fit. The prince had probably told her to spend more time on the bridge. Not necessarily *all* her time. That was definitely open to interpretation.

A slight smile played on Dania's lips. "Fine. I'll rest. Keep that full complement of enforcers with you and contact me if you need anything."

Kile stared at her through the screen. "I will *not* need anything."

"Of course you won't." She bit back a grin as the transmission ended, then she turned to Cal. "To be honest, a good rest sounds like good advice. Let's go home."

Now *that* sounded like the best idea Cal had ever heard. He waved for Alexander to follow. "Come on. I'm sure Alanna will be happy to see you haven't turned into an ice-cold death machine." He almost added 'yet' but managed to hold back the insult. He trusted Alexander to an extent, but not like the rest of his crew.

Dania moved ahead, Cal walking behind her, and Alexander in the rear. It was an odd formation, and in these wide halls, Cal itched to pick up his pace and walk beside her. He was a smuggler, though, on a ship filled with enforcers. He was a criminal here, and it was probably best to let Dania and Alexander lead until they were back in a safe space.

As soon as the three of them had cleared the cargo ramp and entered the *Star Renegade*, Alanna sprinted across the cargo deck and into Alexander's arms.

Tears streamed from her eyes. "I was so worried. I didn't know if you'd be coming back."

The sweet reverence in the way Alexander held Alanna made Cal hate himself for ever worrying about Alexander getting involved with her. Alanna had had a string of hard luck with men. The last thing she needed was another person she cared about turning on her, and in Alexander's case, it would be far worse than the last guy, who'd betrayed her and forced her to help him rob banks.

Of course, like Cal and Dania, Alanna's and Alexander's futures all depended on the whims of a prince who would probably blow a gasket if he knew Dania and Alexander genuinely cared about someone other than His Royally Uptightness.

Cal tapped Alexander on the back. "Why don't you two go back to your rooms and spend a little quality time?"

Alanna mouthed the words, *"Thank you"* before they walked arm in arm up the ramp to the crew quarters.

Hendry came from the rear storage area where most of Zindiria's sick enforcers awaited treatment. He focused on Alexander and Dania walking up the ramp before Bleven stepped out of the same room and moved beside him. Hendry's hair remained flat, while Bleven's hair floated about his head, still charged from his recent feeding.

They both watched as Alexander and Alanna disappeared into the ship.

"Things okay in the back?" Cal asked him.

"Until everyone is healed, they are as good as they can be." Hendry glanced back to the ramp. "I noticed Alexander's scent heavy on the navigator's skin. Are they involved in a physical relationship?"

Cal's gaze rolled over the two enforcers. One of these guys was running on Doc's artificial pathogens. The other was juiced up with the real stuff. This should be an interesting conversation.

Cal folded his arms. "Yeah, they are. I run a very open ship and let people live their lives with whoever makes them happy."

Bleven's hair danced about his head as his crystalline eyes trailed back up the ramp. His expression remained ghostly blank.

"Does the navigator make Alexander happy?" Hendry asked.

Dania nodded. "Very much so. They are each my friends, and I have to say that they are both better for their relationship."

His eyes trailed back to Dania. "Does the smuggler make *you* happy?"

Dania shifted, looking a little uncomfortable.

Cal tensed, waiting for her to deny it. She was a general and had everything to lose and nothing to gain from the enforcers knowing about the way she and Cal felt for each other. That blasted prince could still take everything away from them in an instant.

She lifted her chin. "Yes. Yes, he does make me happy."

Cal gaped. Had she forgotten that Geron had just taken

Bleven as his own? Certainly, he'd run back to the prince with this newfound information.

Bleven's brow creased. "Would you forsake your sponsor for this man?"

Dania's eyes widened. "How could you ask that? My love for my prince is still strong."

Cal startled. He wasn't sure what he'd expected her to say, but it sure as blazes hadn't been that. He knew she couldn't lie to them, and that just drove the knife deeper into his heart. How could she say she loved that monster?

She reached over and grabbed Cal's hand before turning back to Bleven. "What I have with Cal is different than our bond to our sponsor. It's not what we're used to or what we've been brought up to believe, but it's good."

"But taking time away from your sponsor is frowned upon."

Dania lifted her chin. "Maybe, but it makes me stronger."

Hendry glanced at Bleven, then back to her. "How could splitting your time between your sponsor and someone else make you stronger?"

She smiled at him. "It gives me balance. None of us is with Geron every waking moment. Having a life outside our work gives us time to discover new things. It gives us the opportunity to experience joy."

Bleven's head tilted in that strange, robotic style enforcers used before they ripped your head off. "These things are all distractions."

"Maybe, but they're good kinds of distraction. An enforcer simply needs to be strong enough to still do their duty when it's required."

Interesting wording in that sentence... An enforcer...

Their duty. Was she maybe not including herself in that? Did she really not think of herself an enforcer anymore?

"Interesting counsel, General. These are things to take into consideration." Hendry headed toward the *Star Renegade*'s cargo ramp, leading to Geron's ship.

Bleven narrowed his eyes at her, sneered at Cal, and then followed.

"Are those two going to be a problem?" Cal asked.

She laughed softly. "I doubt it. I think Hendry was doing some research of his own."

"What do you mean?"

"Remember when he said he could smell Alexander on Alanna?"

Cal nodded.

"Well, I could smell Bleven on Hendry as far back as when they were both brought to the med bay close to death. And if you hadn't noticed, Hendry has been what some might consider overly-concerned about Bleven. He even tried to get us to drop them off at a trade station to avoid Orion accidentally killing one of them."

Cal watched the two enforcers stepping off the cargo ramp and entering the larger cruiser. "You think those two are involved with each other?"

"Not like you and me. I think they're just close. But something about relationships in general has Hendry intrigued."

"I'm not sure if that's a good or a bad thing."

"I think it's a good thing. The more of them who forgo their feedings while Geron is trying to save the dying enforcers, the better the chances they'll have to find their humanity, just like I did."

"But then what will happen to that humanity when Geron finishes the charity work and starts feeding them again?"

Dania looked down, but he already knew the answer. He'd only asked the question so the stark reality was clear in her head. The prince was playing nice right now because he was too exhausted to do differently. Cal still needed to find a way to get Dania and Alexander as far away from Geron's cruiser as possible before His Royal Highness demanded what he no doubt thought was rightfully his.

CHAPTER 16
DANIA

DANIA RUBBED HER CHEST. Cal's words hurt as much as if he'd stabbed her. "Geron is not the monster you think he is."

"Are you serious? Are we actually going to have this conversation again?" Cal choked out a laugh. "He owns you. He's done terrible things to you and Alexander, not to mention what he may have done to the rest of his enforcers."

Dania closed her eyes and sighed. How could she make him understand? "He might not be what one would consider a good human being, but he *is* a good Kever."

"I don't think there is such a thing as a good Kever."

Dania's eyes burned, and her heart ached, but part of what Cal had said was true. She wasn't sure if her defensiveness was a byproduct of her actual emotions, or programmed emotions, though.

Would she feel this way about Geron if he weren't her sponsor?

Not that it mattered. These were her feelings, and she couldn't control them, fabricated or not.

"Hey." He cupped her cheek. "I'm sorry. I don't mean to

be such a jerk. I've just been so worried about you. I kept expecting the worst, and then when I saw you, I was so relieved—but then the frustration took over, and I got angry again."

"It's fine. I think I just want to get some sleep."

Cal took a step back. "Oh, okay." He shoved his hands in his pockets. "If you want to go back to your own room, that's fine."

Dania startled. "No, that's not what I meant. I want to spend as much time with you as possible." Because Cal was also right that her sponsor owned her, and it was within Geron's rights to take her humanity away at any time. Each moment she spent with Cal could be their last, and she wanted to make the most of it.

His smile melted her fears away as he slipped her hand into his. "Great. Let's go back to my quarters, and we can make something to eat."

Food was one of the wonderful things about humanity that Dania didn't want to give up. She'd always eaten for sustenance, never for pleasure. Flavors and different combinations of spices had excited her in ways she'd never known possible. Making meals for the crew and them complimenting her choices had been an oddly rewarding endeavor. She'd grown up being praised for her ability to destroy. The thought of being praised for creating anything seemed alien and delightfully mischievous.

———

After eating and cleaning up a modest meal, Cal kissed her on her temple. "Do you want to sit on the couch for a while, or would you like to head to bed?"

Her chest fluttered, and a chill settled over her skin. She wanted to be with him every night if possible. But *every* night seemed like an unattainable dream.

Cal frowned. "You okay? You look like something spooked you all of the sudden."

Her cheeks heated. "I'm sorry. You're alluding to being intimate, right?"

He laughed again. "Well, maybe. Yeah. I mean, if you want to."

She looked down. *Wanting to* wasn't the problem.

He ran his hand along her cheek. "Hey, what is it?"

"I know you told me that we'd been intimate before."

"Yeah. We didn't have all-out sex, but yeah, we did a little."

She stepped away from him. "That's the problem. I don't remember. And if we do something now, I won't remember that, either." And once again, Cal would have something to blame Geron for. Which would be true. Her sponsor had placed a shunt in her spine that made her forget deeply intimate moments in her life, and maybe other things as well. She had no idea how many memories had been stolen. "I don't want to be with you and then not remember it."

Cal pulled her into his arms. It was odd, how a single human person with no primordial energy at his beck and call could make her feel so warm, so safe. "I can't even imagine what this is like for you, but like I told you before, we'll figure it out."

She nodded into his chest. She wanted to figure it out *now*, but all her friends' lives, and her freedom, were still at stake. For now, she needed to be the focused enforcer she'd been trained to be. But this time, instead of catching the smugglers, she needed to find a way to set them free.

———

Dania blinked her eyes in the low light as Cal's bedroom came into focus around her. The bed shifted as Cal rolled over in his sleep. She rubbed her eyes. She hadn't remembered lying beside him. Her last memory had been of him holding her in the kitchen.

She ran her hands over her stomach and gasped, finding skin rather than her uniform. She lifted the sheet and stared at her naked body as a deep dread settled over her.

"Good morning." Cal turned on his side and smiled at her. "Sleep well?"

"I-I guess so."

"Do you remember anything?"

"No." A ball lodged in her throat. Her chest constricted. "I suppose we were intimate?"

His smile was dazzling. "Yeah."

"Did I…like it?"

He laughed. "You seemed to."

She pulled the sheet up to her chin, suddenly cold. "Did *you* like it?"

This time, his laugh filled the room. "I definitely liked it." He pulled her into his arms, and she rested on his chest. Everything about him felt comfortable. Right.

The missing memories, though, were most definitely *not right*.

Tears filled her eyes. "I just want to remember. Is that so much to ask?"

"Well, I can tell you everything we did, if you want." He dragged his fingers through her hair. "Or, every time could be exciting and new for you."

That sounded good. In fact, it sounded wonderful, but

how could she look forward to something that she wouldn't remember the second it was over? She closed her eyes and listened to the calming sounds of Cal's heartbeat.

This wasn't fair. Cal was a good, understanding man. This wasn't right. She deserved to remember. She deserved to live her life like everyone else.

She needed to talk to Alexander. They had to find a way to fix her.

CHAPTER 17
ALANNA

ALANNA SCOOTED out from under the lower manual control station for the hydrogen matrix and handed Ethan the soldering gun she'd been working with. "Okay, it's as good as new."

"Thanks. I don't know why they designed that space so small. I'd never be able to do those modifications on my own."

"Well, it's the least I can do after you saved Alexander."

Ethan looked down. He obviously had mixed feelings about playing hero for a guy he didn't like. He could have taken the safer route for himself and left Alex to follow orders when the prince had directed him to go back to his rooms with him. But he hadn't.

"Hey." She squeezed his shoulder. "I really appreciate what you did for Alex."

"Yeah, well, I don't like that he and Dania don't have the ability to say *no* to that guy. It gives me the willies."

She kissed him on the cheek. "Well, thanks."

Ethan shrugged. "Just do me a favor and be careful. I get that you chose Tall, Blond, and Beautiful over me—which was a mistake, by the way—but I want you to know that I'll be here for you when things go south."

Alanna cocked her head to the right. "Things aren't going to go south."

"I know you don't want them to. I also believe that Alex doesn't want them to. But the reality is that there are just so many times that I can pretend that the ship is exploding. We can't postpone the inevitable forever."

The certainty in his eyes left a hollow, expanding hole in her stomach. She knew he was right, but every ounce of her being wanted to scream it wasn't true.

The doors slid open, and Alanna and Ethan jumped back as an opalescent-white uniform filled the doorframe. The tall, muscular female enforcer who'd levitated Miguel's nearly-dead body from the *Star Renegade* after Kile had shot him months ago held on to one side of the frame as she walked into the engine room.

Alanna moved a little closer to Ethan. When Miguel had been shot, Kile had blamed Ethan for shooting him and had executed Ethan for it, only to revive him as soon as Miguel and the female enforcer had been gone. She hoped the woman hadn't come back to do her own enforcing now.

The enforcer scanned the walls and the control panels. "I trust the emergency has been averted?"

Ethan's eyes widened before he covered himself. "Oh, that. Yeah. Our boy Alex knew exactly what to do. He's a wiz with machinery."

She nodded. "It is an unwise use of his time."

"Nah, I don't think so." Ethan folded his arms. "It's Sheera, right?"

The woman flicked an annoyed glance at him. "Shivana."

"Okay, then, Shivana. I don't think it's a waste of time. I

mean, he enjoys fixing stuff and he's good at it. What harm is there in doing something you enjoy when you're off-duty?"

"An enforcer is never off-duty."

"Well, maybe not, but you don't always have an assignment, right? What do you do between missions?"

"I train. I strengthen my body and…"

"And what?"

"Inconsequential." She ran her fingers over the control panel for the very illegal engine modifications. "What does this do?"

"It re-routes energy from the engines to the shields at a moment's notice. Pretty darn effective, too, if I don't say so myself."

"But you did."

"I did what?"

"Say so yourself." She continued running her fingers over the sleek metal. It reminded Alanna of when Rachel pet Max.

Alanna smiled. It was interesting that all the enforcers seemed to experience the same struggle with human vernacular. Dania had said similar things when she'd first come on board. She still struggled with their vernacular from time to time, especially *Ethan-isms*, though she tried to hide it.

Alanna supposed the actual times enforcers spent talking to humans, rather than doling out punishment, were few.

Shivana looked back to the controls. "That sounds like an unwise modification, though. It would leave you dead in space. That would be highly inconvenient in battle."

"True, but it would also be nearly impossible to get through our shield. With that much power, we could sit and wait out almost anything."

She nodded. "That is, in many ways, ingenious. As long

as the other ship isn't big enough to pull you into their cargo hold."

Ethan nodded. "Well, yeah. We're smugglers, remember? We try to avoid big cruisers like this one, when we can."

She scanned the outer housing. "Does this modification really buffer the shield that much?"

"Sure does." He glanced at Alanna, then back to the enforcer as she strolled around the room, stopping at each control panel. Could it be that this enforcer was also interested in ship modifications but had never openly pursued it, like Alexander had?

Alanna inched closer. "Ethan was about to splice the power from the hydrogen matrix. Would you maybe want to help?"

She looked at Alanna, and then to the hydrogen matrix. It was interesting that the enforcer even knew where the hydrogen matrix was.

The woman turned back to Ethan. "Why would you risk splicing power from such an important system?"

To prepare the ship for breaking free from a big, obnoxious prince hellbent on stealing my boyfriend and best friend... But Alanna hoped Ethan knew enough not to admit that.

"It's all about increasing efficiency," Ethan said. "We prepare different systems to do things they weren't intended to do. But then we switch right back before it becomes a problem." Ethan pointed his thumb at the board. "I sure could use some help, if you're interested."

Shivana seemed to search Ethan's face, her expression stony, like Orion's had been every time he'd entered a room on the *Star Renegade*. "Is the modification you are proposing illegal?"

"If it were illegal, would you be able to help me?"

"Definitely not."

"Well, then, it's not illegal. And I love Alanna, but she's not strong enough to hold up the equipment." He pointed at the enforcer's muscular arms. "Looks like you could bench-press a small satellite. What do you say?"

Shivana's stony visage turned to a slight smile. It seemed uncomfortable for her, like she'd never used those muscles before. It was sad, how so many of the enforcers were unhappy, but not even capable of knowing they were unhappy.

Ethan was right, though. All of their enforcer friends were only one feeding away from becoming monsters again. Alanna closed her eyes as Ethan started explaining how diverting the hydrogen could increase power capacity. The enforcer nodded, appearing genuinely interested in what he had to say. Ethan, of course, was eating it up, not even blinking in the face of that opalescent uniform that they all used to fear.

Odd, how they all had started getting used to enforcers being around. It wasn't too long ago that they'd been doing everything in their power to avoid them.

Alanna backed toward the door. "If you two are okay down here, I'm going to get back to the med bay and see how things are going with the pathogens." She looked at Ethan. "You going to be all right?"

"Sure!" He handed Shivana an old-fashioned manual screwdriver. "Me and Shiv are going to have a great time."

The enforcer frowned. "It's Shivana."

Alanna smiled and slipped out the door. The enforcer seemed genuinely interested in helping, and it certainly would be good for Ethan's ego to work with someone who wanted to learn from him. Even if Shivana did discover the modifications were illegal, their current reprieve from Geron would still hold, and this would just be one more item to list on the tally of crimes committed by the *Star Renegade* crew. Hopefully, they would be long gone before any of them needed to worry about the prince passing judgment on them, and maybe in the meantime, they had the opportunity to gain a new friend among the enforcers.

She looked back toward Engineering.

As long as Ethan didn't do anything foolish and tick the woman off.

CHAPTER 18
DANIA

DANIA'S CHEST ACHED. Every time she thought about the missing pieces in her memory, she wanted to scream. Luckily, she could remember cooking with Cal and her newfound friendships. Why intimacy was the only thing she'd lost, she didn't know. Then again, Geron may have erased countless other memories. Unless there was someone close, like Cal, to tell her what had happened, she'd never know.

Alanna's bright smile greeted her as Dania turned the corner.

"Hey, girl." The navigator bit her lower lip. "Have a nice night?"

Dania cringed. She'd probably had the most wonderful night of her life, but it was gone. Erased. Lost forever.

"Whoa. Not a nice night? Didn't you spend the evening with Cal?"

"Yes. It's not that. I'm just not feeling well." It wasn't a lie. The more she thought about it, the more she wanted to puke.

"Well, I'm heading down to the med bay. Maybe Alex or

171

Rachel could have a look at you. You know...make sure all the mojo is mojo-ing?"

Dania nodded. Alexander was exactly the person she needed.

Alanna walked beside her as they headed to the med bay. The woman kept glancing at her as if she wanted to say something but then changed her mind. Maybe it was better that way. Dania didn't want to talk about it. She just wanted to be fixed.

Alanna tapped the entry pad and waved Dania to go in first.

Inside the med bay, Alexander peered at a computer screen while Rachel loaded fresh test tubes into a machine in the back of the room.

Alexander looked up from the screen and frowned at Dania. "You're pale."

"I'm fine." Well, physically at least, she was fine.

Alexander walked away from his station. "Lie down on a gurney." He turned to Rachel. "Can you prepare a treatment for Dania?"

Dania shook her head. "There are people who need pathogen replacement more than me."

Rachel walked up with a vial. "True, but Doc has some set aside for you and Alex. Cal made an executive captainly order that no one is to get those supplies but the two of you." She held her finger to her lips and made a *shush* sound. "Our favorite two enforcers get all the special goodies."

Alanna patted her hand. "It certainly couldn't hurt."

Dania sighed. It wouldn't hurt her, but it wasn't right when so many others were in worse condition. However, they were correct that she *was* starting to feel more tired. Maybe she'd feel better after a small treatment. The problem was she could get called back to Geron's command deck at any time. "I don't have time for a transfusion."

"No problem." Rachel wiped Dania's neck with a cold swab, then placed the injector on her skin.

Dania winced as a chill raced down her neck and into her arms. A slow burn followed before the sensation dissipated.

Alexander ran a scanner over her head. "We can keep doing these small feedings to keep us strong. They don't last as long as the transfusions, but they are working as well as the doctor estimated."

"Until Geron calls us."

His lips thinned. "Yes, of course."

Alanna placed both her hands on Alexander's biceps. "You're still going to try to fight it, right? I thought you wanted to stay."

He kissed her cheek. "Of course I want to stay."

What he neglected to say was the remainder of that sentence...that what they *wanted* was irrelevant. His time with Alanna was coming to an end. As was Dania's time with Cal.

Dania placed her hand on Alexander's other arm. "I need your help."

He smiled. "Of course. Anything."

"I want you to take out my shunt."

The smile melted from his face. "Anything but that."

Somehow, she knew he'd say that. Dania rubbed her face, suppressing a growl. "Please, Alexander. I can't live like this."

Rachel tossed the used syringe over her shoulder. "Max, catch."

The syringe stopped before it hit the floor and hovered

before it drifted across the room and dropped into the recycler.

Rachel looked back to Dania. "What's a shunt?"

Alexander sighed. "It's not your concern."

The med tech placed her hand on her hips. "Hey! If it's Dani's concern, then it's my concern." She flipped her hair as she spun toward Dania. "Where's this shunt thing? I'll take it out for you."

Alexander stepped between them. "No, you won't."

She leaned toward him. "Yes, I will. Dani asked for help and I'm gonna give it to her."

"You can't help with this."

"No? Why not?"

"It is a very delicate surgery."

She folded her arms. "So? I've got talents. I can handle it." She turned back to Dania. "Where is it?"

Alexander sighed heavily, running a scanner over the back of Dania's neck.

Beside them, a screen in the wall came to life, showing an image of a spine with a rectangular object sticking out.

Alexander pointed to the screen. "If you know anything about human physiology, as you claim, then you will see how dangerous removing it will be."

Alanna inched closer to the screen. "Wow. I don't know as much about anatomy as you two, do, but that's horrifying."

Dania lowered her eyes. Her friend had no idea how truly horrifying the device was.

Rachel cocked her head. "Huh. Well, that kinda sucks. Who'd be mean enough to do that to her in the first place?"

Alexander looked down. "I would."

Dania closed the distance between them. "Only under Geron's orders." She took his hands in hers. "But you can fix it. You can take it out."

"I'm your protector, and even more important, I'm your friend." He pointed to the screen. "Taking that out may paralyze you."

"He ain't kidding." Rachel squinted at the monitor. "I can't even imagine how he got it there in the first place."

Alexander had done the surgery because he'd been ordered to, and he'd been programmed to be one of the most talented medical practitioners in the galaxy. She knew that he was worried about her, but he needed to understand that the stakes were higher than any perceived risks. "You can't comprehend what it's like to know you've done something, but you have no memory of doing it."

He sighed. "You're talking about Cal."

Rachel furrowed her brow. "Wait. What? What are you talking about?"

"The shunt steals select memories." Dania looked back to Alexander. "You, of all people, should understand. How would you feel if every time you woke up with Alanna beside you, you had no memory of the night before?"

He lowered his eyes. "Broken."

"Whoa, whoa, whoa!" Rachel held up her hands. "Are you saying that you can't remember having sex? Because that's so not cool!"

Dania inched closer to Alexander. "I don't even know how many memories I've lost. How many things did I maybe learn that I could have built on as a human being, but they're just gone?"

He held up his trembling hands. "Even considering this

makes my hands shake, my vision is skewed, and my head starts to throb." He lowered his hands. "Geron wants that shunt inside you. He's controlling me as much as he's controlling you."

Rachel started rooting through a drawer. "Well, if Pretty Boy's hands are shaky, then I'll just rip it out of you. No problem." She grabbed a long, silver cylinder out of the drawer. "There it is."

Alexander grabbed the cylinder from her hand. "What happened to you agreeing that it's too dangerous to remove it?"

"That was before I found out that she couldn't remember sex." She snatched the device back. "I mean, that's not okay on a whole other level. I mean, I think I'd rather be dead."

Which was interesting, since the last person she'd been intimate with, as far as Dania knew, had left her to return to Geron. And now it seemed like Kile didn't even remember her. If that had happened to Dania, she may have wanted to forget any happiness she'd had with that person.

Alexander grabbed the cylinder back and held it out of her reach. "Not liking that she can't remember does not change that this would be a delicate surgery."

Rachel waved her hands at him. "Aw, I'm plenty practiced. You'd not believe some of the things I needed to do on Hedonaii to help people who'd OD'ed on happy juice. Those were some crazy times, let me tell you."

Alexander's eyes narrowed. "That was nothing like working on a spine. You'd have no idea what to do."

Maybe not, but Rachel had surprised all of them with her abilities before.

Dania squeezed his arm. "Do you think you can talk Rachel through it?"

He pulled the metal cylinder close to his chest. "Allowing Rachel to perform surgery on your spine would be unwise."

Rachel harrumphed. "So would be making her forget every time she got sloppy in the sheets with Cal. 'Cause, I gotta admit, Cally is broody and all, but that's one fine hunk of man, and I, for one, would like her to remember so we can share some notes."

Alexander startled. "Share notes?"

"What? You think girls don't talk? I know all about your skills behind closed doors, Pretty Boy."

Alexander's gaze slowly drifted to Alanna, and her cheeks flashed a deep shade of crimson. She placed both hands over her mouth and giggled like a child before she lowered her hands and shrugged.

The energy in the room shifted, swirling and pulsing like a tidal wave of twisted fury was about to crash on them. Alexander spun toward the entrance a second before the door opened.

Kile stormed into the room, heading right for Alexander. "What did you do to Dania?"

"I checked her vitals."

"Why?"

"She was feeling tired. It's none of your concern."

Kile's eyes drew to the syringe on the sterilized side of the recycler. "You gave her an artificial feeding."

Rachel shoved his shoulder. "He didn't do it. *I* did. Dani wasn't feeling good, and I helped because all of you are so worried about what your precious prince wants that you're too pig-headed to do the right thing when someone needs something." She smacked him again. "And I miss you, you jerk!"

Kile looked past her as if she hadn't just rattled off dozens of words. "Why are you checking Dania's vitals?"

Alexander kept a stoic, enforcer calm. "I'm her doctor."

"That is not a sufficient answer."

"How did you even know I'd done it?"

"We are monitoring everyone's movement on this ship."

That made sense. They had to know that the *Star Renegade* crew would try to get free. The question was, though…how were they monitoring?

Kile spun toward Dania. "You should not allow them to pollute your body with any more contaminants."

Alanna moved beside Dania and folded her arms. "We aren't *polluting* her. We're helping her."

"Yeah!" Rachel punched his shoulder. "We're helping her, so just get off her case. Who asked you, anyway?"

Kile glared at Dania, continuing to act like Rachel wasn't there. "Geron is the only help you need."

Dania rubbed her shoulders. "He can't help me right now. Others are dying and need his assistance far more than I do. These treatments keep me healthy until Geron has saved as many enforcers as he can."

"Those pollutants are not *keeping you healthy*. Never forget that…" He seemed to focus on the back of the room. The fury in his eyes diminished, and the temperature in the room decreased.

"What's wrong?" Dania asked.

Kile didn't even acknowledge her question before he strode toward the back of the room, shoving Rachel out of his way.

"Hey!" she called after him, but he didn't slow his stride.

Kile passed the rows of artificial pathogen mixtures

brewing in the test tubes and stopped at the glass cases in the back of the room.

"Is something wrong?" Alexander asked.

What could possibly be wrong? Kile already knew of all the nefarious work Peter had been involved in. Kile obviously wasn't happy about the production of the artificial pathogens, but Geron had deemed them necessary for the moment. Nothing Kile saw here should have been of any new concern.

Unless Peter was up to something Dania didn't know about, which was entirely possible, since she'd been on the command deck of Geron's cruiser for some time.

Kile opened the glass pane and pushed past several of the white-labeled jars before pulling out a small data pad. He stared into the blank screen before running his thumb over the lock and holding it up until his face had been scanned.

The screen flashed white, and it looked like he was reading.

"What is it?" Dania asked Alexander.

"I have no idea."

They both looked at Rachel, and she shrugged. Alanna looked equally perplexed.

Kile spun, looking directly at Rachel for the first time.

She gulped. "Um... Hi?"

He turned back to the screen and frowned before he threw the data pad at the wall. Splinters of metal exploded from the device as it burst into flames, probably from a surge of Kile's primordial energy, before he stomped out of the room—Dania and artificial pathogens seemingly forgotten.

The flames licked the air around the molten metal until a damp cloth floated across the room and smothered the fire.

Small tendrils of smoke drifted up toward the air vents as Max shook out his fur and became visible.

"What was that all about?" Rachel asked.

Dania's gaze carried back to the melting data pad. She very much wanted to know the answer to that question as well.

THE INFIRMARY ON the prince's cruiser was oddly silent. The doctors barely seemed to speak to each other, and the ship itself didn't have the comforting ever-present hum that the *Star Renegade* did. It was all so...*cold*.

The really-big enforcer lady watched over Ethan's shoulder as he twisted a glob of liquid polymer into place, sealing the wiring system on the rear wall behind a row of beds.

Ethan sat back, rubbing his palms together. "I think this will do it. I just rerouted a little bit of energy from the refrigerant system and reinforced this wiring right here to make sure it'll take the extra power."

A few of the greenish-blue-skinned Kevers tending to the wounded looked at him from over their shoulders. They always seemed surprised to hear his voice. Fallon folded his arms, appearing just as ready to kill Ethan as he always did.

Not that Ethan cared all that much. Grumpy-faced enforcers had become the norm these days. Along the wall, messy globs of polymer dotted the exposed wiring in key places he thought might fail without a little extra TLC. Some of the globs had already dried from dark gray to nearly white.

His methods were unconventional but usually effective. The makeshift repair should work, and all of Doc's new equipment should have power. Whether or not it looked pretty was secondary.

"Are you sure that's safe?" Doc asked.

Safe? He hadn't really considered safe. "Well, I think so. I'm kinda winging it." He rarely worried about safe, come to think of it.

Shivana folded her massive arms. "If you have done anything that may cause harm to this ship, that would be means for immediate execution."

Ethan held up his hands. "Whoa there, Big and Beautiful. I'm just doing the best I can here. Your engineers weren't able to send Doc enough power to run all the extra equipment, so I improvised."

She narrowed her eyes at him. "What did you just call me?"

He pointed to the hardening polymer. "This stuff has, like, a thousand functions. One of them is insulation. It's brilliant, if I don't say so myself."

Shivana squinted, leaning closer to the repair. "You did say so yourself, but this does appear adequate."

"Everything I do is more than adequate, baby."

She furrowed her brow. *"Baby?"*

Fallon cried out, clutching his head and dropping to his knees.

What the blazes?

Shivana raced to him, grabbing his face, forcing him to look at her. "What's wrong?"

Fallon continued to scream.

Ethan backed closer to the wall and the wiring he'd just worked on. Had he done something to make an electrical charge in the air? Could the weird programming-thing that seemed to make the enforcers act like machines get screwed up by something as simple as an electrical field?

Shivana seemed fine, so that shouldn't be the case. Of course, she was a girl, though. A very big, very scary girl, in a cute 'I'm gonna squash you like a bug' kind of way, but still a girl. Could that make a difference?

The enforcer screamed again.

Shivana shook Fallon by the shoulders. "Tell me what's wrong!"

Doc dropped to his knees beside her. "I know what's wrong. I've seen this before." He pulled an injection-thingy out of his pocket and shoved it against the poor guy's neck. Fallon went quiet mid-scream and slumped on the big lady's shoulder. A dribble of blood ran from the guy's nose.

Shivana gaped at Doc. "What did you do?"

Doc ran his fingers through his hair. "I just knocked him out to relieve some of the pain." He looked to the Kever physician, whose eyes seemed ten times bigger than they had been a minute ago. "We're going to need lots of fluids, and let's get a quarter-strength artificial pathogen treatment into him."

"What will that do?" The blue-skinned physician grabbed a cylinder from the back wall and brought it to Doc.

"It's just a hypothesis." Doc grabbed the cylinder and attached it to one of those syringe-thingies. "But I think if we give him a little boost, he won't be in as bad of shape when he wakes up." He pointed to a cot. "Shivana, would you mind getting him onto a gurney for me?"

Shivana picked Fallon up like he weighed no more than a sandwich and placed him on a bed. "What's causing this?"

She looked pale. Well, pale-*er*. Still badass, though.

A deep tone sounded, echoing off the ugly, metal walls.

Ethan flinched. "Are we under attack or something?"

A voice came over several of the comms embedded in the walls. "The human smuggler doctor is required on the command deck immediately."

Doc snorted a laugh and rubbed his face. "Yeah, I bet." He grabbed a medical bag and filled it with supplies before heading toward the door.

Ethan followed. "Hey! Wait up!"

"They didn't call for you, Ethan."

"No, but what kind of friend would I be if I didn't watch your back?"

"You just want to see the command deck."

Ethan shrugged. "Well, yeah, that too."

The halls seemed to go on forever. Doc turned corners like he'd lived onboard for years.

"How do you know where you're going?"

He pointed to the walls. "Omnidirectional color-coded targeting. Follow those little dots in the direction of the dark-purple color to get to the command deck. The blue leads back to the med bay."

"What color leads back to the *Star Renegade*?"

"Either yellow, brown, or black. I haven't figured that one out yet."

"How'd you figure out the way to the command deck in the first place?"

"Alexander explained how it works. I would have figured it out eventually, but Kevers don't think linearly, apparently, so it would have taken a bit longer without his help."

"Hold!" Shivana came up behind them. "You should not be walking through the ship on your own."

Ethan beamed. "Is that the real reason, or did you miss me already?"

She narrowed her eyes at him again. "You are as odd as you are small."

"I bet you say that to all the guys."

Doc elbowed him. "Don't press your luck."

They reached a massive double door about ten feet high with two unfamiliar enforcers guarding either side.

Ethan ogled the large frame. "Who do they keep in there, a Tyrannosaurus Rex?"

"Close. Remember, this ship was built for a prince who is over seven feet tall." Doc turned to the enforcer on their left. "I'm the smuggler doctor. Reporting as ordered."

The enforcer pointed at Ethan. "And him?"

"He's my assistant."

Ethan beamed, saluting them.

Shivana pushed ahead of them. "The doctor has been summoned. Let us pass."

The enforcer was about to speak when a comm behind him blared. Someone shouted in the Kever tongue.

The enforcer grimaced. "Go quickly. They need you."

These Kevers were really impatient. What was the rush?

The door opened to a ridiculously large space. Dozens of stations seemed scattered haphazardly through the room, each with individual monitors, but also facing a wall of blank screens that reached from the floor to the ceiling.

Ethan laughed. "Damn, this place is massive!"

He turned to Doc, but Doc was no longer there. He was on the floor doctoring someone. On the other side of the room, two enforcers were also on the ground. One seemed out cold, while the other one was holding their head, screaming just like Fallon had been.

Ethan's cheeks burned. They'd probably been screaming when he'd walked in, but he'd been too distracted by the pretty tech to notice. He really needed to learn to pay attention to important things.

But those screens were so big! What kind of material were they made of? If they were powered on, would they be different pictures, or all make up one big picture?

"Ethan!" Doc called. "Come here!"

Oh, yeah…medical emergency. "Coming!"

The guy Doc was working on moaned. Blood dribbled from his nose, just like Fallon. His skin was starry-white… even for an enforcer, looking more like an old-fashioned sheet of blank paper than a person's skin. He groaned again, turning more toward Ethan.

Holy sun spots… It was Orion.

"He's been like that for about fifteen minutes," a Kever deck officer with a dark uniform said.

Doc placed an injector-thingy on Orion's neck. "I'm going to say sixteen minutes and thirty-five seconds."

Uniform-guy nodded. "Yes. How did you know that?"

"Because that's exactly the time when Fallon fell in the infirmary." Doc turned to Ethan. "Grab a cold pack from my bag, snap it, and hold it on the back of his neck."

"On it." Ethan rooted through the bag as Doc crossed the room and knelt beside another enforcer rolling on the floor, screaming. Thank goodness Doc hadn't asked Ethan to do something with injections or he may have puked all over the big, pretty, sparkly deck.

The double doors opened, and the prince stomped onto the deck with two enforcers in tow. Damn, Ethan had nearly forgotten, or had blacked out, how tall the Kever actually was.

His Royal Highness shouted in the Kever tongue. At least it *sounded like* he was shouting. Their language *always sounded* like shouting, though.

A translation exploded in Ethan's mind, mixing with the brash Kever words coming from the prince. "What's going on?"

Wow, all those words and all that translated was "What's going on?" Was the translator-guy editing out profanity or something?

The prince crouched beside Ethan. His head was still way above Ethan's eye level.

"You are not the doctor," the prince said.

"No. I'm just a friendly *hold-ice-on-the-back-of-your-neck* kind of person. Don't need much training for that."

The prince frowned, looking down at Orion. "What happened to him?"

"Beats me. I just do what Doc tells me."

"Fallon fell as well," Shivana said. "The smuggler doctor was treating him when he was called to the command deck."

Kile loomed over them. With all the commotion, Ethan hadn't even noticed him. Then again, unless the commander had been a cool piece of alien tech, there wasn't much of a chance of Ethan having seen him—or anyone—when he'd stepped onto a bridge filled with such amazingness.

"Fallon fell as well?" Kile asked.

Shivana nodded, and Kile's gaze carried over the other patients Doc was treating. His face remained stony, but his cheek twitched slightly. In the past, Big Guy had made that face when he'd been worried what Rachel might say or do, but since their bubbly med tech wasn't there, it was more likely he was worried about the enforcers.

Shivana nudged Ethan with her foot. "The ice."

Ethan's grip had loosened. "Oh, yeah!" He pressed the ice onto the back of Orion's neck again.

The last enforcer stopped screaming, and Doc sighed, standing and dragging his fingers through his hair.

"What happened to them?" the prince asked again.

Doc shook his head. "I really don't want to be the person to tell you."

A Kever woman standing at what appeared to be a communications station looked up from the screen on her dashboard. "There is a *green* royal transmission coming through from Keveron." The way she stressed *green* made it seem like that was significant.

"The king?" Geron asked.

Whoa! Okay, yeah, that would be someone significant.

"It's coming from the royal chambers."

Geron straightened his uniform, facing the screen. "Let it through."

Let it through? Ethan stood and backed away from Orion. If he'd gotten a call from the king, he'd want to take it somewhere private. But, as Dania was always trying to explain, the Kever culture was completely different from their own. Still, Ethan didn't want to be within the camera angle.

He looked up. Where *were* the cameras, anyway?

The screen flickered, and a beautiful Kever woman with light-green scales appeared on the screen. Her eyes seemed dark and swollen as she waited for the time delay.

"Mother." Geron inclined his head.

She seemed to force a smile and her lips moved slightly

out of sync with the video. "We expected you sooner, my son."

Ethan flinched. Her Kever voice seemed so much softer and refined from Geron's, yet the translation came through in the same masculine voice of the enforcer translator.

The queen started speaking again. "Our scans show your ship traveled in the opposite direction after you were called home. Are you under attack?"

Geron lowered his eyes. "I am caring for hundreds of enforcers who are not my own. I need supplies to keep them alive. We needed to change course to secure those supplies."

She shook her head. "They are soldiers. Soldiers are expendable. Your father has called you home."

"Did he?" Geron cocked his head. "Did he actually call for me? By name?"

Her gaze hardened. "He did ask for *the Eighth*." She lifted her chin. "I corrected him and reminded him of your name." She moved closer to the camera. "I assure you, he knows your name *now*. You are now Prime Three."

The prince balked, gaping. "What? Keza is Prime Three."

Her already thin Kever lips got even thinner. "Keza is now the high prince. Your oldest brother's ship was just lost in defense of Simerellion."

Geron gaped, glancing at the two enforcers Doc was treating on the floor to his right, and then to Orion on his left.

"Hol-ee-shit," Ethan whispered.

The prince returned his attention to the screen. "That's impossible."

"I wish that were true." The queen's eyes glistened despite the harshness of her tone. "You will take your place at your father's side immediately."

The prince's attention flipped back to her. "But...Prime Three? Why isn't Meda taking Keza's place?"

Her eyes narrowed. "You don't know."

Geron's hands twitched. "Know what?"

"Meda has been gone for quite some time. His enforcers fell and died not long after we lost Zindiria."

The prince's lips tried to form several words, but instead, he closed his eyes. "Are you telling me that five of my brothers and sisters are dead?"

She lowered her eyes. "Six. We lost Igezen four days ago."

"There're only two of us left?" Geron held his temples and walked a few steps from the screen before turning back to his mom. "This can't be true. This must be a ploy to get me to come home."

"It's not. You are to come home now. You need to be protected. Keza is already bolstered with your father. At full speed, you can be here in a few days. The three of you will command your enforcers and the military from a secure location."

Geron's thin, alien lips twisted at an odd angle. "You want me to just abandon all these ships that came to me for protection? Most of them are disabled and none of them are fast enough to keep up."

"They are not a concern. Your bloodlines are. Leave them."

He cocked his head to the left. "I can't do that."

She held up her hand. "Leave them. That is an order from your king."

The transmission winked out. The prince leaned his head back and screamed at the ceiling. The lights flickered. The crew cowered as the center screen where the queen's face had been exploded, raining shards of glass-like material across the deck.

The entire crew eased away from Geron.

Kile took a tentative step toward his sponsor. "Ada, please."

"Please what? Don't be upset? Over half my family is dead. And for what?" Three more screens exploded behind him. "He is impossible. He has no reference for anyone's lives outside of what *he* considers important." Geron held up his hands, staring at his palms. "Bane bloodline...that's all he's worried about. Everyone else can freeze and suffocate in the void of space." His hands formed fists and he screamed at the ceiling again. One of the computers near him exploded in a flash of sparks before the metal frame started dripping to the decking.

This guy was going to blow up his own ship, and it didn't look like anyone was willing to stop him.

Ethan stepped forward. "Hey, hey!"

Geron spun toward him, eyes blazing. The heat coming off him felt like standing in front of a faulty fusion reactor.

Ethan held up his palms. "Hey, I get it. Your dad is an asshole. That's no reason to wreck your ship."

Two of the enforcers approached, their hands getting all blurry, like when they were about to do something really-not-nice to someone who probably didn't deserve it.

Doc grabbed his shoulder. "Ethan, are you nuts?"

"No. I'm perfectly sane." He turned back to Geron. "I get you. My dad was an asshole too. That's why I'm out here in space." He shrugged. "Well, I'm out here in space because I had a bad gambling debt, and Cal saved my hide...but the point is, you don't need to let your dad run your life. Believe me. I'm better off without my dad. I made friends and learned to be my own person. I mean, I'm not the greatest person, but I get by, and I think I live a pretty good life on my own."

Geron narrowed his eyes. "You are a crewman of a ship wanted for breaking multiple laws. You are a criminal."

"And I wouldn't change a thing. I don't need my old family. I found a new one out here, and I wouldn't give them up for anything." He pointed at the screen. "So what if your dad is an ass? Live your own life. Suck it up and be your own man."

Kile grabbed Ethan's arm. "Enough."

"Hold." Geron kicked the broken shards at his feet.

The commander lifted his chin. "But he spoke ill of our king."

Geron shook his head. "He spoke the truth. I cannot fault him for that." He turned back to Ethan. "I do not know what an *ass-hole* is, but I trust it is something bad?"

"The worst," Ethan said.

Geron nodded. "My father is, and always has been, an *ass-hole*."

A blue-skinned Kever guy in a dark uniform with an important-looking seal on the right shoulder stepped forward. "Do we change course to Keveron?"

Geron shook his head. "My father's impatience does not change the fact that we have wounded. Stay on course."

"Good for you!" Ethan punched the prince's arm.

The two enforcers nearest Geron reached out and their hands erupted in flames.

Kile stepped between them and Ethan. "This smuggler is not worth the primordial energy. He's harmless."

Ethan peeked around him. "But capable, right? You always said I'm the capable one."

Kile appeared bored, as usual. "Indeed."

Doc ran a scanner-thingy over the last of the three unconscious enforcers and then pointed his thumb at the door. "I'd like to get the injured back to your infirmary for monitoring."

Geron nodded. "Proceed." His gaze seemed to focus on the broken, smoking screen where his mother's face had been only moments before.

Ethan didn't like his own brother. Honestly, he couldn't care less if he never saw home again. But he didn't want anyone in his family dead. It was an odd feeling, hating someone but loving them at the same time. Were those the same strange, conflicted feelings going through the prince's head? Did Kevers even have emotions like that?

Shivana narrowed her eyes at Ethan. She seemed to do that a lot when Ethan was around. She leaned closer and spoke softly. "You stood up to a Bane."

"Yeah, I guess I did."

She continued to stare, as if taking his brain apart piece by piece. "I cannot decide if that was incredibly foolish or interestingly brave."

Ethan shrugged. "I'm not really sure which one it was, either."

Doc stood, scratching his head as he looked over his new patients. "I guess if your brother is dead, all these enforcers will need to be recoded to you as well."

The room started to heat up again. The prince lowered his eyes and walked toward the doors, the translation-guy following.

Ethan leaned toward Doc as the doors closed behind the prince. "He didn't answer you."

Doc nodded. "Yeah. I noticed that."

CHAPTER 20
DANIA

PETER HAD SAID that Fallon had simply dropped to his knees, screaming, just like Zindiria's enforcers had back on the *Star Renegade*. All of this loss seemed unthinkable. Zindiria had been incredibly strong, but the high prince had been even stronger. Most said his power had rivaled the king's.

Power was a moot point, however, if he hadn't projected himself into space before his ship had been destroyed. She rubbed her eyes, turning down the hall that led to Geron's rooms. When the Banes had made an alliance with Earth and driven the Carteks out of Earth's space, the battles had been over quickly. The king had been praised as a savior in most of the colonies.

Of course, that opinion had changed over time, but that didn't change the fact that the enemy had been defeated easily. That had only been thirty-eight years ago. How could the Carteks' tactics or technology have improved so much that they'd be able to do such catastrophic damage to the Bane line?

She stopped several yards from Geron's door and took a deep breath, not even looking at the enforcers stationed there. The tides of the war were not her immediate concern. Geron had lost six of his siblings. The deaths may have happened over a long span of time, but he'd found out about them over a number of days. This was too fresh and painfully new.

To worsen the blow, not long ago, Geron had been Prime Eight. Only his brother Igezen had ranked lower in the Bane line. Now her sponsor was Prime Three, the third most powerful Bane alive, and second in line for the throne.

Peter had told her Geron had left the command deck without comment when Peter had mentioned that the former high prince's enforcers would now have to be recoded like the others. Had that realization been too much for him emotionally?

She wasn't sure how he felt about his brother, but the news had to affect him somewhat. The former high prince's enforcers were battle ready. They'd been trained to attend to and protect not only a king, but all of Keveron. Geron had never aspired to any of that.

She approached the door, and both enforcers standing guard lowered their eyes to her. She was thankful that they all acted like she still had power. Any one of them could rip her in two in her current condition.

The door opened, and Geron's voice sounded from within. "Enter, Dania."

She stepped inside. As usual, the lights were lower within. Geron paced, his hands clasped behind his back. He reminded her oddly of Cal when he was nervous about something.

"The high prince is dead." He continued pacing, his eyes on the floor.

"*Your brother* is dead."

"They are one and the same."

"True. And you have decided not to return home."

He nodded. "I made my decision to save these people before this news. It was the right decision. I cannot allow my father to force me to change my mind."

Interesting. Was he doing the right thing because it was right, or because he wanted to purposely go against his father's wishes? If it was the latter, it wouldn't be the first time. Of course, there was the genuine possibility that he might be afraid. That would make sense, knowing his highly trained and incredibly powerful brothers and sisters may have been targeted.

She moved closer, but not so close as to get in the way of his pacing. "If it is any consolation, you did the right thing by doing your best to save those in your care."

"I have a feeling that there is a 'however' hanging on the end of that sentence."

Dania smiled. "*However*, I do fear that this will increase your father's wrath exponentially. Your family is in crisis. He may want to be surrounded by his children."

"My father cares nothing for us. He sent a communication to find me less than twenty minutes after my brother died. That means he barely blinked. He just thought of the military implications." He faced the wall, breathing heavily. "We are pawns in his game. I guarantee you, he's worried about Keveron and about staying in power—not his children or any sense of a familial bond." He ran his fingers over his scalp. "None of that matters, though. My father's wrath is the least of my worries."

"Oh?"

"Keza is now high prince. That means he is next in line for the throne."

She tilted her head, searching for understanding. Being next in line was the definition of being a high prince. What point was he trying to make?

Geron pointed at his chest. "That means I am next in line after that." He started pacing again. "I've never been good at rules or paying attention or doing anything the way others expected my brothers and sisters to do." He stopped pacing. "To be honest, in many ways, I was glad my father ignored me. I was free to have my own life, just like the odd, little human said."

Odd, little human? He had to have been talking about Ethan. That was a story Peter had only touched on. Dania would need to get the details later.

Geron turned to the window screen. Like many high security rooms in the cruiser, there were no true windows, but large screens were in place to show the stars outside. Today, the view was diluted with dozens of ships hanging close to the cruiser like a gaggle of *prias* goslings scurrying around their mother for protection.

Geron's reflection shone back in the screen. "How could all but one of my siblings be gone?"

Dania wished she had an answer for him. It still made no sense. The galaxy had been at peace her entire life. She wasn't sure how to compute or even force herself to comprehend what had happened.

"I think you should rest, Ada. You've had quite a shock."

He held out his hand to her. "Stay with me. I've been neglecting you for too long."

The air between them tingled, but she didn't feel the need to jump into his arms and accept what he was offering. That must have been the product of her artificial feeding earlier that day. She was thankful she was able to keep a clear head.

"Everyone is just as confused as you are now, Ada. You told me once that you felt safer with me in command. I think it's best if Kile and I remain in charge while you sleep."

"You are always thinking of others, but you'll need to be taken care of soon, no matter how stubborn you are."

She bowed her head. "Yes, Ada."

Dania backed out of the room. If he hadn't been so preoccupied with his own thoughts, he'd probably have pressed the issue. She wasn't sure she'd have been able to keep a level head if he had.

It was a possibility that they could use Geron's preoccupation to their advantage. She'd need to discuss this with Cal. First, though, she wanted details of Geron's initial reaction, and what had led to him damaging parts of the command deck.

She headed back to the *Star Renegade* and as soon as she'd stepped off the smuggling ship's ramp into the cargo hold, the comm in the wall flicked on.

"Hey there! Welcome home," Ty's voice said. "Are you still you?"

Dania laughed. "Yes. No need to sound the alarm."

"The boss is in his office. Should I tell him you're coming?"

"Sure, but I want to chat with Ethan first."

"Okay, I'll let Cal know you'll be there in a little bit."

The halls seemed smaller but comforting. As much as the cruiser was home, it would never have the sense of emotional attachment as these dented and blast-marked surfaces.

She knocked on Ethan's door. "It's Dania." There was movement inside, but the door didn't open. She knocked again. "Ethan, it's Dania."

The door opened, and Dania froze when she looked up into the eyes of the last person she'd expected to see. "Shivana?"

The enforcer lifted her chin. "I'm sorry, General. I had a moment of weakness."

Ethan peered around the door, shirtless. "Hey, give me some credit. It was a little more than a moment."

Shivana scowled at him. "Quiet. This does not concern you."

"Sounds like it does."

"I instructed you to be quiet."

Ethan held up his hands and walked back into the room. "I guess we're back to enforcer-mode again. That's okay. I'll be here when you're done working, dear."

Dania gaped. Had he just called Shivana *dear*…and lived to take a second breath?

Shivana grimaced, closing her eyes and stepping into the hall. Her uniform was partially fastened and hung slightly off one shoulder.

She held her head high. "I am fully prepared for any punishment, General."

"Punishment? For what?"

"I have forsaken my sponsor."

Dania tilted her head. "Forsaken? How?"

"The human engineer. I…" She sighed. "I was weak. I'm not sure what came over me."

Interesting…none of her male enforcers ever apologized

for seeking human company between missions. Had this been Shivana's first time, or was this a product of programming? Could Geron have tried to quell human desire from all his females? Not that this mattered at the moment, but it would be something interesting to explore.

The woman stood at partial attention, waiting for her general's decision.

Dania folded her hands behind her back. "Are you aware that many of my male enforcers have taken human company after missions?"

"Yes, General. And so have I."

Well, that answered that question. "Then why do you expect to be punished now?"

"We are not between missions. We are on our sponsor's cruiser. And this is not a random human. This was a smuggler. Someone who will soon be executed for his crimes."

Dania tilted her head. "How do you feel about that?"

She frowned before looking down. "It will give me no pleasure."

Dania wondered if executions had given Shivana pleasure in the past. She'd been robotic about passing her judgments, but precise. Her executions were over quickly, not drawn out with screaming like Miguel's or, unfortunately, Dania's.

She had to wonder, though. "What would you do if you were ordered to execute Ethan?"

Her eyes widened. "Please don't make me do that. I understand it would be a suitable punishment for this infraction, but..."

Dania held up her hand. "It's okay. I have no intention of ordering anyone's execution."

Shivana closed her eyes and released her breath.

Dania touched her shoulder and Shivana jumped, gaping

at Dania's hand. Dania realized the touch might have been foreign to her. "It's okay to explore your humanity."

Shivana shook her head. "Not with someone you know. And definitely not with a criminal."

"Why not? Do you like Ethan?"

She looked back to the closed door. "He is small. He is odd. But something about him..."

"Something about him what?"

Shivana rubbed the base of her neck. "He is not intimidated by my size. In fact, he doesn't appear to be intimidated by anything."

That was a very valid representation of Ethan.

Shivana raised her eyes to Dania. "He called me 'beautiful.' No one has ever said that to me before." Her lips thinned. "But that is a lie. I am built for strength and fortitude. I am made to be imposing. I'm not beautiful. Not like you. Not like Alexander."

Not like most enforcers. Shivana had definitely been molded differently, unless she'd been larger from the start, and Geron hadn't seen the need to change that.

Dania smiled. "Does Ethan give you joy?"

She looked at the door again. "He was adequate."

Dania laughed. "Not like that. I mean, do you like just spending time with him, listening to him, and speaking to him?"

"He speaks excessively."

"And?"

"No one ever speaks to me as long as he does. He doesn't try to get away from me. He showed me around this ship's engineering area and explained the different modifications he's done on the ship." She frowned again. "He treated me... like anyone else."

It sounded like Ethan being Ethan.

"His modifications to this ship are impressive," Shivana continued. "Kile is right. He's highly competent."

Dania smiled. "Well, it sounds like Ethan likes you, and you like Ethan. You just took your relationship to another level and enjoyed each other in a new way. There's nothing wrong with that." It was human. It was real. Not like the modified, rigid life they'd been forced to live.

Shivana lifted her chin. "It was wrong. I don't want to upset Geron the way you did."

Dania had upset Geron? She supposed she *had* upset him. She'd never really thought about it that way. "That may be true, but it is wrong of Geron to be upset if any of his people find happiness."

"Happiness outside the relationship with your sponsor is inefficient and makes you weak."

"I disagree."

Shivana stared at her, but it wasn't the usual glare the woman had when she didn't approve of something Dania had done. She lowered her eyes. "I think I disagree as well."

Her eyes reddened and she looked back to Ethan's door. "I will forget him the next time I feed, won't I? Is this why you have been avoiding being made whole again?"

Dania nodded. There was no use in trying to dance around the subject. "Yes, it is. I've found the same comfort in the captain."

"Yet you are still connected to Geron. You still need to do his will."

"Yes."

Shivana cocked her head to the left. "This is highly inappropriate, but since we are having an otherwise inappropriate conversation, may I ask a personal question, General?"

Dania nodded.

Shivana gazed into her eyes as if searching for answers she desperately needed. "What are you going to do?"

Again, there was no need to even try to lie. "I don't know."

CAL HAD NEVER BEEN good at taking orders. The only thing different about today was he didn't have a choice to comply when the prince called and asked to speak to him in person. The imposing enforcer woman who'd been spending an odd amount of time in Engineering with Ethan walked him through the halls of the prince's cruiser.

Every time he was 'escorted' through the ship, he found himself preparing himself for the *final* walk. The prince had kept his word, though, at least for now. Even Ethan and his big mouth hadn't warranted an execution.

The enforcer looked over her shoulder. "Your engineer."

That sounded like the end of a sentence, not that start of one. And how strange was it that she'd asked about Ethan when he'd just thought about him?

She looked over her shoulder again as they went around a corner. "Would you consider him a trustworthy person?"

Interesting question, from an enforcer. "I know you people don't think much of smugglers, but I'd trust my life to any member of my crew."

She stopped and spun toward him. "What about Dania's life? Would you trust Ethan with *her* life?"

Why would she even ask such a thing? The truth was, he'd rather be the one to protect her. But if he couldn't be there… "Yes, I would trust Ethan with Dania's life, too. Why do you ask?"

She turned, continuing her stomping gait. "Curiosity."

Why did Cal think there was more to the question than that?

They arrived at a Kever-sized, sealed archway, and the guards standing on either side of the entrance inclined their heads to the large enforcer lady.

As the door opened, she grabbed Cal's arm and nearly dragged him inside.

What was with the change in demeanor? Oh, yeah, because there was an even bigger, badder person in the room who she needed to impress.

She released him in the middle of the chamber. "The smuggler captain, as requested, Ada."

Cal stumbled into what may have been a small meeting room. Two chairs sat on either end of a small, metallic, rectangular table hovering above the floor with no visible supports. The prince stood behind the table, slightly to the left of a broken, burned monitor. It seemed like Ethan and Doc hadn't exaggerated about the prince having a meltdown. How many computers had the guy fried today?

Cal pointed at the broken screen. "I have a really great engineer who can help fix that, if you want."

Geron nodded. "It seems your engineer is as brave and honest as he is efficient."

What was with all the sudden interest in Ethan? Not that it was a bad thing. Any possibility of someone in the crew getting a reprieve was good. He just didn't expect the one person he'd had to order the other members of the crew to hang out with to get them past all that *Ethan-ness* to make a good first impression on anyone, let alone notoriously hot-headed royalty.

The prince gestured to four screens making up a single picture to the left of the larger broken monitor. "I trust you recognize this planet?"

A little blue-and-brown circle glowed on the screen. "At this distance, no. But I'm guessing that's Themyscira?"

"Yes. This planet has scoffed at any recommendations of a treaty, and they've already pinged us five times warning us not to come closer."

"It's nice to see that you're complying."

He turned toward Cal. "I have no choice. While I could take this as a personal offense, fly to the planet, and obliterate half their colonies, that would serve no purpose, and it would put many of the weaker ships under my care in jeopardy."

Cal nodded. Themyscira did have one of the largest militaries outside of the Earthan cradle, with maybe the exception of Keveron. It was good the prince recognized that and didn't let his ego take over. Which was a surprise, after all Cal had heard about the guy.

The prince looked back to the screen. "Despite their insistence that we come no closer, we still need their supplies. That's where you come in, Mr. Espinoza."

"Me?"

"As you pointed out, you've traded here before, and despite Kile embarrassing their inadequate soldiers before your last departure, scans of their data stores show that your ship is still in good standing."

That was actually a relief. After all the damage, and Kile throwing the Themysciran guards around like they were part of a light exercise routine, he hadn't been all that sure they'd ever be welcomed back.

"You will transfer your entire crew to my vessel. Then you will fly your ship out, land on the planet, procure the needed supplies, and return to the cruiser."

Cal's stomach bottomed out. "I'd have a better chance of things going well if I had my crew."

Geron perused the edges of his fingernails. "You'd have a better chance of forgetting the supplies and running if you had your crew."

True. But hey, he couldn't blame a guy for trying. But maybe he could lobby for one of them at a time. "I get your caution, but Doc would be intrinsic to the supply run. He knows what supplies he needs and can make sure I get the right stuff."

"Your doctor remains here. He can inspect the supplies when you return, and if you didn't get a correct item, you can go back to get more."

Well, that hadn't gone as planned. "My pilot would be helpful."

"You are perfectly capable of piloting the ship on your own."

It sounded like this guy had recently had a long conversation with Kile. Cal shouldn't have been surprised. He probably knew what kind of toothbrush was in Cal's bathroom.

Cal held up his hands. "Hear me out. What do you know about Themyscira?"

"It is a defiant military world known for starting problems in this region."

By *problems*, he probably meant keeping the Banes as far away as they could. "What about demographics?"

"The population's age range is moderately similar to any world of its size. Population growth is smaller on average, and the inhabitants are predominantly female."

"Do you know why this is?"

"There is no data on this."

Probably because the Banes had very little understanding of humanity as a whole.

"Let's just say it would be easier if I had women on board. Most of the population doesn't take kindly to men in any way, shape, or form. Alanna would be helpful, along with Dania."

"You may have your female med tech. Not the navigator, and definitely not Dania."

He could have Rachel? "Why not Alanna and Dania?"

"Because all information on you confirms that you will no doubt try to escape the first chance you get, forcibly removing Dania in the process. However, data also confirms that you place the lives of your crew, especially the members of your crew who have been with you for some time, before your own. You will not leave them behind to secure your own escape. So, the only way I can guarantee your return is to hold the lives of your crew in my hands."

"You're going to execute them all when this is over, anyway."

"True, but humanity is odd. They cling to every last moment with hope and treat every second of their lives like it is important, even if those seconds are moments before their demise."

"You act like this is a bad thing."

"In your case, it is. You'll do everything I ask. You will go to the planet and obtain my supplies. Then you will return under the slim hope that you will be able to one day set your crew free. Your profile shows me that you would not be able to live with yourself if I executed them in anger if you escaped without them."

This guy had definitely been talking to Kile, and the commander had spent far too long on Cal's ship—apparently studying more than just schematics and modifications.

But maybe Cal could lobby for his people one at a time. "Rachel fits the bill as far as being a woman, but I really could use another pilot. If something happens to me, she'll be stranded, and you won't get your supplies."

The prince cocked his head slightly to the right. He had that bored look on his face that really made Cal want to punch him. "Please don't take me for a fool, Mr. Espinoza. That would be an egregious error."

Cal frowned. He wasn't taking anyone for a fool. It was the truth.

The prince looked at the translator-guy and shook his head. "Certainly, one or more of the pirates hiding behind closed doors in your ship has some piloting abilities."

Cal closed his eyes and sighed. None of the enforcers entering the ship had even glanced in the direction of any of the storage areas where the pirates had been hiding. He'd thought, or maybe hoped, Orion had forgotten about them. Apparently, they hadn't been important enough to worry about until now.

Cal sat back. "Yeah, Chris is a good pilot." And the others would probably round out a decent crew. A crew who—other than Chris—Cal had no emotional ties, which Orion probably knew.

The prince folded his hands on the table. "Ah, yes,

Christopher Columbus. An interesting pseudonym. Christopher Columbus will stay behind as well. I'm sure you can find a pilot among the others."

"What? Why do you want Chris, too?"

"Because there are documents linking the two of you across the span of several years. You've known each other long enough that you will most likely have a similar attachment as you have with your crew. Disembark your pirate friend, your doctor, your pilot, your navigator, and your engineer tonight, and I will expect my supplies before tomorrow's late-day meal."

Sweat beaded Cal's brow. The pirates were barely keeping from killing each other with Chris around to keep them in line. Without him, they'd probably regress to the cutthroats Cal expected them to be. Why Cal had ever thought being charitable and saving their lives would change them, he didn't know.

Still, he didn't like the idea of him and Rachel being outnumbered on a ship with a bunch of guys who killed for a living. "How about I just take Iggy with me? He used to be Victor's pilot. He'll be fine."

A small, slight smile played on the edge of the prince's lips, but his eyes were cloaked in hate. "I think *all of the* pirates would make the perfect choice."

Ice rolled over Cal's skin. That slimy son of a…

Cal's hands clenched into fists. He couldn't even come up with a slur bad enough. "You're hoping I don't come back." And maybe Rachel, too, if he'd found out about her relationship with Kile.

Geron shrugged. "Untrue. It would be easier to procure the supplies if you return with them peacefully, but if things should go amiss, I could always take them by force."

So, no matter what happened, Geron would win. He'd get his supplies, and he could also get rid of Cal *by accident*, which would take the blame off Geron if Dania wanted answers. When the dust settled, the Kever would probably unleash Dania to kill the pirates, and she'd be thankful for the opportunity to pass judgment, making this crazed prince look like a hero.

Cal, as usual, was royally screwed. And either way, Cal's ship, and his crew, were at the mercy of a prince who probably had no comprehension of what mercy even was.

Cal rubbed his face. The Kever had him cornered, and he knew it. If Cal said *no*, the enforcers would start executing the crew. If he said *yes*, he was walking into a possible nightmare with only Rachel at his side.

Of course, there was a slim chance that the pirates were still grateful to Cal for saving their lives. That was at least a chance.

Cal hated this, but there was nothing left to say. The prince was making this sound like he had a choice, but there simply wasn't one. "How do I know my friends will be safe?"

"I will leave their temporary living arrangements to Dania. Is that agreeable?"

Cal sighed. At least Dania would make sure they were comfortable. "Yeah, I guess it will have to be."

And just like that, one more chance at escape had disappeared. And now Cal had to place his trust, and his and Rachel's lives, in the hands of people who murdered for a living.

DANIA FOLLOWED one step behind Geron as he made his way to the infirmary. He'd been oddly quiet on matters concerning his siblings, and his outright defiance of his father. This was not unlike him, though. He tended to make decisions without considering all the possible negative outcomes, only dealing with them when the time came.

His brother's death was not a simple, boring family matter, though. It was a travesty of intergalactic proportions. Did he realize this, or was he more upset than he let on? Was he blocking it out like it hadn't happened or simply putting on a false face, making it seem like he didn't care?

She wished she could tell. She used to be much better at analyzing his moods. Of course, the link to him had been stronger then…and that link had ramifications she needed to avoid as long as possible.

The infirmary door opened as they approached, and Geron walked inside. As usual, there were close to a dozen enforcers lined up for his arrival. Several more beds were filled with the former high prince's enforcers.

Peter adjusted the IV on one of them and checked the

readings. "A few of our new, unexpected patients are still in shock. The ones who are awake I've heavily sedated and put on painkillers. They are not happy, but they're stable. It's your choice, of course, but I'd say the enforcers they brought in from the ships before all this happened are in the worst shape, and you should take care of them first." He held up his hands. "Again, it's your choice, of course."

That was a good call, on Peter's part, to make sure that hadn't sounded like an order. The last thing he needed was a full-blooded prince getting angry with him.

Geron strode to Orion's bed. The commander's eyes were heavy, and his skin drawn and pale.

Orion blinked his bloodshot eyes. "Your brother was a great man. It was an honor to serve him."

"I'm sure."

"He would have made an excellent king."

Dania had to agree. In many ways she—and others, no doubt—had been looking forward to the day he ascended to power, although no one would have ever voiced such treason out loud. No one should ever make it sound like they were unsatisfied with their king.

Orion shook his head. "He shouldn't be gone. It shouldn't have been him."

Now *that* was an interesting thing to say. Those words suggested that it would have been better if another life had been sacrificed in his place. But whose? He obviously didn't care much for Geron, but no one would have been foolish enough to insinuate they'd want a Bane dead. Especially the one standing over their bed.

Geron leaned over him. "I can feed you if you want. It may take away some of the pain."

Orion shook his head. "I wasn't there to protect him. I deserve this pain."

"You have not committed a crime. You do not deserve pain."

Orion closed his eyes. "His final order to me was to find his sister and bring her home. I failed him. I didn't even recover a body."

"That wasn't your fault. You made an attempt."

"By making an alliance with smugglers. It was foolhardy."

Geron's expression remained blank. If he harbored any animosity toward Orion for the death of his sister, it didn't show. "I've been told by several of Zindiria's enforcers that after the initial shock of being absorbed by another sponsor abated, all the guilt and pain they'd experienced after her death vanished. I can do that for you now and add you to my fold."

Orion's eyes widened, the thick veins growing more pronounced. "I was meant to serve the high prince. He was going to be king."

Dania balked. That was another odd thing to say. Was he insinuating he was too good for Geron?

Her sponsor didn't show any signs of annoyance. "I can ease your pain today, and you can take your place as an enforcer. You can join Kile as co-commander in charge of the newly-absorbed enforcers.

"And belong to *you*?"

Geron frowned. "Of course."

Orion grimaced. "I'd rather die."

Dania struggled to contain her gasp. Had he just said that to a member of the royal family? The same family he'd pledged his life to serve?

The air about Geron heated slightly before her sponsor

took a deep, cleansing breath. "It is illegal for an enforcer to willfully die unless they are protecting their sponsor. Are you telling me you want to break the law?"

"I will wait until we return to Keveron. I will offer my service to the new high prince or the king."

Geron's lips thinned as the true meaning of Orion's words set in. The commander had foreseen himself protecting a future king. Now that future king was dead. It seemed he was only interested in serving the new high prince or higher.

Geron took a step away from the bed. "I won't force you to serve. You are not dying, but if you come close to death, like the others, you will no longer have a choice."

Orion continued to look away. "I will take my chances."

Dania's lips parted in shock. She'd never seen such insolence in an enforcer. Hopefully, this was simply grief—and not outright treason.

Geron turned to Peter. "Give him an artificial feeding."

Orion jolted. "No! I will not be polluted with that filth."

Geron looked bored. "And I don't care. I offered you a feeding, but apparently, I wasn't good enough." He walked to the other side of the room, where the patients closest to death awaited him. "Knock the commander out if you need to, Doctor, but give him a treatment."

Orion pulled against the special bindings meant to keep him from hurting himself after his sponsor died. "Don't you dare touch me with your illegal concoctions."

Peter shrugged. "No worries. You'll fall asleep eventually."

He winked at Dania and headed to another patient.

Peter obviously had no trouble giving the artificial pathogens to anyone. To him, this *concoction* was a miracle meant to save lives. Obviously, Orion thought differently. It would be interesting to see how the commander felt about the treatments after he woke up and started to feel better… and maybe even started to think like a human again.

She headed for the door.

"Dania?" Geron called from the back of the room.

She returned to him. "Ada?"

"Have you spoken to the smuggler today?"

Her chest cinched. Had he found out she'd spent the night before last with Cal? Had they been monitoring her rooms?

She took a steadying breath. If Geron knew, or if he cared, he would have addressed it already. He hadn't asked about *yesterday*. He'd asked about *today*.

In that case, the answer was simple. "No, Ada. I left the command deck this morning and came straight here with you."

"Good. Send an enforcer to extract the *Star Renegade* crew from their ship. I need you to find them temporary accommodations."

Accommodations? They'd decided it would be easier to house them in the *Star Renegade*, rather than converting the brig—which had been used as storage for years—back into habitable cells. "Why, Ada?"

"The smuggler and the med tech are making a supply run to Themyscira for me. The others are remaining behind."

"Captain Espinoza agreed to this?"

"Yes. I told him that you would see to the comfort of the crew while he was gone."

She nodded. That made sense. Cal would know they'd be safe with her. "All of them but Rachel?"

His gaze seemed to search her. "Yes."

That meant Ethan, Peter, Alanna, Ty, Chris, and the seven pirates. They had more than enough accommodations in the lower decks, but she'd have to arrange guards on the rooms...especially for the pirates. "I'll see it done."

"Not you personally, though. I want you on the command deck immediately. You may give direction from there."

He's afraid I'll try to escape with Cal. But he was smart enough to know that Cal would never leave his crew behind.

There was something in Geron's eyes...an air of annoyance, or was it a challenge?

She bowed. "I'll head to the command deck immediately and send someone to extract the crew." She started for the door.

Geron called from behind. "And do not leave the command deck until the *Star Renegade* has launched."

Another odd command, but she bowed her head again. "Of course, Ada." His commands were oddly precise today, like maybe there was more to this than he was letting on. But he did say that Cal had agreed, so she needed to do the only thing she could do for her friends...take care of them while they were on a ship filled with enforcers who saw them as criminals.

"Dania!" Orion shouted as she passed his bed.

She kept her eyes on the exit.

"Dania, do not ignore me!"

Orion should have known better. She wasn't able to *not* ignore him. She had orders from her sponsor, and orders took precedence over everything. Luckily, she had Alexander, who was the only one she truly trusted with her friends' lives.

TY PUNCHED the wall near the door of the lounge. "This is bull, Cal, and you know it."

Cal rubbed his face. "It may be bull, but it's the way it is. We don't have a hell of a lot of options."

Alanna wrapped her arms around her midriff. "I don't want to leave the *Renegade*."

"Hey." Cal squeezed her arm. "He said Dania was going to take care of you all. She'll keep you safe."

Victor snorted. "Anyone heard from your girlfriend lately? Is she still team *Star Renegade*?" He shook his head. "It would be just like a Bane to be walking them all into the arms of their executioner."

Cal's jaw tightened. He hadn't thought of that. But the prince certainly wasn't above killing them one at a time until he complied. Cal had to believe Dania was still with them and that she'd keep their friends safe.

The door opened and Doc slipped inside.

"What's going on out there?" Alanna asked. "Have you seen Alexander?"

"Yeah, girl. He's coming." He turned to Cal. "I looked up

the rooms designated for us. We're not staying in a Hedonaii luxury suite, but it's not a dungeon, either. Our illustrious host is holding to his word."

Alanna looked at the exit and smiled, wiping unshed tears from her eyes.

What was she smiling at?

The door opened and Alexander walked in.

"Alex!" Alanna jumped into his arms, and he kissed her forehead.

Had she heard him walking up to the door or something?

Not that it mattered at the moment. "Where's Dania?"

Alex stroked Alanna's back. "She's on the command deck. She's been ordered to stay there until you depart."

An unfortunately good call on Geron's part because even if they weren't ready, Cal might have tried to come up with a way to escape. The prince kept proving he wasn't as gullible as they'd assumed.

"When do they want us to leave?" Victor asked.

Alexander released Alanna. "You're expected to depart immediately. The Themyscirans are getting more insistent that we come no closer. Geron tires of their impudence. The sooner we depart this system, the safer the Themyscirans will be." He turned to Cal. "Geron should let everyone return as soon as you deliver the supplies."

Cal gritted his teeth. "I don't like that word *should*."

Alex flicked a glance at Alanna. "I don't like that word, either. But Geron is conflicted at the moment. We can give him counsel and try to steer him to do the right thing, but nothing is a certainty."

Cal sighed. "Are my people really going to be safe?"

He nodded. "For now, yes. Kile continues to advocate that

the crew has value as long as Geron needs to control you and the doctor."

Cal snorted a laugh. He was certainly right about that.

Victor clapped his chubby-fingered hands and rubbed them together. "All right. I guess we should get this party started. I, for one, am tired of sitting in the dark. I'm ready to see some stars again." He turned to his men. "If we're going to be the temporary crew, I need to dole out assignments."

Iggy raised his hand. "I'm the pilot."

"Like hell," Victor said. "*I'm* the pilot."

"Why can't I pilot?" Jasper asked.

Victor waved them to the door. "Come on, you dolts. Maybe we'll have a little fun and let you fight for it." He ushered them from the room.

Alanna's eyes turned glassy and she hugged Cal. "I have a really bad feeling about this. Something just seems wrong."

What seemed *wrong* was Cal leaving without them. The *Renegade* hadn't taken off without her full crew in years. "Hey." He leaned back and looked into her eyes. "I'm coming back. I'm not leaving anyone here."

She nodded but didn't meet his gaze again.

Cal's stomach flipped as he shook hands with Doc, Ty, Ethan, and Chris.

This was temporary. There was no doubt in his mind that he'd come back for his friends. But a dark pressure pressed in on all sides, warning him that this might be the last time he saw any of them.

As the rest of the crew left to pack their bags, Cal held Alexander back. "Dania agreed to all this?"

Alex pursed his lips. "She asked me to prepare accommodations for twelve."

Cal's stomach sank. "She doesn't know the pirates are staying on board."

"It appears not."

"Can you tell her?"

Alex shook his head. "A few moments after she asked me to help with the crew, Geron ordered me to only take Peter, Ty, Ethan, Christopher, and Alanna from the ship, and not to speak with Dania until the *Star Renegade* had left the cruiser."

So, the prince was as good at talking around the truth without lying as the enforcers were. *Fabulous.*

"I trust you have weapons stored throughout the ship for this sort of eventuality?"

"Yeah, we're smugglers, but I want to give Victor the benefit of the doubt."

"I wouldn't."

Cal dragged his fingers through his hair. "Yeah, you're probably right." The problem was, Cal and Rachel would be outnumbered. "I'll have to wait for them to make a play and then figure things out."

"Don't let your guard down for a moment."

Cal nodded. Hopefully, Victor remembered who'd saved all their lives back on that tanker. If not, this might be a very unpleasant trip.

THE BRIGHT LIGHTS in the cruiser's hangar grew dim as Cal backed the *Star Renegade* out of the megalith's gaping maw. As they drifted farther away from Geron's ship, Cal shivered. It still seemed hard to fathom that something that big could fly, even in the depth of space.

Victor sat in Ty's chair on Cal's right, tapping keys as they leveled off. "I still can't believe they let us go."

"They didn't *let* us go. They've kept a pretty big security deposit on our return." Cal spun the ship toward Themyscira. "We need to move away from the cruiser slowly so we blend in with the fleet. Then we'll whip around and make it look like we're approaching from the pirate sector."

Victor glanced at Iggy standing beside Ethan's station. With the guy's history of fighting, Cal would have preferred anyone else running Engineering, but Victor had insisted Iggy was the best pirate for the job.

Urvin and Degal were downstairs prepping the cargo bay for supplies, while Freddy, George, and Jasper were in Engineering. Ethan had made them swear not to touch anything, which, of course, was ridiculous.

Cal checked the ship scans. So far, everyone was where they were supposed to be. If anyone strayed from their posts or tried to get through the security on the weapons lockers, he'd know about it.

Chris and Cal had gone over all the possible scenarios and decided the pirates would most likely make a break for it as soon as they hit the ground on Themyscira. Chris doubted his pirate brethren would want to discuss options, but Cal hoped to talk them out of leaving, just in case the prince used it as a reason to start trouble. Deep down, though, Cal knew they'd be better off without their newest passengers.

Rachel scanned the screens on the nav and comms station. Alanna had gone over things with her before they left, and Rachel had sworn that she could handle the job. That didn't make Cal feel better, though. He was used to… Heck, he'd *learned to* depend on the cohesiveness of his crew. This should be a pretty cut and dry trading run, but he'd learned to never take for granted that anything was going to be easy.

Rachel sat on her foot. "So, what's the plan? Do we just tell the Themyscirans that the prince has our friends? Do you think they'll help us?"

Victor huffed a laugh. "Yeah, that's ripe."

Unfortunately, Cal had to agree. "The only people the Themyscirans hate more than men are the Kevers. They might kill us if they even thought we'd *spoken* to a Bane."

"Huh," Rachel said. "Well, that's inconvenient." Her screen flashed. "Hold on a minute." Rachel tapped on the screen. "What the heck?" She turned to Iggy. "Did you just send out a comm?"

The pirate pursed his lips. "You bet I did. You want to approach the pirate sector unannounced when there's a

Kever cruiser larger than most colonies threatening the planet next door? I don't want to be blown out of the stars as a precaution."

"Good call, Igg," Victor said. "Let's just keep it slow and steady, and we'll be fine."

Cal glared at him. "This is still my ship. I'd like to clear any communication from here on out."

Victor saluted, then shook his head. Cal supposed the guy hadn't followed a chain of command in years. Not that Cal's own crew was better in that respect, but at least Cal trusted them.

The stars sparkled and danced in the distance. They usually calmed him, like being wrapped in the arms of an old friend. Today, though, their sparkle seemed more distant than ever, reminding him that the people he cared about most in the world were no longer onboard.

"Um, Cally?" Rachel squinted at the nav screen. "I'm pretty sure we've got some ships heading right for us."

Cal looked over his right shoulder at her. "What?"

"I'm sure it's nothin'." Victor scratched his nose, leaning back in Ty's chair.

"I don't think it's nothing." Rachel tapped on her screen. "If it's nothing, there're even more nothings out there now."

Victor spun and pointed a gun at Cal as Iggy drew a gun on Rachel. Victor's small, black handgun was standard street issue—the kind that was nearly impossible to trace. They must have brought them onboard from the tank without Cal even knowing about it.

Cal held his hands out to the sides. He hated being right, but it would probably be best to act surprised. "What the blazes is going on?"

Victor eased out of his seat, keeping his weapon trained on Cal. "We ain't going to Themyscira."

What? That was the nearest planet. "We have to. We made a deal."

Victor pointed his chin at Cal. "*You* made a deal. Not us." He called over his shoulder to Rachel. "Get over here where I can see you, Red."

She sneered at him as she passed. "I never liked you."

Cal, unfortunately, had to back her on that one. He pulled her closer to him and whispered in her ear. "Take it easy." Then to Victor, he said, "If you're not on the *Renegade* when we get back, I don't know what that star-blasted prince is going to do."

"Not our problem."

Iggy sat at the nav station. "I've got a skipper approaching the cargo bay door now. Urvin is there, prepping the seal."

Cal folded his arms. "That's your plan? You're going to pile into a skipper and run with your tails between your legs?"

"Not quite." Victor waved his gun at them. "*You two* are going to pile into the skipper and run with your tails between your legs. Me and my boys are going to get comfy in the crew quarters you were so selfish about sharing."

Cal lowered his arms. "You want the *Renegade*? No way."

Victor snorted a laugh. "I ain't thinking you got a choice, my friend." He stood. "Let me tell ya, it would be easier to shoot you, but I'm feeling charitable 'cause you were nice enough to get me and my boys off that exploding tank. But my charity only goes so far." He pointed at the door. "Now make like a good, little smuggler and do what you're told." He pointed the gun at Rachel. "Or I blow a hole in Red's pretty little face."

———

After securing the skipper to the *Star Renegade*'s hull, Urvin had been kind enough to meet wiry, thin Degal halfway to the cargo bay. Degal pulled Rachel along ahead of Cal while Urvin walked behind them with the business end of a gun pressed into Cal's back, just in case Cal happened to forget that they might get shot at any moment.

Rachel remained uncharacteristically quiet, which was probably a good thing. It gave Cal a chance to think, although he wasn't sure he'd be able to come up with a plan before he and Rachel got herded into another ship.

Degal took a bite out of a bar of chocolate that Cal was fairly certain had been in his private stash for cooking. "Don't look so glum, Espinoza." He tossed the wrapper on the floor. "The boss was in a good mood. The original plan was to put a bullet in both your heads and we'd just clean up all the blood once we reached a port. I'd say you're getting off easy."

Getting off easy? These guys were planning on stealing their home. There was no getting off easy when they were leaving most of the crew to be executed and shoving the remaining two people into a skipper and leaving them to explain to a prince what had happened.

Static crackled over the speakers above, and Iggy's raspy voice came over the comm. "Hey, Espinoza, here's a little going away music for ya."

A shrill guitar and heavy drumbeat filled the halls, erasing the *Star Renegade*'s normal calm. The walls trembled from the volume. If the speakers blew out, Ethan would have a brain aneurysm, but Cal figured that was the least of his worries at the moment.

The open hatch leading to the skipper loomed off to Cal's right as his feet hit the bottom of the ramp to the cargo hold. Degal still had the gun squarely pointed at Rachel's temple. Cal had no idea how itchy the guy's trigger finger was. He couldn't take any unnecessary risks, but he also couldn't get onto that ship.

Degal shrieked and spun, releasing Rachel. Blood streamed from his eyes, and he flailed his hands and his gun about his head.

"What the—" Urvin pulled Cal to his chest and pointed the gun at his temple. "Whatever that is, make it stop."

The drumbeat thumped through the hall as Degal fell to his knees. Rachel stumbled back, gaping.

Degal held his head. "I can't see! I can't see!"

Cal didn't doubt it. There wasn't much left of his face.

Urvin twitched, looking around the cargo bay. "What the hell is going on?"

Cal felt the *whoosh* of a fluffy, invisible tail whip by his face. When Urvin gasped, Cal shoved the pirate's gun hand away from his temple a micro-second before it went off. Cal's ears rang as Urvin started screaming, thrashing in circles.

Rachel scrambled to Degal and grabbed his gun.

Cal ducked as Urvin shot his own pistol into the air, trying to dislodge the invisible menace. Thank goodness there were no major computers down there. A dull ache pressed against the back of Cal's eyes. He gritted his teeth and willed it away. Now was *not* the time for a migraine.

Urvin clawed and punched at the air above his head as deep gashes sliced across his face.

"You okay?" Cal slid beside Rachel, keeping his head down in case Urvin fired blind again.

She held up the gun. "I am now."

Another voice echoed through the chamber and a third pirate came running from the direction of the skipper holding a metal bar over his head.

Dammit! Cal had forgotten about the skipper pilot!

The new guy howled, "Keep still!" as he swung the metal bar at Urvin.

Rachel got up on one knee and aimed the gun at the pirates.

A dull *thunk* filled the room, like the metal rod the pilot had been swinging had intercepted something in the blank space over Urvin's head. Rachel gasped as Max's limp, fluffy body materialized and slid across the floor.

"No!" Rachel fired.

The pirate turned toward her, and his eyes widened before he fell to the deck.

"Max!" Rachel scrambled to the unmoving pile of fur while Cal sprinted to Urvin, grabbing the gun out of his hand.

The guy screamed, clawing at his eyes. "I can't see!" Blood dripped down his face.

Max's attack had been calculated and effective. No wonder the Trellan colonists had a problem with their fluffy, indigenous neighbors. They knew exactly how to disable a human.

The music still drummed from the speakers above. Iggy had actually done them a favor. Without the music, the gunfire and screaming would have echoed throughout the ship.

Cal grabbed a few cable ties from the supply cabinet and started tying up Urvin.

"You're dead, Espinoza. I swear it!" The pirate spat at him.

Cal ripped up a rag and tied it around the pirate's mouth to gag him. "Not yet, I'm not."

Across the room, Max rolled over and whined, hobbling to Rachel as she cable-tied Degal's wrists behind his back. She pulled tightly, making him arch his back and grunt.

Degal twisted when she pulled him to his feet. "When I get out of these, I'm going to kill you."

"Yeah, right. Whatever." She shoved him forward. "What do you want to do with them, Cally? I think the nearest airlock would be a perfect way to get rid of the trash."

He quirked a brow at her. Cal wasn't too fond of the guys trying to take over his ship, but killing two nearly blind, defenseless men was out of the question.

She rolled her eyes. "I was only kidding. How about we shove them in there?" She pointed to the skipper craft still attached to the cargo entrance.

"I guess that will do." Cal grabbed the back of Urvin's jacket and dragged him, then Degal into the skipper. When Degal struggled, Cal accidentally hit him on the head, and he fell into a heap. Urvin followed suit.

Rachel kicked Urvin with the edge of her boot. "Neither of them looks as menacing when they're unconscious." She puffed out a breath. "Now what?"

As usual, he was expected to have a plan. By now, they should all have known that most of the time, he was making stuff up as he went along.

Cal dragged his fingers through his hair. "Well, they're expecting us to leave in this thing."

"Yeah, so?"

"So, let's make them think we're leaving."

"What do you mean?"

"We used to have a medical cadaver named Bessie. We

shot her into space once, and two entire fleets of ships took an initial scan and figured she was Dania."

"*What?*"

There are two of us, and two of them. If Victor does a scan, he'll find two people on board and be none the wiser."

"Will that work?"

"Like I said, it worked with Bessie." Cal called up the autopilot and programmed the ship into a wide arc that would land them in the shipping lanes of the pirate sector. Worst-case scenario, someone would pick them up for salvage within the next day.

He hit a thirty-second countdown, and they slipped out of the ship before closing and sealing the airlock.

Cal pointed at the dead pilot. "Let's stuff this guy in a cargo container for now."

"That ain't gonna hide the blood."

"No, but it'll at least not give anyone a reason to see him on the ground and come down here to check it out."

A moment later, the secondary seals released, and the skipper drifted a few yards before the engines engaged, shooting Urvin and Degal away from the *Star Renegade*.

The music lowered and the comm went off beside them. "Good work, Urv. Now get up here." The music blasted again, even louder.

Rachel stormed toward the comm. "I'm gonna give him a piece of my mind."

"No, you won't." Cal grabbed her hand, stopping her from tapping the comm. "It worked. They think we're on the skipper."

Her eyes grew wide. "That means..." She turned toward the ramp to the upper levels.

"That means they won't be expecting us." Cal looked at

the floor until he found a bloody, small paw hanging in the air—and nothing else. "Max, are you feeling good enough to help?"

The little guy shook out his tail and became visible. He ran in a circle three times…probably a little slower than he had in the past, but still faster than a pirate.

Cal nodded. "Okay, then. It's three of us against five of them. Let's use surprise in our favor."

CHAPTER 25
CAL

CAL LEANED AWAY from the window in the door to lower Engineering. "It looks like just Freddy and George in there."

"Two of them, three of us. I like those odds." Rachel stretched out her arms like she was about to work out in the gym. "I think our best bet is to enter from upstairs. If we're looking down on them, we'll have better visibility, and they won't see us as quickly."

"That's...*actually* a good idea."

She placed her hands on her hips. "I get good ideas sometimes. I was a thief before I was a med tech, remember?"

A thief, a med tech, a hospitality agent, and a host of other interesting things. Rachel was definitely a wealth of unexpected knowledge.

They made their way upstairs, easing around corners with their guns raised. There were two pirates in Engineering, but that still meant that Victor, Iggy, and Jasper were somewhere else on the ship. At least one of them was probably sitting in Cal's chair on the bridge, but the other two could be lurking anywhere, ready to ruin the surprise.

The drumbeats and shrill guitar solos echoed through the halls as Rachel placed her back against the wall outside upper Engineering. "All right. They'll probably hear the door open, but we'll have a solid one or two seconds before they look up. What's the plan?"

Interesting that she had honed her skills to know how long it took someone to look at a door after it had opened.

She glanced at him. "Normally, I'd be sneaking in, not shooting. So, I need a little direction here."

Good call. "When I looked in the window downstairs, Freddy was by Ethan's workstation. George was back by the air recycler. You take the one by Ethan's desk."

She nodded. "I get the one on the right. You get the one on the left. Got it."

Something scratched at Cal's leg. Cal looked down but wasn't surprised to see nothing there. "You're hurt, Max. You stay in reserves. You'll be backup in case anything goes wrong."

The little guy chittered, and Cal took that as understanding before he took a deep breath and met Rachel's gaze. "Ready?"

She adjusted her grip on the gun. "Let's kick some pirate tushy."

Tushy? She must have been hanging out with Alanna too much. "Okay. Let's go."

Cal placed his palm on the controls. The door slid open, and Cal moved in first. Two seconds wasn't long. They needed to make this count. He scanned the area around the air recycler, but no one was...

George walked out from the lavatory and looked up. The pirate pulled out his gun and got off a shot the same time Cal pulled the trigger. Cal ducked as George's blast hit the wall behind him.

On the other side of the room, a laser fired. Rachel cursed and screamed, "Ow!" a second before George's body hit the floor.

A chill ran over Cal's skin. Rachel hadn't been carrying a laser.

Down below, Freddy cried out, circling, clawing at his head like something was attacking him. Max, no doubt.

Rachel sat with her back against the wall. "I'm so out of practice!" She hissed, holding her arm. "It's only a scratch. I'm fine. Go help my little buddy!"

Cal gritted his teeth. He hated leaving her, but if Freddy reached a comm, the rest of the pirates would come in guns blazing.

He bounded down the steps. Freddy was still swinging and punching at his head while blood dripped down the sides of his face. Cal aimed at the guy's chest, then his legs...but Max could hop anywhere and Cal wouldn't even have known it.

"Max!" Cal leveled his weapon on the pirate. "Jump clear."

A high-pitched bark filled the chamber. Freddy stopped swinging his arms and his eyes widened when he saw Cal. Freddy cursed and raised his laser-rifle, but Cal pulled the trigger, and the pirate thumped to the deck.

Cal pointed his gun left, then right, not breathing until he knew they were alone. "Max, are you okay?"

The floor blurred and the little guy appeared, scraping his claws on the ground, probably trying to clean off the blood from scratching the pirate's face.

Cal stroked the back of the animal's head. "Good job. You're like a miniature tornado."

"I'm alive if anyone cares." Rachel stepped off the last rung of the ladder. "Would you mind grabbing the medical kit?"

Cal tucked his gun into the back of his pants and grabbed the metal case from its hook on the wall. "How bad is it?"

She sat on the floor, opened the lid, and started unpacking supplies. "It's not bad. It just stings like blazes." She ripped a package open with her teeth and applied a salve to her right shoulder. "I probably need a few stitches, but I'm kinda thinking we don't have time for that. This will numb it for a few hours."

"Stitches?" That didn't sound good.

She waved her left hand at him. "It's not like my guts are going to fall out or anything. I'll just have a nasty scar." She pressed a bandage on the cut and pulled her sleeve down. "I guess I won't be wearing strapless dresses anymore."

Cal frowned. Girls thought of the strangest things when they got hurt. He helped her stand.

Rachel looked at her own gun and then the one on the floor. "Huh." She tucked the one in her hand into her waistband and grabbed Freddy's laser-rifle. "Okay. We've got three nasties left, right? That's three of us, and three of them. That's pretty good odds."

Cal started walking toward the exit. "It is, as long as we keep the element of surprise."

The door opened as he neared the archway.

Jasper bounded into the room. "Hey, guys, Iggy said..." He skidded to a stop when he saw them.

The music stopped and the comm on the wall went off.

Victor's voice filled the room. "George, we have a situation up here. Where the hell are you?"

Jasper leapt for the comm control and Cal grabbed his arm. The pirate swung with his other arm and dug his fist into Cal's side. Cal coughed, wincing as he swung around with his other hand and caught Jasper in the jaw. Another punch came in a blur, slamming Cal in the temple. He stumbled back a step, and a laser shot echoed in the chamber.

A hole appeared in the wall beside Cal's head and Rachel cursed, lowering the laser-rifle in a shaking hand...her *left* hand. Wasn't she right-handed?

Stars shot around Cal's eyes and his head exploded in throbbing pain. He fell to his knees, grabbing his head. *Shit! Not now!* He reached behind for his gun, but the room started to spin.

Max growled, and Jasper flinched like something had jumped on his shoulders. He backed up, slamming into the wall and Max yipped before the pirate lunged for Cal again. Cal ducked, but the room swirled. He dropped to the deck and puked. When he looked up, the pirate was pointing the gun at his face.

"Nighty night."

The gunshot reverberated through the room. The echo danced, careening through Cal's brain, digging and clawing until he vomited again. He stared at the trail of yellow goo hanging from his lips.

There was no blood. And he was still breathing.

He squinted, blinking.

Rachel stood over him. "Ew." She held out her blood-splattered shirt. "I don't know what's grosser. This—or you."

Cal squinted again, his eyes barely making out the body on the floor before the room started spinning again.

Rachel crouched beside him. "Migraine?"

Cal could only grunt as he slipped to the floor. The cold tiles felt glorious. If he let that chill seep into his skin, maybe he'd stop puking. But he couldn't stay there. Victor was taking the *Star Renegade* stars-knew-where, and he needed to get to Themyscira and get those supplies. If Geron killed his family because Cal couldn't stand up straight...

Rachel appeared beside him again. "I've got you, Cally." She pressed something against his arm, and a needle lanced his skin before a burning spread down his biceps.

Cal took slow, steady breaths. "What was that?"

She looked at the cylinder. "Suma something-or-other. Doc put these miracle injections in all the med kits and showed us how to use them. He said it would take about twenty minutes to turn you human again."

The only problem was, they didn't have twenty minutes.

Rachel moved to the wall and started stroking a gray, fuzzy blob on the floor.

Cal took for granted that was Max. "Is he okay?"

The gray blob moved—but slowly.

"I think he's okay," Rachel said. "But hurt. I guess that's something we all have in common."

And Victor and Iggy were still on the ship, and they were probably fine. The playing field may have just tipped a little in the bad guys' favor.

THE EXPLOSIONS RIDDLING Cal's skull had dulled from nuclear to atomic. His vision had cleared enough that he could see the hallway leading to the bridge. The damn lights still felt like knives in his eyes, though.

Rachel placed her hand on his shoulder. "Cally, I think you need more time to rest."

Yes, he definitely needed more time to rest, but they couldn't give Victor the opportunity to figure out that his pirate buddies weren't simply off on a drunken bender.

"We need to hit them while luck and surprise are still in our favor."

"Luck? I have a slice in my arm, Max got hurt twice, and you just looked like you were gonna die. I'm not lyin', Cally. I thought Ethan was exaggerating when he said he shot you for your own good, once—but after seeing you spewing like that, I kinda understand where he was coming from."

Cal rubbed his eyes, and the hall came into focus. "I agree that we're not at our best, but I'm getting better, and we have no idea where Victor is taking us. For all we know, he's—"

A dull boom echoed through the walls, and the ship shook.

Rachel stumbled before righting herself. "Is someone firing on us?"

Cal grabbed the wall, closing his eyes and taking a few steadying breaths as a wave of nausea rolled over him. "It sure as hell sounds like it. We need to get to the bridge."

The floor rumbled again as they sprinted down the hall. Cal concentrated on his breathing as the pressure in his head eased to a dull ache. He had to get back in the captain's chair and get the *Star Renegade* back on course. How he was going to do that, he had no idea. Victor was no fool. He'd have the bridge locked tighter than a—

At the end of the hall, the door to the bridge slid open and Cal skidded to a stop. They couldn't possibly have gotten that lucky.

Iggy stepped out, cursing and muttering under his breath. The pirate gaped when he looked up, his eyes widening. "It's Espinoza!"

He ducked to the right as Rachel shot her laser-rifle. The blast burned a hole in the wall above his head as he dove around the corner.

"Dammit!" Victor shouted from within the bridge as the door shut and the locks engaged.

Rachel groaned. "Next time, remind me to get shot in my left arm rather than my right!"

She walked toward the corner.

"Wait!" Cal pulled her back as a laser blast singed her hair. "Don't make yourself a target."

An ashy smell filled the hallway. "I didn't see a gun in his hand." She patted down the smoking edges of her hair.

"It's the guns you *don't* see that get you killed."

The sound of nails scraping on the floor tiles grated through Cal's brain like a million needle-like claws gouging his temples before Iggy started to curse and scream somewhere down the hall.

A laser shot off. Then another.

Rachel bolted for the corner again. "Max!"

Cal sprinted after her and turned the corner to see Iggy swiping the air about him and shooting at what looked like nothing.

Rachel held up her gun. "I don't know where to shoot!"

Not only that, her aim with her left hand was almost as bad as Ethan's.

Cal blinked until his eyes refocused, seeing a small spot of blood floating in the air just above the deck plates. *There you are, Max.*

Iggy spun, pointing the gun at Cal. "Screw you, Espinoza!"

Rachel's weapon shot a microsecond before Cal's. Iggy's body jolted then hit the floor.

"Max, are you okay?" Rachel ran down the hall as Max shook out his tail. He held up a bleeding paw.

She perused the wound. "It's not bad. Are you good to keep going?"

Max nodded, licking his wound. The deck rumbled again.

Rachel sighed, standing. "One bad guy left. Victor is a jerk, but he isn't an idiot." She pointed at the entrance to the bridge. "That door's gonna stay locked."

"Yeah, but the sensors let us into Engineering, which means he never disabled general controls."

"So?"

"So, I have a private entrance to the bridge in my quarters."

"Well, that's handy."

"Captain's privilege." Cal took a deep breath and scanned the deck. The lights hurt but no longer stabbed his retinas. Doc's magic injection was working wonders.

"What's the plan?" Rachel asked.

The ship rumbled. "We need to find out who's shooting at us." They needed to sneak onto the bridge to do that, though, which wasn't going to be easy with a room that small, and the secret door being just off the captain's left periphery. "You stay out here with Max. Keep making it sound like you're trying to get in."

Rachel frowned at him. "You're going to go in there alone?"

"It's a ladder straight up to the bridge. One person gets through at a time."

"Cally, that doesn't sound like a good idea."

"Victor has been too busy to look around. He may not even know the door is there, and if he thinks we're still outside trying to break in, I'll be able to surprise him."

Max limped a few steps then waved his front paws, garbling and growling.

Cal cocked his head. "I'd love your help, but you're already hurt."

Max barked at him.

"That better not have been a curse."

Rachel snorted. "I gotta agree with him. He's good in a fight."

That was definitely true, but Max's fur was bloodied, and his paw was shaking. Not to mention that limp. The little guy had heart, but Cal would feel better if both Max and Rachel were out in the hall, where they couldn't get hurt any worse. Not to mention, they'd be able to watch each other's back if anything else went wrong.

Cal certainly wasn't going to admit to Rachel that he was afraid she'd get hurt, though. She might accidentally on-purpose shoot him for his honesty.

He also wasn't all that excited about breaking into his own bridge without backup. This wasn't the greatest situation, no matter what they did.

Max formed a miniature fist and waved it at him. He looked surprisingly like Mel, giving one of her famous lectures from the doorway of her kitchen on Kirato.

Rachel winced, holding her arm. "Please take Max with you, Cally. I don't want you going up there alone."

Max yipped, shaking his tail. He faded out, then reappeared. At least his camouflage still worked. That had to amount for something.

"All right, I'll take Max." Cal wiped the sweat from his forehead with the back of his arm. "You stay out here and every once in a while, bang on the door like you're trying to break the locks."

Rachel saluted. "Got it."

Cal looked down at his partner in crime. Max shook out his tail and disappeared again. Hopefully, that little trick would be enough to keep luck tipped in their favor.

CAL REACHED the top rung of the ladder and paused on the small landing. He took a deep breath, released it slowly, and pulled his gun out of his waistband. He checked the chamber: only two bullets left. He'd need to make them count.

A deep boom sounded through the walls and Cal lurched backward. He grabbed on to the upper rails to stop from falling back down the tube leading to his quarters. Whoever was out there pummeling them was relentless. Either that, or Victor was a lousy pilot.

Someone warm and fuzzy brushed up against his leg.

Cal reached down and patted Max on the head before adjusting his grip on the gun.

Best-case scenario, he'd open the door and Victor wouldn't even notice. Cal would be able to get a single shot off and it would be over. Worst-case scenario, Victor would be waiting for him, ready to shoot as soon as the door cracked open.

The floor jolted again, and a chill raked over Cal's skin. Victor waiting for him *wouldn't be* the worst-case scenario.

The worst case would be if Cal shot, missed, and hit one of the panels or the main screen. *Stars!* The room was wall-to-wall critical systems, and most of it was already being held together with spit and love.

The platform rumbled beneath his feet, and Cal grabbed the wall beside him. One misplaced shot could leave them dead and drifting, and Cal still had no idea who was out there, shooting at his ship.

He tucked the gun back in his waistband. He'd just have to do this the old-fashioned way, and hope that Victor either wouldn't have time to pull out his gun or was smart enough to calculate the risk of using it.

Max scratched lightly against Cal's pant leg.

"Yeah, buddy. Slight change of plans," Cal whispered. "We're going to have to do this with fists and smarts."

Max's ears perked up. He stood on his hindlegs and bared his teeth, holding up curved claws while growling. The little guy seemed to lose his balance, and his eyes widened. Max yipped before he fell to the side, whimpering as he started licking at his injured back leg.

So much for their secret weapon. "Maybe you should stay here, buddy."

Max stopped licking and sat, holding up his claws again, this time on his haunches rather than standing.

"I get that you want to help, and you're without a doubt the bravest Trellan I know." But Cal couldn't ask a wounded member of his crew to fight. If it were Doc or Ethan, he'd feel the same way. The number of legs they had shouldn't make a difference.

Max growled something and made punching movements with his paws.

Cal smiled. The little guy certainly had spirit. But maybe he could use his skills in another way.

"Have you been studying comms?" The little guy had been making everyone think the ship was haunted for quite some time, setting off recyclers, forcing doors to bounce back, and making people feel like they were being watched. Mainly because they *had* been being watched.

Max looked at the door and then nodded. This was a long shot, but it was worth a try.

"When the door opens, I want you to sneak over to Alanna's station. See if you can type out a comm to whoever is out there and tell them to stop trying to poke holes in my ship."

Max's eyes grew slightly wider, but he nodded. Cal had learned quickly not to underestimate the smallest member of his crew. He'd typed out messages to them on data pads already, so he had a solid understanding of how to communicate in typed English, even though his voice box wasn't capable of making the sounds.

Cal switched the dial on the wall to manual and slowly slid the door open. Victor sat in Cal's chair with sweat dripping down his face as his hands swiped over the controls. The man's larger girth hung slightly over the edges of the seat as the pirate wiped his forehead with his sleeve.

A few streaks of bloody hair—and nothing else—crept past the backs of the captain's and pilot's stations, barely visible if you didn't know someone was there.

Alanna's chair turned slightly as an invisible Max climbed up and started pressing the keys. Cal smiled. When stealth was necessary, size really did matter. Hopefully, Max didn't type the wrong thing and piss off whoever was out there even more than they already were.

Outside, Rachel pounded on the door with something that sounded like it was made of metal. Hopefully, she didn't dent the door past what they could repair...which was pretty foolish to worry about all things considered.

Cal eased the door open a little more and took half a step inside.

Victor startled and looked right at him, his eyes filled with raw, red fury. "Espinoza!"

Victor stood while Cal lunged, jamming his shoulder into the pirate's chest.

They skidded toward Ty's chair before Victor grabbed Cal and slammed him into the door, knocking the air from Cal's lungs.

Rachel's muffled voice came through the metal frame, calling Cal's name. Maybe it would have been a better idea if they'd all come up the ladder together.

Over the pirate's shoulder, five ships shot past the view screen. Three were worn, battle-hardened, and highly modified skippers. The others were state-of-the-art, barely blemished black ships with red lines. Those had to be from Themyscira. The common ships could have been anyone, but they were most likely the pirates Iggy had called right before this little mutiny had started.

A red warning icon flashed on the upper-right of the screen.

The comms were down. *Dammit!* Max's message wouldn't go through!

Victor tightened his grip and Cal tried to struggle, but the larger man punched another fist into Cal's stomach.

"I ain't going back to be executed." The pirate spat. "And if you had any common sense, you'd be running, too."

A growl filled the air and Victor cursed as a deep gash

appeared on his cheek. He reached over his shoulder and grabbed what looked like nothing before throwing Max across the bridge.

Max yipped when he hit the wall but shook out his fur and bared his teeth.

Victor gaped. "What the hell is that?"

Cal punched, and the pirate grabbed his fist, yanking Cal toward him.

Max barked and his fluffy tail flashed in and out of existence as he gnawed at Victor's leg.

Cal spun out of the larger man's grip and managed a cross punch to the pirate's side. "I have family on that cruiser. I'm not leaving them."

"Then you're going to be just as dead as they are."

Victor kicked his foot and Max thudded against the main entrance before sliding to the floor in a pile of gray, fluffy fur.

The pirate seethed. "You ain't taking me down with you, Espinoza."

He swung at Cal and Cal dodged, swinging around and avoiding another hit.

The little guy struggled to get up. Cal should have left him with Rachel.

Behind Victor, a bright-yellow flash flew across the screen, and the ship rumbled beneath their feet. Cal needed to get to those controls.

Victor charged him again, and Cal ducked right, slamming Victor with a firm upper-cut. The pirate drove his own punch down, slamming Cal to his knees.

Stars riddled Cal's vision before Victor's hands wrapped around Cal's neck.

"Don't worry, Espinoza." The weapons firing on the

skipper in the viewscreen lit the pirate up like a vengeful angel. "I'll take good care of your ship."

Cal bet he wouldn't. He clawed at Victor's hands trying to get free.

The pirate leaned closer. "Or maybe I'll just scrap it for spare parts."

Heat flushed through Cal that had more to do with protecting his home—his *family's* home—than it did with lack of oxygen. Closing his eyes, he mustered all the strength he had and punched Victor between the legs.

The pirate flinched but barely moved. Did the guy have balls of steel or something?

Cal punched again and Victor jolted enough for Cal to shift his weight. A flush of adrenaline raced through his veins as Cal kicked his knee into the guy's groin.

Victor groaned and took a few steps back, clutching his crotch and struggling to breathe.

Cal jumped to his feet, coughing as he waited for the explosion of a migraine to make this even worse, but his vision cleared with each breath. Whatever had been in that injection Rachel had given him really was a miracle.

Cal took a deep breath. "You can't have my ship."

Victor righted himself, breathing heavy, like it still hurt. "I already..."

A clang reverberated through the bridge. Victor's eyes widened and his mouth fell open before he slipped to the floor.

Rachel stood behind him, spinning a metal frying pan in her left hand. "I had about enough of him."

Cal shook off the shock. *"A frying pan?"*

"Yeah, I was thinking that my aim ain't all that good with my right arm all bandaged up. I didn't want to blow a hole in anything important, so I looked in your quarters for a weapon." She spun the pan again. "The kitchen was filled with useful stuff."

Cal leaned over, placing his hands on his knees as he laughed. "Good job."

Max limped to Cal and licked his hand.

Cal scratched behind the little guy's ears. "Thanks, buddy."

"You got anything to tie Big and Ugly up with?" Rachel asked.

Cal pointed under Ty's station. "Zip ties in the repair kit."

She reached underneath the panel. "On it."

The floor rumbled again as two ships shot over the *Star Renegade's* bow.

Rachel looked out the viewscreen. "Whoa."

"You're not kidding." Cal sat in the captain's chair. "Get on nav and see if you can find out where we are." Cal banked up and over two ships in a dogfight.

She tossed the zip ties on the floor. "Here, Max. You can do the honors."

Max grabbed the ties as Rachel sat in Alanna's chair. "It looks like we're not far from where we were, Cally. Themyscira is off to your right."

"Roger that." He eased the ship right and the planet came into view. Cal had never been happier to see that blasted, annoying world in all his life.

One of the pirate ships exploded into a fireball before space muffled the flames. The black-and-red ship circled back and headed straight for the *Star Renegade*.

"Rachel, send out a comm. Tell them we're friendly."

"I'm trying! We've got some kind of blocky-thingy on our comms. Nothing is going out."

Great. "They must have earmarked us as the command ship. Victor must have been giving the pirates directions."

A spray of artillery shot toward them, and Cal spun around it. He'd rather have Ty piloting in a life-or-death situation. There were too many ways to make a mistake. But Cal had come this far, and he wasn't about to get blown up after just getting his ship back. He swerved up and over a second ship, then around a third.

"Two more are heading right for us. All the other little blips on the screen are gone, so I'm guessing we're the only thing left to shoot at."

Max climbed into Ty's chair and growled, pointing at the screen.

"What did he say?" Cal asked.

"I don't know. I can't speak Trellan."

That had never stopped her from understanding him before. Cal banked down, taking a wide loop around the three approaching ships.

A tone sounded.

"Was that the comm?"

"It looks like they wanna talk now." Rachel tapped her fingers on the panel. "You're live, Cally."

Cal took a deep breath. "This is the *Star Renegade*. We're friendly. Cease firing. Repeat. Cease firing."

The screen flickered and a woman with light skin and long, dark, straight hair appeared on the screen. "The only reason you are still alive is because you suddenly started flying better and stopped firing on us. Explain yourself."

"We were hijacked by pirates."

The woman frowned. "Hijacked?"

"Yeah, by this ugly jerk." Rachel got up and grabbed Victor by the collar, grunting as she hoisted him into view.

"He can't talk right now. He had a run-in with a frying pan." She let him go and his head bounced on the floor.

Cal turned back to the screen. "My name is Calvin Espinoza. This is the *Star Renegade*. We were en route to Themyscira to trade when our passengers decided to stage a mutiny. We're back in control, and all unfriendlies have been detained or eliminated. There are two tied up in a small skipper that we shot off into the shipping lanes if you want to pick them up."

The woman nodded. "We've already arrested the ones in the skipper. They were decidedly uncooperative." She looked to the side of her screen, like she was reading something, before she returned her gaze to Cal. "I am sending you an approach vector. You will be escorted into Themysciran space. Any deviation will be dealt with harshly."

Cal nodded. "Understood. Thank you for the escort." Cal tapped off the comm.

Rachel shifted her weight and sat on her foot. "They're not really being nice with that escort, you know. They don't trust us."

"I realize that, but if they stop playing nice, the only way to avoid firing on them would be to run, and we can't do that. So, I'm willing to be sugary sweet if I need to be."

"Gotcha." She stood and tapped her thigh. "Come here, Max. I'm going to sit there for a bit."

Max jumped off Ty's chair and Rachel took his place.

She leaned back. "Hey, this chair is really comfortable. No wonder Ty doesn't mind hanging out up here." She pointed at the control panel. "What does this yellow, flashing light do?"

"Don't touch anything."

"Hey, I just proved I know my way around a cockpit."

"That was nav and comms, not piloting. I don't *need* you to know your way around anything. I'll do all the flying."

"Aw, you're no fun."

Themyscira grew larger in the view screen. The comm pinged and the picture faded into Veronica's face. "Well, hello there, *Star Renegade*. That was a pretty exciting approach. I have to say we were a little puzzled."

Cal bet they were. "I'd like to extend a hearty *thank you* to your pilots for not blowing us up. We were headed your way to do some more trading."

"Really?" She glanced to Cal's right. "Where's that delicious copilot of yours?"

"Ty's not with us on this trip."

She looked down, and her eyes moved like she was reading something. "It looks like *none of* your crew is on your ship. There are a couple of bodies, as to be expected if what you say is true, and someone…" She squinted at the screen. "Someone is either asleep on your bridge or unconscious."

"He's tied up," Cal said.

"Roger that, *Star Renegade*." She looked up. "No one else is there with you?"

"Hey!" Rachel sat up. "I'm sitting right here."

"We're just here for a very fast trade," Cal said. "The same items as last time, so we'll go right to see Yonid and then head right out."

Veronica stared at him through the screen. "*Really?*"

Rachel muted them. "She's not buying this."

"Quiet."

Veronica's smile returned, but it seemed a little more rehearsed. "Send me your wish list, *Star Renegade*. We'd like to see what you'll be shopping for today."

This was bad. She didn't trust them. Cal knew he needed

to have his crew on board. Maybe Ty could have flashed that million-dollar smile and distracted her enough to not care the others weren't on the ship.

He tapped a few buttons on his console and unmuted himself. "Sending now."

"Received, *Star Renegade*. We'll get back to you." The screen blanked out.

Rachel turned Ty's chair toward him. "Cally, we're in trouble. That woman doesn't believe you."

"We're fine."

"No, we're not. Believe me, I'm a woman, and I know that look on her face."

"We need to play it cool and calm. If she doesn't let us land, we're out of luck."

The screen came to life and Veronica appeared again. "Captain Espinoza, this order is five times what you picked up last time. Can you confirm those numbers?"

Cal tapped the comm. "Yes. If you haven't heard, there's a war going on. We're stocking up on supplies."

She nodded slowly. "Yes, there is a war going on, which makes it odd that you were approaching from the Z8 region." She leaned closer to the screen. "Can you tell me anything about that area?"

She was testing him…searching for lies. "Other than the fact that there was a massive blockade, and we turned and headed here instead?" He leaned on the console. "Look, last time we were here, we cleaned Yonid out. I knew this was a huge order, so we tried to fill it in Z8 first. Since we couldn't get there, we turned around and decided to drop in on our good friends on Themyscira. I'm not sure what the big deal is."

"*The big deal* is that we have a squid blockade on one side, and a small armada of snake ships on the other side. Not to mention our navy just engaged a small squadron of pirates too close to our own airspace." The screen flickered slightly. "We're surrounded by enemies who don't like us, and we are between two enemies who probably hate each other more than they hate us. You'd be a little cautious, too."

Cal nodded. "Understood. I'm sorry, Veronica, but honestly, we don't want any trouble. We want to land, get our supplies, and get out as fast as we can, nothing more."

The sincerity in his voice should have been palpable—because it was the truth. He'd left his family back on Geron's ship. Their lives were in danger, and Dania was one step away from being turned into a monster. Geron had been right about one thing. Every moment of every day was important when you had the opportunity to spend it with someone you loved.

Veronica's face changed, showing what may have been a combination of relief and understanding. "All right, *Star Renegade*. You're cleared to land. Same slip as last time. A guard will meet you on the surface to escort you to your destination, and we'll send a complement to get rid of your unwanted guest and help you clean up the trash."

The screen went blank before changing to stars again. Interesting that Veronica had called the bodies *trash*. Cal wondered if a different term would have been used if they'd been women, or not pirates.

Cal looked over his shoulder to Victor on the floor. Part of him wanted to drag him back to the cruiser, just in case. But the smuggler in him understood Victor's desire to run. The pirates had a chance on Themyscira. Victor, Degal, and Urvin could serve their time in a state-of-the-art prison that was probably cleaner than the tanker they'd been living on, and then maybe start a new life. The chances of Geron showing mercy anything near that were slim.

"Are you gonna let the guards take him?" Rachel asked.

Cal nodded. "Less for us to worry about."

"What about His Royal Pain-in-the-Derriere?"

"We tell the truth. The pirates mutinied. We killed a few and tied up the rest. And then the Themyscirans took them off our hands." There was no reason to lie. It wouldn't do them any good, and the truth, in this case, was better than any lie Cal would have been able to come up with.

Rachel leaned her elbow on the dash as they headed into the atmosphere. "A guard escort doesn't sound too friendly."

"That's their regular protocol. This planet doesn't have an overall trust in men."

Cal maneuvered the ship down to the surface and landed. As promised, a complement of guards awaited them.

Rachel leaned over the console to see the landing pad below. "They don't look so friendly. They kinda look like a boarding party."

"I'm sure that's the plan. They'll check things out, probably confirm there are signs of a fight or two, and then they'll take out the trash, as promised."

She looked out the window again. "What's to stop them from stealing stuff?"

"These people can be difficult, but they're not thieves. Anyway, we'll have someone watching them." He called into the air. "You with us, Max?"

Three streaks of bloody, matted fur launched from the floor and hovered in the air over Ty's station. The air about the console grew blurry and solidified into gray fur with paws matching the surface below him. Max shook out his tail and wiggled his nose at Cal.

Someday, Cal was going to get Doc to figure out how that camouflage worked.

Cal leaned on the back of his chair. "Okay, Max. Your job is to make things difficult if they try to do anything to the ship. And if they do put a tracker on us or take anything off the ship, you'll let me know, right?"

Max gave an overexaggerated nod of his head before disappearing.

Rachel folded her hands by her chin. "Aw, that's my little dude! Such a handy, little guy."

Cal stood. "Okay, let's go."

Empi was waiting for them at the base of the ramp. The large, imposing guard stood at attention, holding her long, knife-shaped gun beside her like a walking stick. Half the guards headed up the ramp into the ship as Cal and Rachel exited.

Cal waved at them. "One body in the cargo area, three in Engineering, one in the hallway outside the bridge, and the ringleader is tied up on the bridge."

The last woman gave Cal a curt nod but kept walking.

Rachel looked over her shoulder at them. "Not a very chatty bunch, are they?"

"We're probably better off that way."

When Cal and Rachel stepped onto Themysciran soil, Empi grabbed Rachel and placed the edge of her weapon at the med tech's throat.

Rachel's eyes widened. "What the heck? Chill, lady!"

Cal held up his hands. "Whoa! What's going on?"

Empi glared. "Is this woman holding you hostage?"

Cal gaped. "What? No!"

Empi shook Rachel. "Does she have something to do with the mutiny?"

"Ow!" Rachel tried to pull away. "Get your grimy mitts off me!"

Empi ignored her. "Is she an emissary for someone holding your crew hostage?"

An emissary? "No. You have this all wrong. Rachel is a new member of my crew. She signed on not long after the last time we traded here."

Empi narrowed her eyes. "I am giving you a chance, Calvin Espinosa. If this woman is threatening you or extorting you in any way, we will take care of it."

He held up his hands. "No! I swear. She's a friend."

Empi let her go.

Rachel stumbled to Cal. "Wow, that wasn't a very nice greeting. You know, I used to work on a welcoming committee—I can maybe give you some pointers on making someone actually feel *welcome* when they arrive on your planet. Sheesh!"

Empi waved her gun-sword like it was an extension of her arm. "Last time you were here, Calvin Espinoza, an enforcer threw my guards around the deck. We tended to bruises and broken bones for weeks."

Cal raised his palms again. "We had nothing to do with that."

She glared at him. "Yet you let that monster on your ship."

"I had no choice. He'd blocked us in with his own ship."

"Yet you survived. Did you lose your whole crew in the process?" She flared her nose at Rachel. "Did you pick up this one after that? The pink-haired one was prettier."

Rachel put her hands on her hips. "Hey!"

Cal elbowed her. "Listen, Empi, we're just here to trade. I

promised Veronica we'd land, trade, and get out. I'd really like to make good on that promise."

Empi nodded. "Very well. Follow me."

They made their way through the main trade center, receiving the same angry looks Cal had gotten every time he'd stepped foot on Themyscira.

"Gee, Cally, these people really don't like you."

"Yeah, I get that a lot here."

They stopped at Yonid's place as a woman stacked a box on top of two others at the door. Another woman handed her a credit tablet before turning to Cal and flipping her long, black hair over her shoulder. "You must be the infamous Calvin Espinoza."

He took a step forward. "Yeah. I'm here to see Yonid."

"She's not available. I'm her sister, Morgan. I'll be taking care of her transactions."

Cal frowned. Doc had warned him it was imperative to get perfect-grade supplies. He didn't want to take the chance of working with anyone else. "Is it possible to wait for Yonid?"

She leaned on the cartons. "Sure…if you want to wait two months. She's on a government-mandated holiday in the woods, away from all forms of stress and distraction."

"*Government mandated?*"

"Sure. We take pregnancy very seriously here. It's not all that common and the health of the mother is imperative."

Rachel gaped "Wow, really? Government mandated? That's unbelievable. Half the worlds I've visited are like, '*You're nine months pregnant? That's okay. You've still got time to work on the production line. Did your water break yet? You're okay, then; you can work one more day.*'"

Cal elbowed her again. "This is not the time. Get in, trade, get out, remember?"

"Oh, yeah. Sorry, Cally."

Morgan smiled at her. "No worries, she's fine. That's just another reason this planet is here. We cater to equitable rights to all."

Cal held back his smirk. Equitable rights as long as you were a woman. There was a reason most of the men who were born there left as soon as they were of age.

"You know," Morgan said to Rachel, "you are more than welcome to stay. We have plenty of free housing, and the government pays for all necessities deemed a human right."

Rachel's eyes widened. "Really? Like what?"

"Housing, education, air temperature control, food, and water."

That was another reason Themyscira had very little crime. There was no poverty to drive people to desperation.

Rachel made a *pft* sound. "Wow. That sounds like paradise."

Cal leaned closer to her. "The catch is: no men."

Rachel gaped. "Oh, wow, sorry, that's a nice offer and all, but that last one is a hard *no* for me."

Cal snorted a laugh. "I figured."

Morgan shrugged. "Your loss. Anyway, Yonid's trading center is technically closed for now, but they called and asked me to take care of your order." She tilted her head. "Which is quite large, by the way. I had to call in some favors." She tapped the crates behind her. "Like these, for instance."

"How do we know those will be as good a quality as last time?"

"Because this is Themyscira. We have a reputation to

keep. If people want to risk cheap, poor-quality goods, they can pass by and go to Z8."

"When there's not a blockade."

"True, however Z8's squid problem hasn't been as good for trade as one might expect. We've found that most traders would rather travel greater distances than come so close to the blockade." She tapped her fingertips on a data pad, typing something. "As for your trade, this is going to cost you. You're clearing out three different supply stores, and with the Carteks walling off the pirate sector…"

"Yeah, blockade price increases. We've heard that before." He handed her the money card Geron had given him. "Run that. It will be covered."

Cal didn't bother to worry about the price. He just needed to get back to his people…to Dania.

Morgan took the card. "Feel free to check out the inventory while I run the payment. I have three hover carts inside, and we'll get these new supplies loaded up for you."

Cal nodded. "Thank you." He tugged Rachel inside.

"Wow," she said. "This place is really hard core."

"You're not kidding."

"Do you really think these supplies will be okay?"

Cal considered the sealed boxes. "I sure hope so because I'd have no idea if they were giving us dirt and water and not medical supplies."

Morgan came inside. "We ran your card for a million ducets, and it cleared."

Cal gaped. "A million?"

"Yes. I thought it was strange that a poor smuggler had that much on his card, so we ran it again."

"For two million? I thought you weren't crooks?"

She narrowed her eyes. "The point is that it cleared again,

Captain Espinoza. Which makes me concerned about what kind of people you've gotten wrapped up with who have these kinds of funds on a payment card."

That was the question of the hour, and one that could get them arrested. Thankfully, Rachel kept her mouth shut.

Morgan handed the card back to him. "What kind of trouble are you in, Captain Espinoza? And where is the rest of your crew?"

"How did you know about my crew?"

"Veronica is monitoring everything. She's the one who authorized the second million."

Great. They were falling deeper and deeper into a pit of half-lies.

"They're on shore leave."

"Veronica said you'd say that. She finds that doubtful. Are they alive?"

"Yes, they're fine." At least, he hoped that was still true. He had to believe at least some of the trust that Dania had in her sponsor was warranted.

Morgan cocked her head. "You don't seem all that concerned that we charged your account for two million."

"Can we go? I made a promise to Veronica to get in, trade, and leave."

She nodded. "You can go."

The carts started to hover through the door, meeting the last fully-loaded cart outside. They needed to get off this planet before anyone asked more questions.

"Mr. Espinoza?" Morgan followed them outside. "Is that brilliant doctor whom my sister was so excited about still a member of your crew?"

Cal nodded. "Yes. The supplies are for him."

She nodded. "Good. Please let him know that Yonid's

pregnancy is going well. She mentioned once that he'd wanted to know."

Under other circumstances, Cal would have asked more questions. But all he could think about was getting out of there before they got arrested. "Thank you. I'm sure he'll be thrilled."

Rachel placed her hands on her hips. "Wait a minute…"

Cal grabbed her arm. "It's time to go."

"But I have questions!"

"It's nothing that can't be answered later."

"Was this Yonid lady an old girlfriend of Peter's? Because if so, I had him all wrong. I mean, I never met the lady, but I don't think she sounds like the type I had pegged for him. Like, you know…at all."

Cal stopped, and Rachel nearly ran into him. "Let's discuss this another time."

"Okay, okay. Wow, you're extra grumpy today, aren't you?"

Empi escorted them back to the landing platforms, and when they got back to the *Star Renegade*, three guards stood at the base of the cargo ramp. One had blood dripping from her fingers. Another whispered, "Demon ship" as they passed.

Cal smiled. It sounded like Max had done his job.

Rachel headed up the ramp as the cargo started loading. "I'll make sure everything looks okay." She disappeared into the *Renegade*.

Cal stopped by the guards at the base of the ramp. "Can I assume all the pirates are off my ship?"

The woman who was bleeding scowled.

The taller woman nodded. "The bodies and the prisoners have been removed."

"May I ask what you're going to do with them?"

Empi moved beside him. "That is none of your concern. They hijacked a trader in Themysciran space. They will be dealt with according to our laws."

Cal nodded. Whatever it was, the alternative would have been an execution when they got back to the cruiser. There was really no good choice for the pirates, no matter what happened.

Cal gave her a salute as the last of the containers floated up the cargo ramp. "Well, thanks for the escort."

She gave a curt nod, but her expression remained stern. Cal couldn't really blame her. Cal seemed to bring trouble to the planet each time he arrived.

A deep dread settled over him as he gave a friendly wave and closed the ramp.

The pirate threat had been taken care of, and the trade was done. Cal was ridding the planet of his male-ness as soon as he could. For some reason, though, it didn't seem like Empi felt as happy about his departure as she should have.

CAL

CAL FLEW OUT of the atmosphere and headed toward free space in the opposite direction from Geron's fleet. They needed to get far enough into free space to make Themyscira believe that they didn't want to go anywhere near the Banes, while also not going so far to make Geron start executing people—and there was a fine line of error between the two.

Rachel fidgeted in her seat. "I have a bad feeling about this, Cally, and one thing I've learned is to always trust my bad feelings."

Cal nodded. The radars weren't picking up any other ships...not even a distant ping. Normally, he'd have found that comforting, but this close to a major trade world, and also close to the always-busy pirate sector, itched at everything that was wrong in the galaxy. The silence could have been the blockade. It could have been the war in general. Or something worse.

"I don't like it. I'm heading back to the fleet." Cal adjusted their course.

"Yup. Your copilot is with you a hundred percent."

Too bad that was in spirit only. Cal wished Ty were here. Cal could get by as a pilot, but Ty had skills at the helm that Cal could only dream of. Of course, half those skills were the kid's inane optimism that he could get out of everything, which had worked, at least most of the time. Maybe if Cal could stop being so cautious, he'd be a better pilot, too.

"What's that?" Rachel pointed to the screen.

Cal frowned at the rows of neatly-lined stars hanging between them and the fleet. A few moved out of line and then returned—not stars at all, but ships. Hundreds and hundreds of ships.

Rachel moved to the nav station and punched some buttons. "This…probably isn't good."

"What isn't good?"

"Those ships are from Themyscira." She looked at Cal. "Could they be crazy enough to go head-to-head with an actual prince? I mean, I don't know much about war tactics, but I think that would be a pretty bad move, even if most of those ships huddled around Dani's cruiser are being held together with planetary-grade adhesive."

"How do *you* know about planetary-grade adhesive?"

"I hang out with Ethan. Listening is the best way to learn stuff." She shifted, pulling her knees to her chest. "What people teach you in school isn't really all that helpful. I mean, why do I need to learn three different versions of the history of Hitus? One year, they made us learn about this historian who—"

"How about we focus on right now?" Cal stared at the ships. Rachel had been right. It *would* be a bad move for Themyscira to attack, no matter the outcome. This little planet had avoided the wrath of the Banes from the onset of the alliance. Most of that was by them being so far away from the Earthan Cradle that they could avoid contact. Forcing a military action would push them into open war that the Banes might try to finish quickly so they could move on to more important adversaries, like the Carteks.

Rachel placed her feet back on the floor and folded her arms. "Okay, then, Captain-Man. How do we get past them?"

He sat back in his chair and tapped on his console. "The bigger question is: How do we get past them without being seen?"

Rachel squinted at the screen. "Looks like we'd have to go pretty far out of the way. They've made their own miniature blockade."

And here Cal was, out in space without his pilot, without his engineer, and without his star jumper. He didn't even have Doc on board to analyze the situation and give him the idea with the best statistical possibility of success. Even Dania, who'd had trouble finding herself after losing her powers, had realized that her training and instincts were still an asset. And Alexander, of course, was not afraid to project his body into space and give anyone hell to protect his general.

Cal had none of these traits, though. He was just a guy with a ship. He'd be the first person to admit that he'd be nothing without his crew.

"Cally?" Rachel bit her lip. "What are we going to do?"

He wished he knew. When he'd started this journey as a kid, it had been just him. The first time he ended up in a bind, Chris Columbus had saved him. Then he'd ended up on Kirato, and Mel and Stanley had taken him in. Ultimately, they'd given him the *Star Renegade*, and Ty had jumped on board as a pilot. They'd picked up Ethan by accident not long after that, and about a year later, Doc, and then Alanna a few weeks after Doc. Cal couldn't think of any time in his life when he'd done anything on his own and had it work out okay. He owed everything to someone else.

Rachel slapped him on the back of his head. "Snap out of it! I don't know what you're thinking, but I know it ain't good."

"I'm thinking that I don't know what to do."

"What do you mean, you don't know what to do?" She pointed at her chair. "We have to get from here." She pointed at the Kever ships in the distance. "To there. How hard can it be?"

"Did you see the ships between us and them? Those people hate the Banes. It's illegal to trade with them. If they realize we're heading for the armada, they'll probably open fire to make sure that their goods don't end up in Bane hands."

"So what? This is the *Star Renegade*. We'll just outfly them."

"Without Ty and Alanna?"

She pointed at her chest. "You've got me."

The air on her lap grew fuzzy and Max appeared. He chirped and growled something and pointed at his own chest.

"Max says you've got him, too."

Great. Cal had a former thief turned med tech, turned hospitality worker, and an intelligent alien animal...up against one of the most advanced militaries in the galaxy.

"Come on, Cally. We've got this."

Cal scanned the lines of ships. If they got any closer, the

Themyscirans would definitely see them. If they headed away from the fleet again…

The stars started to shift. Rachel ran her hands over the copilot's controls.

"What are you doing?" Cal asked.

"Enough thinking, more doing."

Max growled and jumped into the navigation chair.

"You got to be kidding me. Neither one of you is qualified to—"

Navigation coordinates popped up on the main screen, and circles appeared over certain ships.

Cal gaped and looked over his shoulder at Max. "You know how to run nav?"

Rachel banked them left. "I told you he was a quick study, and also that I knew my way around a cockpit."

She may have known her way around a cockpit, but they were spinning in circles.

"Woohoo!" She punched her fist in the air. "This is fun!"

Cal pulled the controls back to him. "This is not a Hedonaii amusement park, Rachel. This is real!"

"Which makes it safer. There's no ground out here to hit."

Was she actually basing her training off ride simulators at parks?

Three of the Themysciran ships turned and headed straight for them. So much for not being seen.

"See?" Rachel said. "Now they know we're here. No need to sneak around."

"You did that on purpose?" Cal banked away from the oncoming ships.

Rachel grabbed the armrests of her chair, keeping herself steady as the stars shifted. "Where are you going?"

"Looking for a way through that won't get us blown up."

Directions started flashing on the screen, and Max growled and barked off to Cal's right. A small section of space opened up right where the little guy had marked.

"Good job!" Cal aimed for the opening. Maybe he needed to give Max more credit.

The ships closed in on them again.

Cal growled, banking up, only to be met by more ships. "We're getting squeezed."

Rachel pressed a few buttons and the munitions control rose from Ty's panel. "Should I start shooting?"

"No, you definitely should *not* start shooting!"

A beam of light shot across their bow.

"What was that?" Cal adjusted his path, moving away from it.

"It's coming from Dani's ship."

Cal maneuvered up and over the beam, and the Themysciran ships scattered. The light winked out, and another replaced it.

"Is that a weapon?" Cal asked.

The words "can't tell" appeared on the screen. Max, no doubt, relaying the information from nav.

The Themyscirans swirled away from the light, giving them a clear path toward the cruiser.

"Here we go!" Cal punched the controls and they sped forward.

The words "ships chasing" flashed on the screen.

"Thanks, Max." Cal had figured the Themyscirans would be ticked. They'd traded with him in good faith. Morgan had said she hoped he wasn't involved in anything bad. From their perspective, nothing could be worse than trading with a Bane. They'd probably rather destroy the *Star Renegade*, and everything on it, than let those supplies get into the hands of their enemy.

The ship rumbled.

"Sounds like they hit us," Rachel said.

"That was just a love tap. They're playing nice." Hopefully, they'd keep playing nice until they got within range of the cruiser.

Another beam of light shot from the cruiser, then another.

"They're gonna hit us!"

Max growled and chittered, but no translation came across the screen.

Cal grabbed the manual controls and pressed hard, pulling on the engines as much as he could without having Ethan to reroute power.

He clipped one of the light beams, and the overhead lights flickered off, then on again.

Rachel tucked her hair behind her ear. "You probably shouldn't hit those beams, Cally."

"Thanks for the warning."

Three more bolts of light blasted from the cruiser, one just missing them on the left.

"Fly straight, Cally! Fly straight!"

"I see it!"

The words "stop chasing" appeared on the screen.

Cal looked at Max. "They stopped chasing us?"

"Stop chasing" faded to "yes."

"Okay, good." Cal kept the engines hot until he slowed and slipped into the prince's cargo hold.

Rachel pulled back her hair. "Well, that was exciting. At least we got all of Peter's supplies."

Hopefully. Cal honestly had no idea *what* they had.

Cal stood. "You stay on board with Max. Check out his cuts and make sure he has no broken bones."

"Yeah, okay." She followed him through the door. "Where are you going?"

"I need to find out what's going on."

A group of Kever deckhands met him at the base of the cargo ramp as the supplies hovered down toward the deck.

Cal patted the top of one of the crates. "Make sure this gets right to the infirmary."

"Of course." The deck officer waved over two technicians to help.

Cal allowed himself one cleansing breath. He'd done his job. Just barely. Hopefully, the prince wouldn't be too pissed he and Rachel had made it back alive.

Alexander strode toward him. His expression was unusually grim, even for Alex.

"What's going on?" Cal asked.

"Things are bad."

"Tell me about it. We got hijacked."

Alex nodded as he turned and escorted him into the cruiser. "We saw. We were unable to assist without breaking Themysciran space. Dania was perturbed, to say the least."

"I bet she was. I hope she had some choice words for your prince on the matter."

Alex pursed his lips. "Geron explained to us that he gave you a capable crew to facilitate the mission. He said he trusted that the infamous Calvin Espinoza would have no trouble with a change of personnel."

Cal skidded to a stop. "That was it? That's a bold-faced lie, and you know it."

"Is it a lie? You had Ms. Quirky running communication

and navigation, plus three capable pilots and two engineers on board."

Was he serious? "We had seven cutthroats onboard. Eight if you count the pilot of the skipper they hooked up to. We barely got out alive."

"Nonetheless, you are both alive."

"Are you even listening to yourself? Your precious prince tried to kill us."

"Geron gave you a capable crew. It's not his fault they mutinied."

Cal's stomach clenched. "Hold on a minute. Are you even capable of believing your prince set me and Rachel up?"

Alex didn't meet his gaze before he pointed them around a corner. "Both Dania and Geron wanted confirmation of your condition. I'm taking that to mean they want you on the command deck."

"The prince was probably hoping for a confirmation of my death."

Alex stopped and faced him. "You are still on borrowed time, Cal. You've only been absolved of murder. All of your other crimes hold death sentences as well."

"Why are you telling me what I already know?"

"Because you're acting like you have inalienable rights. You don't. You know as well as I do that there are only two ways you get out of this: You either escape, or you'll be executed. Don't be a fool and go into that room half-cocked and pointing fingers at a prince who can execute you in an instant. No matter how much he cares for Dania, believe me, he won't hesitate to end your life."

"Dania would never forgive him."

"You still don't understand. He would simply *order her* to

forgive him. She and I are just as much prisoners on this ship as you are."

The heat in Cal's veins turned to a chill. The enforcers all came and went as they pleased. At least, it looked like they did. Cal hadn't really considered them prisoners, but that was exactly what they were. That was what Dania had been fighting for all this time: freedom. Deep down, he'd known that, but the scope of it hadn't really sunk in until now.

Cal continued to follow Alexander down the hall. "Do you really think they'll welcome me on the command deck?"

"Probably not. However, bringing you to them is a reasonable deciphering of their request." He picked up his pace. "And I don't think Dania will stop worrying until she actually sees you."

And Cal wouldn't stop worrying until he saw her. This entire situation was getting to be too much. He needed to get his crew back on board, and they needed to step up their plans.

Of course, now those plans were down seven people. Before the mutiny, the pirates, despite being a royal pain with all the spitting, fighting, and general bad attitude, had been fairly adept with the modifications.

Speaking of the pirates, Geron had obviously had ulterior motives for sending the murderous bunch on the mission, but hopefully, Cal wouldn't be blamed for them not coming back. "We left the pirates who survived on Themyscira. Is that going to be a problem?"

"I doubt Geron will even notice nor care. We're dealing with worse than pirates."

"What do you mean?"

Alexander paused his gait. "Didn't you see the outright

defiance of authority? The lineup of ships threatening a member of the royal house?" He started walking again.

The Themyscirans. Cal had assumed once he was onboard the cruiser would leave and that would be the end of it. Apparently not.

Cal quickened his pace to keep up. "It wasn't really a defiance of authority. They just asked you to back off."

Every few dozen feet, a light flashed green. Cal doubted green on this ship had the same "everything is okay" connotation that it had for humans.

"They told us not to come closer. We stayed out of their immediate space. Geron is looking at this current aggression as an act of war."

"An act of war? It's nothing of the sort. They're just protecting themselves."

"I agree. Dania is trying to calm him down."

The last few times the prince had needed to be calmed down, he'd melted an ambassador, nearly burned Orion alive, and blown up several of the screens and computers on his ship. Cal wasn't sure he wanted to know what *calming down* meant this time.

As Alexander and Cal turned a hall, Doc came running from another direction. "The comms are going crazy. Everything is flashing green."

Yeah, Cal had noticed. "What's green?"

"Highest priority. In this case, we're battle ready." Alexander picked up his pace.

Cal cringed. That sounded very bad for the Themyscirans.

Doc struggled to catch up to Alexander's longer gait. "They can't attack Themyscira."

"They certainly can." Alexander's gaze remained fixed on

some point down the hall. "If you mean they *shouldn't*, then I agree, but I think it's too late to stop it."

After some finessing, the guards let the measly humans on the command deck. Geron stood in the center of the room, facing the now-repaired screen with his back to them. His fists opened and closed in what looked like an animalistic, preparatory motion—like a raptor preparing to strike. Which was, unfortunately, exactly what he, and the considerable power of this cruiser, were about to do.

CHAPTER 29

DANIA

DANIA GRITTED her teeth as the small fleet of enemy ships began to multiply. Kile stood behind the navigation officer, glaring at the screens. The Themyscirans were known for a strong military, but they'd never faced a fully equipped cruiser. They were about to waste their lives. It was unfortunate, but Dania had witnessed this kind of tomfoolery far too many times to count. The outcome was always the same.

The doors opened and Alexander walked in with Cal and Peter behind them. Cal's hair was disheveled, and bruises were forming along his jawline. Relief swept over her, but her joy abated as a stinging wave of anger carried through the air around Geron.

While she was happy to see Cal, Alexander bringing them here was a huge risk. Civilians should have been in the lower levels during a military exercise, definitely not on the command deck.

Doc pushed past Alexander and approached Geron. "Don't do this. You can't attack Themyscira."

Geron gave him a disinterested glance. "You should be in

the infirmary. You now have an adequate number of supplies."

"I can't stay down there knowing what may be happening up here."

"Your job is to save lives. Nothing more."

"That's exactly what I'm doing."

Geron continued to face the screens as several Bane battle skippers came into view, drifting away from the cruiser and inching ever closer to the Themyscirans. The ships looked exactly like the skipper craft Kile had parked behind the *Star Renegade* the last time they'd been on Themyscira. That interesting maneuver had kept the *Renegade* from taking off while Kile had demanded their assistance with saving Alexander.

Dania could see the recognition in Cal's eyes as he realized that those ships were not only lethal, but they each had an equally-lethal enforcer pilot on board. He grew pale, no doubt realizing the Themyscirans would be annihilated. Her heart ached. This was a side of her life she never wanted him to see.

Cal eased beside Peter. "Doc's right. They're just protecting their home. You don't need to destroy them."

Kile pointed at the screens. "They are doubling their numbers. It is an outright show of aggression."

"Then just back off. We have what we need. Let's just leave."

Geron narrowed his eyes. "You expect us to run?"

"No. I expect you to do the right thing and not cause unnecessary bloodshed."

The air heated around Geron. "I consider the Themyscirans' actions a personal offense."

There was more to the situation to consider, though. A

thickness settled in Dania's chest, making it hard to breathe. "I-I do understand that, Ada, but Peter makes a good point."

Geron straightened slightly and the room seemed to shrink. He spoke through clenched teeth. "They. Are. Threatening. Me."

But were they, really?

The pressure in the room pressed in on her from all sides. What were the Themyscirans thinking? They had to know there was no way for them to overcome a Bane cruiser, even one as small as Geron's.

Her sponsor's eyes bored through her before he looked over his shoulder. "Kile, take command. Dania is in far worse need of a feeding than she's admitted to."

Dania stepped forward. "No!" She refused to have her command stripped from her.

Cal's gaze fell on her as Dania's past life and her new one each latched on to half her soul, fighting for control. She wanted to call off the attack, run to Cal, and find somewhere to hide together, away from the horrors of war. But her prince's anger rolled over her, seeping into her skin. These people were breaking the law, and all crimes were punishable by death.

In the viewscreens, the Themyscirans drifted closer, baring their throats to be cut.

Was she that general anymore, though, or had she become something *less*?

"Dania?" Geron hissed.

She blinked.

No, she was no longer that general, but she refused to think her time on the *Star Renegade* had made her something *less*. If anything, it had made her stronger.

She clenched her fists—a muscle memory from when she

would have grabbed hold of her power—and turned to the screens. People were going to die today, but maybe, possibly, she could reduce the body count.

She kept her eyes forward to avoid the disappointment she knew would be in Cal's and Peter's eyes. "If they make a move toward our ships, cut a hole through the center of their defenses and scatter them."

"No!" Doc stepped between her and the screens.

Dania's heart clenched, but she kept her attention on the screens behind him. "If they have any common sense, a single, direct strike will remind them of whom they are facing, and they'll retreat." Then, hopefully, she'd be able to convince Geron not to hunt the survivors down and slaughter them for their insolence.

"Dania?" Peter's eyes were on the verge of tears.

Her own chest ached. He'd stood up for her when others in the crew had wanted her gone, including Cal. Peter had been the catalyst to bringing out her humanity. She wanted to prove to him how far she'd come. Killing a few to save the others was her humanitarian solution, even though he'd probably think it insufficient.

Peter's face reddened. "So help me, if you destroy a single one of those ships, I'll stop making artificial pathogens."

Dania glanced at Alexander, who looked as shocked as Dania was. Was he threatening her and Alexander, or the sick enforcers as a whole? The more important question was: How would Geron take it?

Doc was certainly not the type to ever look for a fight, but his protective instincts probably had everything to do with one of their previous trades, which had been paid for not in credits, but in a donation of a more personal kind. Was he concerned that the woman, or women, who'd received his expensive gift were on any of those ships?

Geron folded his arms. "You are not in a position to negotiate for anything."

Peter lifted his chin. "I sure as hell am. You're all very fond of reminding us that we're all facing death sentences. I'm going to die at the end of this, anyway. I'd rather save innocent lives than enforcer lives."

Captain Quaren turned from his station. "The hostiles are advancing in a formation typical of a gridded assault construction."

Geron glared at Doc. "They are attacking. They have sealed their own fate."

"You know nothing about war," Peter said. "You've never been in a battle."

"But I do know that a Bane never retreats."

"Well, that's probably why your brother and sister are dead."

Geron spun on him, eyes blazing. The temperature in the room spiked.

"Go ahead and kill me," Doc said. "And all those enforcers in the infirmary will die. Even the ones you might be able to save. You can only flip so many in a day, remember?"

"The Themyscirans are coming within range," the captain said. "The skippers are awaiting the order to engage."

Cal pointed at the screens. "The Banes are already at war with the Carteks. You don't need to start a war with Themyscira, even though this ship could easily wreak havoc on the planet."

Alexander moved beside Cal. "Ada, the smuggler is right. Starting a war in this climate would be unwise."

"They are provoking us." Kile pointed at the screens. "It would be detrimental not to make an example out of them."

Geron opened and closed his hands, staring at the screens. "Dania?"

Outside, the Themyscirans continued to bolster their numbers.

Dania understood Cal's and Peter's points. Even Alexander's. War was never kind. She'd rather avoid it. But how?

The general inside her clawed through her chest, slicing through that part of her that wanted to save lives. The Themyscirans were being defiant. They'd given up their right to breathe the moment they'd decided to threaten her sponsor. "Kile is right. If this insolence isn't answered, other colonies may rise up."

That horrible truth seized her from within. Maybe this was why Geron had kept such tight control of her in the past: so her decisions to do the right thing wouldn't be hampered by emotions.

But *was this* the right thing? She reached up to grab her head, hoping to quell the debate raging within, but stopped herself. She couldn't be seen as weak. She still had some autonomy, but Geron would take it away in an instant if she couldn't prove herself competent.

Doc gaped at her.

"I'm sorry, Peter. I need to look at this from a military perspective. We're about to be attacked without provocation."

Doc pushed past Cal. "Then pull on your humanity at the same time. Drop back. It won't be a sign of weakness. It will be a sign of mercy."

Geron turned back to the screens. "I disagree. Instruct the ships to defend the fleet."

Doc pressed his hands together, pleading. "Dania, all I hear about is what a great general you are. You're not just a killing machine. You're a tactician. Is this tactically a good move?"

"From your perspective, no. But not answering this attack, or letting our own people die, is not an option." She looked away again. "I'm sorry, Peter. Sometimes, no matter what decision you make, people will die." It was a horrifying truth, and probably the reason Geron had kept such tight control of her. Emotions only got in the way. Her training, and probably her programming, pushed her to do what was right for the Banes, no matter the cost.

Deep down, though, part of her died. This was just...*wrong*. Like murdering children who'd broken laws that they weren't even capable of understanding.

She gave in and rubbed her temples, trying to stop the war in her mind.

Cal moved between her and Geron. "Your king needs those blasted enforcers in the infirmary. You can't let them die, so you can't let those ships be destroyed. There has to be another way."

"One minute to conflict," the captain announced.

Kile folded his arms, his eyes fixed and expectant. "Prepare wide scatter cannons and remove the smugglers from the command deck."

Dania blinked, shaking off her fog. Wide scatter cannons? That wasn't what she'd ordered. That would destroy half of those ships in one sweep.

Kile flicked a glance at her, then returned his attention to the screens. At another time, she would have had him on the floor, begging for mercy. But now?

From an enforcer perspective, he was doing the right thing, but the right thing was so egregiously wrong.

Alexander grasped Cal's shoulder. "Come on. You've done all you can."

But had they? She looked out over the advancing ships. Peter had given them an ultimatum. He'd refused to make artificial pathogens if they *destroyed* any of the advancing ships.

Did they need to destroy them to show their might, though?

That was the enforcer way...a swift strike meant to inflict terror in the masses. Maybe she could show their might in a different way...a new way that would command respect, rather than outright fear and loathing.

Dania moved to the center of the screens beside Kile. "Belay both those orders."

Her commander scowled at her. "You want us to stand down? We are the superior power here."

"Thirty seconds to conflict," the captain said.

She nodded. "Yes, we are." She turned to Geron. "The doctor's arguments have merit. We have a chance here to show mercy."

"With weakness?"

"No. With superior strength and skill." She pointed at the screen. "All my pilots are lethally practiced marksmen. They can kill from great distances."

"This, I already know."

"If they can kill from distances, they can also shoot less lethal blows." She spun toward the captain. "Who is in the lead ship closest to the enemy?"

"Shivana in Ship Nine."

Perfect. She couldn't have asked for a better pilot, or a

better person to enact this plan. "Give me comm to Ship Nine."

"Granted."

Dania approached the screens. "Shivana?"

"Yes, General."

"Take out the propulsions systems of the closest attacking ship without destroying it."

There was a momentary pause. "It will be easier to target the fuel cells directly, General."

"Five seconds," the captain called.

Dania closed her eyes and took a deep breath. "I'm aware of that, Lieutenant." That was protocol in matters such as these. A quick, definitive kill, and then move on to the next.

There was only one way she could think of to make Shivana comply with no further question. Luckily, she wouldn't even have to lie. "I heard several pilots say yesterday that they were better shots than you. I thought you'd like the opportunity to prove them wrong."

A circle appeared around three ships on the screen, and three bolts fired from Shivana's skipper. The bolts winked out on contact, and three Themysciran ships veered away and started to drift.

Three simultaneous shots, and three ships disabled. Shivana never disappointed in the cockpit.

Dania spun to Geron. "We make this a game. Target practice. It will be a show of skill, and no one has to die." She pointed at the screens. "You will avoid a war, my pilots will have some entertainment, and I guarantee you, your father would *not* approve." This one act would make him less of a renegade prince, and more of a renegade guardian. It was a win for Geron, and a win for the planet.

A smile touched Geron's lips as he glanced at Peter, then

to the screens. "I want zero casualties. The pilot with the most ships disabled will be rewarded."

Cal's smile dazzled and Dani's heart leapt in her chest. "As you wish, Ada."

The order went out and space became alight with weapons fire. The Bane skippers scooped up and over the smaller Themysciran ships, leaving a graveyard of floating enemy ships in their wake.

The last shots fired, and the Bane ships headed back to the cruisers.

"Casualties?" Geron asked.

"Two Bane ships damaged. Pilots are reporting minor injuries. Themysciran ships are disabled, but most seem repairable. Each enemy ship is communicating with the others, so we are assuming zero casualties." The comm officer turned to Dania. "They are all reporting confusion that none of their ships have been destroyed."

Geron nodded, his attention fixed on the screen. "Excellent. Report to the planet that they have my permission to collect their ships and wounded. We are moving on. Do not wait for a reply."

"Destination, sir?"

Geron grimaced, like he had a bad taste in his mouth. "Keveron."

CAL LEANED back in his chair and laughed with his crew —minus Dania and Alexander—as Doc walked around the table in Cal's personal dining room, waving his hands as he described the battle they'd witnessed on the command deck.

Today had definitely been a win, but it could have gone far worse. Geron obviously still had too much control over Dania. If Cal and Doc hadn't been there to anchor her to her humanity, the body count would have been unthinkable. Not to mention the fact that Alexander, and apparently Dania as well, from the looks of it, had been unable to comprehend that their star-forsaken prince had set both Cal and Rachel up to be murdered.

Cal gritted his teeth and took a deep breath. In the grand scheme of things, that probably wasn't the worst of his troubles anymore. Alexander was right: The important thing was that Cal and Rachel had survived.

Max sat in the seat between Rachel and Alanna, holding a half-eaten roll, occasionally growling or barking while Doc talked.

"You should have seen it!" Doc said. "There were ships

weaving in and out no farther than a few feet from each other, and the enforcers were disabling the Themyscirans like it was nothing!"

Cal pressed his lips together, trying to hide his smirk. They'd seen plenty of battles, but he supposed it was more entertaining when the combat wasn't actually aimed at the *Star Renegade*.

Alanna fidgeted in her seat. "It's a little strange to be so excited about this if they really destroyed Themyscira's military."

"Only a few hundred ships," Cal said. "And it sounds like they're repairable." The important thing was that no one had died.

Ty leaned back in his seat at the other end of the table and put his feet up on the empty chair to his left. "From all our research, that was only a small part of Themyscira's arsenal. Maybe one squadron."

Doc walked around to the far side of the table and sat beside Ethan. "It was a strange show of force on the Themyscirans' part, though. They had to know they would be decimated. I wonder what their endgame was?"

"Probably just to prove that they weren't going to take the king's crap," Ethan said. "I mean, those ladies are really hard core."

The doorway opened and Dania stuck her head in. She met Cal's gaze and smiled. "Are we too late for dinner?"

Cal stood. "Not at all. We have places set for you."

Alexander walked in behind Dania, followed by the huge enforcer who'd been helping Ethan in Engineering.

Cal's breath caught in his chest. What was *she* doing here?

Max's eyes widened, and he shoved the last of the roll into his mouth before he winked out of existence.

Cal knew the little guy was still there, maybe even sitting in the same seat. He shook his head, marveling at the newest member of his crew.

Ethan jumped from his seat. "Shivana!"

The enforcer gave him a quick nod. "My apologies for the intrusion."

Had that enforcer just…*apologized*?

Shivana looked at Cal. "I won a competition. My general offered me a special request as a boon." Her gaze found Ethan. "Your engineer mentioned how much he enjoyed group meals, so I requested to attend. My general didn't think you'd mind."

"You're right," Ethan said. "You're totally welcome. Come sit by me. Doc will move."

Doc laughed, slipping down to the seat next to Ty. "No problem."

This was going to be interesting.

Cal chewed the inside on his cheek as Dania took her seat on Cal's left next to Ethan. Alexander seemed to consider the seat between Rachel and Alanna that Max had been seated on before kicking Ty's feet off the other chair next to Alanna and sitting beside her.

Rachel glanced at the empty seat where they'd last seen Max. "We have room for one more." Rachel leaned across the table toward Dania. "Did you, by any chance, invite the Big Guy?"

Dania pursed her lips. "I don't imagine Kile will be paying anyone social calls any time soon."

Which definitely hurt Rachel more than the rest of them.

Cal would die a happy captain if he never had to lay eyes on the guy again.

Cal placed his hand over Dania's. "Can you help me put together a few more plates?"

"Of course." She walked to the other side of the table, grabbed the dish with Max's second roll on it, and followed Cal into the kitchen. Good call on her part. If that roll had started to float, and then a bite disappeared out of it, that would be a little hard to explain.

Once inside, she grabbed the roll. "Max, are you here?"

The creature's tail, and nothing else, morphed into existence.

"Here you go." Dania handed the roll to the tail, and the bread seemed to magically float to the side of the room before a bite disappeared from it.

"Sorry about this," Dania said. "But it's probably still a good idea to hide from everyone you don't know."

Cal served up three more plates of food. "What's with the huge enforcer lady?"

"Shivana is slowly discovering her humanity. And she's not the only one."

"But does that mean we should invite her to dinner?"

"We had Kile here when he was fully charged."

Cal sighed. "I didn't really have a choice in the matter."

"Hey." Dania brushed her lips over his.

She was soft and warm and everything that made him want to forget about dinner and pull her into the back room.

"Give her a chance." Dania leaned away. "I think this will be good for her."

Cal handed her a plate. "You're the boss, General."

She walked outside and placed the plate in front of Shivana.

The enforcer's eyes widened. "You should not be serving me, General."

"We are all equals at this table."

The enforcer pushed a potato around with her fork before scooping it up and taking a bite. She glanced left and right, shifting her weight. She'd probably never been an equal in her life.

Ethan grinned at Shivana like a kid who'd just gotten a fresh bowl of canna berries. The woman dwarfed him in both height and shoulder width. She made Ethan look like a gangly teenager.

"So, you won a contest?" Ethan leaned his elbow on the table.

Something warm brushed up against Cal's leg, and he passed his roll under the table to Max. That was easier than having one suddenly disappear from someone's plate.

The enforcer placed her fork down. "Yes. I disabled the most ships in the contest today, with zero casualties." She turned to Dania. "An interesting strategy, General."

Dania took a sip of water. "So, you agree with my decision?"

"At first, I was confused, but as time went on, I had an odd feeling." She looked down at her plate. "I felt...*relieved.* And after a short time, I realized I was...having *fun.*" A smile nudged at the edge of her lip. "And I enjoyed proving I was the best."

Dania sat back. "Well deserved. You're an excellent pilot."

The woman gave a curt nod. "Thank you, General."

Doc wiped his mouth on his napkin. "So, Ms. Shivana, I'm going to take a wild guess and say that you haven't been fed recently."

The enforcer shook her head. "You, more than anyone

else, understand that we all must go without regular feedings for the good of our sponsor." She grimaced. "I hate seeing how weak he's been getting over the past several days."

"How many enforcers are acting..." Doc waved his fork around. "Somewhat out of character?"

Shivana picked up her fork again. "Most of his own enforcers, other than possibly Kile, are starting to feel the strain. I must admit, I find myself..." She stared at her plate. "Making interesting choices."

"Choices are good," Dania said. "As long as they don't interfere with your work."

"So you keep telling me. It still feels...*odd*."

"Is the food odd?" Dania asked.

Shivana forked a potato and held it up to the light. "No. This is quite enjoyable. I'm not used to such flavors."

"Right?" Dania smiled. "There are many things on this ship that are quite enjoyable."

Ethan leaned close to the enforcer with the widest grin Cal had ever seen on the guy. Shivana's cheeks turned pink. Was the food too spicy or something? Because Ethan, with all his Ethan-ness, wouldn't be foolish enough to hit on an enforcer. Would he?

Dania looked away from Shivana and Ethan, placed her fork down, and frowned at her plate.

"Is the meal okay?" Cal asked.

She nodded. "It's fine."

But Cal had a feeling something else *wasn't* fine.

Doc leaned his elbows on the table. "Our guest pointed out something that I've noticed, too. Our royal host seems to be getting weaker and weaker." Shivana narrowed her eyes at him, and Doc held up his palms. "I'm just pointing out the truth. He's been taking on a record number of enforcers every day. As a doctor, I should be raising a red flag. Are his natural pathogens constantly replicating? Can he run out?"

Shivana straightened. "Our sponsor's primordial energy is limitless."

Alexander placed his fork down. "Peter means no threat to Geron. He is many things, but he's not a fool." He turned to Doc. "I have noticed he's been retiring early and sleeping more. I've suggested he should consider staggering his absorption, but he's determined to help these enforcers. It is, admittedly, uncharacteristically selfless of him."

Shivana opened her mouth as if to argue but then looked at her plate. Maybe she realized that she was incapable of lying, even to defend their blasted sponsor.

It was interesting, though, that she probably felt the same way about the prince. If Cal had had all that power, let alone an unlimited payment card, he'd have used it to save lives. Yeah, they were all under the prince's control, but even so, how could they all worship a guy who apparently had a history of caring about no one but himself?

Ethan stabbed a few carrots with his fork. "I don't think the prince is all that bad. He's doing the right thing now, right? I mean, we all did something stupid in our past that brought us here. Isn't the *Star Renegade* all about second chances?"

The room became uncharacteristically silent.

Second chances were hard to consider in this instance. They were all still at the mercy of a guy who thought nothing of owning people and manipulating them at a genetic level.

Dania stood, startling everyone. "I can't..."

Cal reached over and grabbed her hand. "You can't *what*?"

Her lower lip quivered, and Cal's heart ripped in two. Whatever it was, he wanted...hell, he *needed* to make it right.

She took a deep breath, and her gaze trailed to the opposite side of the table, where Alanna and Alexander were gaping at her. She closed her eyes and took another breath before looking down at Ethan and Shivana beside her.

The enforcer slowly rose from her seat. "General?"

Dania held up her hand, silencing her. "I-I can't." She muttered something under her breath as she started walking toward the door.

Cal followed, grabbing her arm. "Dania, what's wrong?"

Her eyes seemed to look through him. There was love there, but something about the way her lower lip quivered hinted at a deep, painful loss.

She pulled out of his grip. "I can't live like this anymore."

Live like what? "What does that mean?"

She lowered her eyes and continued through the door. "I just can't."

"Wait." Cal started to follow, but a hand locked on to his shoulder like a vise.

Alexander pulled him back. "Let her go."

Cal tried to break free, though he knew it was fruitless. "I need to help her."

"I know this is hard for you to hear, but you *can't* help her."

Cal closed his eyes. Nausea roiled through his core, as he imagined who she might *think* could help her, and *why*.

DANIA STOOD outside the infirmary door on Geron's cruiser. Her sponsor had been inside most of the day, and if Geron *had* absorbed a record number of enforcers, as Peter had stated, then now would be the safest time to speak with him.

The door opened and Miguel exited, followed by their sponsor.

Dania lifted her chin. "I will escort Geron back to his rooms."

Miguel inclined his head. "I will call guards to watch his door." He bowed to Geron and headed down the hall.

Geron walked slower than normal. "It's always good to see you, Dania. Is there an issue I need to be aware of?"

"No, Ada. The ship is running as usual. We're on partial engine power to save energy and also to run as silently as possible, in case we encounter any enemy crafts while we pass through the Earthan Cradle."

"The center of the Cradle is still clear, correct?"

She nodded. "As far as we know, your father has managed

to keep the Carteks out of the immediate vicinity of Earth. The other colonies…"

Dania took a deep breath and released it. Several of the other colonies had been deemed complete losses. Refugees were scattered in ships, making ragtag fleets that were mostly heading toward Earth, for lack of anywhere else to go. But all of this, of course, Geron already knew.

They reached his rooms and he stepped inside. "Now that we are here, will you tell me what you really came to discuss?"

Dania smiled. Her sponsor knew her well. She followed him inside.

Being alone with him was dangerous, but Geron's eyes were swollen and his head hung low. He needed sleep and didn't appear capable of much else, just as Peter had observed.

She should reiterate the doctor's fears for Geron's health, but in this one instance, his exhaustion benefitted her. "I discovered something recently that disturbed me, Ada."

"You haven't been fed in months. I'm sure many things disturb you."

He ran his palm on her cheek. Small trickles of energy sank into her. Her cells drank them in and screamed for more.

He lowered his hand. "I promise, when this is done, you will be the first I bring back to full strength."

Dania gulped. How could she explain that she no longer wanted that?

He walked toward the bed and sat. "What is it that has disturbed you so?"

"There's something inside my spine that makes me forget things."

He sneered. "How did you even find out? The smuggler's doctor?" He shook his head. "Or maybe the smuggler himself." His lips turned with disgust. "Kile warned me about Espinoza. I wanted to dispatch him right away, but Kile suggested the rest of the crew might rebel if I did so."

Kile had lobbied for Cal's life? "That was good counsel on Kile's part. They would not have cooperated. In fact, they would stop cooperating if any one of them was harmed."

He nodded. "Alexander gave similar counsel. But it may be best if you don't spend so much time with anyone on that ship."

That wasn't an order. More like a suggestion. This was good.

She took a deep breath. "When you are well, you will make me whole. My connections to them will no longer matter."

"This is true."

She flinched. She'd expected no less, but his callousness still stabbed at everything she'd become. "With that in mind, I ask a small favor."

He smiled, holding out his hand to her. "You want your feeding now? I'm sorry, but I don't think I have that kind of strength to give you."

She laughed, grabbing his hand. A small amount of energy again passed from him to her. Was he even aware of it?

"Ada, I asked Alexander to remove my shunt. He said he couldn't do so because you ordered him to implant it in the first place."

"Why would you ask him to undo something I wanted?" He drew his hand away and stood. "You may need a feeding more than I thought."

"You're correct, Ada. I do, but I'm not in danger of dying, so I ask this one favor of you. Please allow Alexander to remove it."

"It makes you stronger, Dania. It keeps you focused on your goals and responsibilities."

"It makes me forget things I want to remember."

"It makes you forget what I *want you* to forget."

So it was true. He'd been controlling her, even from afar. "You haven't done this to your other enforcers."

"Because you are my only general."

She lowered her eyes. That was true. It didn't make it fair, though. "When the time comes, I will not have a choice to return, whether or not the shunt is in my spine. I only ask that you allow me to have my memories until that time comes. I don't think that's an unreasonable request."

"I cannot give you back your memories. They are already gone."

"But you can allow me to remember for the next few days or week or however long it takes you to help the rest of the ailing enforcers."

He glared at her. "We are headed for Keveron. I'm taking care of those in the worst condition. When we get there, I will pass them off to lower-ranking Banes. I don't need these extra enforcers, nor do I want them."

She grabbed his hands again. "Then I implore you: Allow me my memories for the next few days until we reach our home world."

He shook his head. "I need you strong when we get there. I need to show my father I have control."

"And I will be there for you." Oddly enough, she meant it. Deep down, even when she'd dreamed of living a life of her own, she'd always known that she'd have to come back someday. She dearly wanted to be with Cal, but the most she could offer the crew was a head start before she started hunting them down again. How she would be able do that for them before she'd been fed, she wasn't sure.

"Please, Ada. You have no idea how much this means to me."

His lips twisted again. "Why do you want this human so badly?"

It wasn't just Cal, although he was a big part of it. It was a need for control of her own life. She'd never realized how little of a person she had been until she'd been accidentally freed. Now she didn't want to give that up.

However, at the same time, she still wanted her sponsor. The contradicting desires in her head were driving her mad… which was probably why Geron had ordered the shunt in the first place. In her previous life, she'd never been in one place long enough, or close enough to a person that she would have noticed losing memories before.

"Please, Ada. Just give me these few days. I will still serve you. You know I cannot lie."

"The smuggler is a criminal and will die for his crimes. Memories will only hurt you."

"Would you give me the honor of allowing me to hurt, just this once?"

He frowned at her. "You want me to allow you to hurt?"

She wiped away tears burning her eyes. "Yes."

He tilted his head and his eyes filled with sorrow. "Has this really cost you so much pain?"

Dania pressed her palm to her chest, trying to combat the burning sob struggling to break free.

He held out her arms to her. "I'm so sorry, Dania."

Her sob broke free, and she folded into his embrace.

"Don't be sorry, Ada. You were trying to do the right thing. You always try to do the right thing."

"But this time, I made a grievous error."

She leaned away from him. "Ada?"

Geron ran his fingers through her hair and around the back of her neck. "I never should have left you alone for so long."

His grip on her tightened, and he drew her closer. His hand heated on the back of her neck, scorching her skin. She opened her mouth to scream, but nothing came out.

Geron's lips moved closer to her ear. "I should have done this the moment I found you. I'm sorry I let you suffer for so long."

His hands turned molten and something dark and alien reached inside her, probing and searching for something to grab on to.

She wanted to scream, bang at his chest, and push him away, but she stood there, clinging to him, unable to move. The jagged, invasive claws inside her eased back, stroking and kneading, caressing until a sigh escaped her lips.

"There you are," he whispered into her ear. "It's okay. I have you."

Tingles of warm, glorious energy coursed through her veins. She breathed deeply, like she was tasting air for the first time. The room brightened, or maybe she could simply see better.

She groaned, clinging to him. This was everything she'd ever wanted. How had she stayed away so long?

Geron's body became stiff in her embrace, and he grunted. The warmth running through her cooled, then abated as the tingling left her skin. Geron started to sway.

"Ada?" She leaned away as his eyes lost focus and his

head lolled back. "Ada!" She eased him onto the bed, touching her fingers to his neck, his face.

What had happened?

She shook him. "Ada!"

His breaths were shallow and his eyes fluttered closed.

"Alexander," she whispered.

Geron's skin grew pale and his head fell to the side.

Dania looked at the ceiling and screamed, "Alexander!"

CHAPTER 32

ALEXANDER

ALEXANDER NEARLY DROPPED the vial he had been handing a technician in the infirmary when Dania's voice exploded in his mind. Her fear raked through his soul, and he called on his power, focusing on her until a yellow light flashed in his eyes and he appeared beside her.

He blinked, shaking off the primordial energy and ascertaining his surroundings.

"Alexander, help me!" Tears streamed from Dania's eyes as she leaned over a bed where Geron lay prone with his lips parted and his head fallen to the right of his sleeping slab.

A surge of primordial energy flooded Alexander again.

"Ada!" He moved to Geron's side. "What happened?"

Dania choked out a sob. "He was feeding me."

Alex noted the edges of her hair floating about her face in his periphery, but he was incapable of looking away from Geron as he traced his fingers over his sponsor's skin. Geron's energy sparkled, calling to him, but not nearly as strong as it should have been.

"Help him," Dania whimpered.

An interesting request, being that she'd been trying to avoid Geron for the past several months. But she, like Alexander, was incapable of letting their sponsor fall.

Unfortunately, neither one of them had fully tasted true Bane strength in far too long, leaving them both far too weak in a situation as dire as this.

Alexander placed his hands on either side of Geron's face and glanced at Dania. "I need to siphon your energy. Place your hands on the back of my neck."

She nodded. "Of course. Take all you need."

Alexander intended to do that and then some. When she made contact, he used the pathogens Alanna had given him and lassoed Dania's primordial energy, stripping it from her cells and drawing it into his own body.

Dania screamed, but he sent a flux of power into her muscles, forcing her to grip on to him harder. She screamed again until the swirling energy under her grip abated, and she slumped onto his back.

Alexander separated the dark, frigid power of the Banes from Alanna's sweet, comforting joy and thrust the Bane energy through his hands and back into Geron. Their sponsor twitched and furrowed his brow before he groaned and then his face grew placid.

Alexander steadied his breathing before sending a release to Dania's muscles.

She slipped to her knees, crying. "You took it. You took my power."

"He needed it more than you."

"I know." She pulled herself from the floor and reached for Geron.

Alexander swatted her hand away. "He gives us energy

without even realizing it. You can't touch him. He can't spare any more until he replenishes himself."

Dania nodded and stood, holding her chest and breathing heavily.

Drawing out the power Geron had given her had probably been a shock, especially after being without strength for so long. However, Geron hadn't fed her long. If their sponsor had brought her to full strength, she'd still have been every bit the monster she had been before boarding the *Star Renegade*, even with the power Alexander had siphoned.

"Do you still have memories of the *Star Renegade* crew? Can you remember the last several months?" he asked.

She nodded. "Yes, it wasn't like before. I was hazy when Geron started feeding me in the cargo bay. This time, everything's still clear."

Interesting, and he'd like to study why. The temporary haze may have been the artificial pathogens reacting with the real primordial energy. But that would be a study for another day.

He ran his hands over their sponsor, testing the energy ebbing and flowing around him. Dania had been lucky Geron had run out of energy. This could have been far worse.

Alexander scowled at her. "What were you thinking, coming here alone? That was foolish beyond measure."

Her lips parted, and she lowered her eyes. "It *was* foolish. What was I thinking?" She covered her lips with her hand. "I *hadn't been* thinking. I kept coming back to his room over and over again, despite the danger." She looked up. "Alexander, he's still controlling me. Every other time, I managed to talk him out of feeding me, but this time…"

"What happened?"

"I asked him to allow you to remove my shunt." She rubbed her shoulder, like she was overcome with a chill. "He fed me instead."

How could she have even dreamed that he would have agreed? Geron almost never changed his mind unless the outcome benefitted him in some way. However, there had been cases where he had changed his mind, especially concerning the care of his enforcers.

Alexander placed his hands on her shoulders. "Think carefully. Did he say anything before he fed you? When you asked the question, did he say *no*?"

"He didn't have to. He just started feeding me. He gave me my answer."

"But he didn't actually answer. That's the important thing."

She narrowed her eyes. "What do you mean?"

Alexander walked over to their sponsor and ran his knuckles over Geron' forehead. Primordial energy tingled beneath his fingers, but he pushed it back. Geron was exhausted, and Alexander wouldn't accept such a gift when his sponsor needed it so much more.

"Ada?" Alexander whispered.

Geron stirred slightly. "Alexander."

Alex leaned closer. "Dania is in pain."

"I know."

Alex glanced at Dania. "May I treat her?"

"Of course."

Alexander drew in a deep breath and released it slowly. The treatment she needed to stop this pain was the removal of the shunt. All he needed was Geron's permission. He could take Dania to the *Star Renegade*'s med bay, give her a sedative, and…

A deep pain lanced his temples, no softer than if a pirate had driven a knife through his head. His hands trembled, like he was in the last stages of many ancient, eradicated human illnesses.

Apparently, agreement to treat Dania was not enough to sway Geron's intent in this instance.

Dania placed her hand on his arm. "Alexander, let's go before he wakes up."

Alexander held up his hand. "Wait." He moved closer to Geron again. "Ada, to treat Dania, I need to do something I don't want to do." It wasn't a lie. The surgery would be dangerous. "I need to remove her shunt."

Geron's nose crinkled in his sleep. "Can you replace it afterward?"

Alexander's eyes widened before he shook off the shock. "Yes, of course."

"Then do what needs to be done."

Dania covered her mouth with her palms again.

Alexander held up his hands and imagined doing the surgery. Nothing happened. His hands remained still, and no pain exploded through his mind.

He bit his lip to keep from shouting with joy. He leaned down and kissed his sponsor's forehead. "Thank you, Ada. Now sleep."

Alexander tapped on the keypad, calling for Hendry and Blevin to stand guard over their sponsor. He backed away a step and waited for Geron to take a deep, settled breath. He'd probably sleep most of the day and through the night. Which suited Alexander perfectly.

He grabbed Dania and pulled her from the room, hugging her as the door closed. "We need to get back to the *Star Rene-*

gade now, before Geron realizes he didn't tell me *when* afterward I need to put the shunt back in."

If Geron had given a timeframe, Alexander would have had to comply. *Afterward* was generic. A day from now or fifty years from now would both be *afterward*...and if the *Star Renegade* managed to escape before he gave a time, that meant Dania would be free.

CHAPTER 33

DANIA

ALEXANDER PUSHED into the *Star Renegade*'s med bay, dragging Dania behind him.

Rachel gaped, holding a white cloth. "What's going on?"

"We're doing surgery," Alexander said. "Do you have a spinal immobilization table?"

Rachel took a step back. "A what?"

"A surgical table with a hole in it so the patient doesn't smother when they are face down."

"Oh, a massage table. Yeah." She pulled a sheet off the table on which they'd laid Ethan not long after Dania had boarded the *Star Renegade*. The engineer had been hit from behind with a particle beam, and they'd asked for Dania's help to save him. She never dreamed that she'd be the next person to lie there, hoping for salvation.

Alexander pointed Dania to the table. "Take off your shirt and sit on the table so I can insert a catheter in your arm."

Rachel held up her hands. "Whoa there. You're serious? Dr. Pete isn't even on the ship."

Dania tossed her uniform top to the side. A chill skated over her skin despite the protection of her undergarment.

Alexander helped her onto the table. "Time is critical. You may call the doctor, but we're starting now." He turned to Rachel. "Are you able to assist?"

"Well, yeah, of course." She tapped on a comm pad. "Shoot! I don't even know if Dr. Pete will get this in time."

Alexander wiped Dania's arm with antiseptic. "Get all standard surgical items prepared."

Rachel sucked air through her teeth as Alexander placed the catheter in Dania's arm. "Oh, boy. Okay, I'm on it." She raced to the back of the room.

Alexander tapped the head of the surgical bed. "Let's get you situated."

Dania's chest fluttered, but she nodded. There was no possible way to mentally prepare herself for surgery. All she could do was trust in her friend's skill.

He helped Dania place her face through the hole in the table. The cushioned edges acted like a pillow as Alexander pulled Dania's hair away from her neck.

"Holy moon rocks," Rachel said. "You're gonna remove that shunt thing, aren't you? I thought it was too dangerous?"

"It *is* dangerous, but we have one chance to do this. If we don't take it, the opportunity may never return."

Dania took slow, steady breaths as someone wiped the base of her neck with a cold cloth, and the smell of antiseptic filled the room. Alexander had warned her that this surgery would be dangerous, no matter the circumstances. That alone should have given her pause. This was why she'd gone to Geron, though: to get his permission. To make it possible for Alexander to hold a scalpel with steady hands and wield his primordial energy with a focused mind. Part of her had never dreamed it would actually happen.

Her heart fluttered as tears filled her eyes.

"Easy, Dania," Alexander said. "Are you ready?"

She gulped. "Yes."

One of them adjusted her arm, and she felt a slight warming sensation spread up her shoulder.

Alexander rubbed her back. "You'll be asleep in a moment, and then we'll begin."

She took a few unsteady breaths as a sob threatened to break free. Below her, the tiles blurred, and Max appeared. He looked up at her and waved.

She coughed out a laugh as darkness crept in on all sides.

CHAPTER 34
DANIA

DANIA'S EYES FLUTTERED OPEN. A bright light swung over her head as Alexander leaned into her view.

He shined a light in each of her eyes. "How do you feel?"

"Sleepy." She tried to reach for her face to push away a stray hair, but her hand didn't respond.

Her stomach sank and she started to sweat. Why couldn't she move?

Alexander swiped the hair away for her.

Dania tried to raise her other hand, but nothing happened.

Her heart started to beat erratically, and she choked on a sob. "I-I can't move." He'd said the surgery was dangerous. He'd tried to convince her it hadn't been worth the risk.

He ran a scanner over her. "I have you partially immobilized. It's only temporary."

She tried to control her erratic breathing. "A-Are you sure?"

"Of course." He looked to the side. "Someone wants to see you."

Alexander slid away, and Cal's bright, smiling face

replaced him. The overhead light cast a glow about his hair, making him appear angelic.

He smiled, his eyes glistening slightly, like he'd been crying. "Alexander said you're going to be just fine."

Dania gasped. "It's gone? The shunt is out?"

Cal leaned down and placed his lips over hers. He lingered, his kiss soft and inviting, before he drew away. "Do you remember that?"

She laughed, but it sounded muffled in her ears. "I never seemed to forget kisses."

"Then we'll just have to try something else the first chance we get." He smiled again before stepping aside.

Alexander's face returned, blocking out the overhead light. "All scans show the surgery was a complete success. But please move your toes for me."

Dania tried, but it didn't seem to work.

"Good. Can you move your fingers?"

She tried to clench her hands, and tears started to flow. "Am I paralyzed?"

"No. Both your hands and feet twitched. That's all I expected."

"So I'm free?"

He patted her shoulder. "For now."

For now… The words hung on her soul, threatening to drag her into the abyss. Cal was probably joking about being together the first chance they got, but she needed to get out of this bed and make the most of this unprecedented gift while she still could.

———

Warmth surrounded her, a deep sense of comfort and... home. Everything felt right. Like she belonged. She opened her eyes and Cal came into focus, lying on his side on the bed beside her and looking right at her, in exactly the position he'd been in when she'd closed her eyes.

"Didn't you sleep?" she asked.

"Not a wink. Do you remember anything?"

A smile flowed across her lips as visions of Cal pulling her into his arms, easing her onto the bed, and his lips trailing kisses over her entire body raced through her mind, rekindling all the same sensations and aches from the night before.

A tear dripped from her cheek and splatted on the pillow.

His eyes widened. "You can't remember?"

She wiped her eyes. "No. I can. I remember it all."

He laughed. "Aw, come on. It wasn't that bad, was it?"

She forced a smile through her tears. "Of course not."

"Good to hear." He pulled her into his arms again. His kiss was like fire, even stronger and more certain than it'd been the night before as he gave her even more wonderful memories that were hers.

All hers.

She clung to him, but her joy faded, replaced with a deep dread as her last conversation with Geron replayed in her mind. Geron would remember his conversation with Alexander. He would know that she no longer had the shunt.

Her shoulders tensed, and she pushed Cal away.

Cal frowned. "What's wrong?"

She pressed her palms on her temples. "I shouldn't have done this."

"Why? You remember. That's what you wanted, right? You're finally free."

She shook her head. "Geron said I'd feel pain if the shunt was removed, and I told him I wanted to feel pain." She closed her eyes. "Cal, I'm afraid he'll do something to you and the crew to prove how bad pain can be."

"He won't do that. He still needs us."

Her eyes started to burn with tears. "But what about when he doesn't need you anymore?"

CAL GRIPPED DANIA'S HAND, probably harder than he needed to, as they walked toward the lounge. Dania, at least for the time being, was free. Now Cal's singular goal was to keep her that way.

Getting her shunt out had never been a certainty. It had been more of a hope. But it *had been* the last thing he'd truly wanted before seriously enacting their plan to escape. Luckily enough, she'd managed to get that memory-sucking thing out just as they'd come close to finalizing modifications to the ship. Now there was nothing to keep them here under the control of that blasted prince.

Her gait slowed the closer they came to the lounge.

"You okay?" Cal asked.

She stopped walking. "Yes, it's just that last night was wonderful." She rubbed her face with her palms. "It's hard to explain, but knowing that my memories won't be taken away anymore…it's a little overwhelming." She placed her hand over her heart. "I'm free, Cal. I'm actually *free*."

He pulled her into his arms. Somehow, she felt warmer.

More real. Maybe for the first time, he actually believed they could make this happen.

He kissed her and then held the sides of her face. "I'm getting you away from that prince. We're going to run like hell, find a nice, quiet place to lie low, and you're going to live your life the way you were meant to." Hopefully, that would be with him, but even if it wasn't, he'd die happy knowing he'd given her the life she deserved.

"That sounds amazing."

He kissed her again. "Then let's rally the troops and make it happen. I'm more than ready to get out of here."

"Me, too."

He placed his hand on the control pad for the lounge door, and they stepped inside.

Chris Columbus leaned against the rear wall by the window while Ty, Ethan, Alanna, Rachel, and Doc stood shoulder to shoulder, watching them expectantly.

There wasn't a sound in the room. It barely looked like any of them were breathing.

Had something happened?

"Come on!" Rachel tossed up her hands. "Don't keep us waiting, Dani. Do you remember or not?"

A laugh burst from Cal's mouth. This was about Dania's memory?

A bright smile exploded on Dania's face. "I remember!"

The crew erupted in whoops and hollers. Max jumped into Dania's arms and licked her face. She laughed before placing him back on the floor.

Alanna pulled Dania into her arms. "I'm so happy for you."

Rachel pushed Alanna away and gave Dania a hug of her own. "This is so great! I can't wait to hear everything."

"Not *everything*," Cal said.

Rachel snorted a laugh and whisper-spoke to Dania. "You're gonna spill it, right? 'Cause I wanna know all the juicy details."

Dania grinned and nodded like an excited schoolgirl.

As much as Rachel getting too much information was the furthest thing from ideal, this was all probably regular girl stuff, and Dania deserved to know what a normal life, and normal friendships, were like.

Doc patted Cal on the back, then pulled him to the side. "Fantastic news. Sorry I couldn't be there to help with the surgery."

"No worries. Once Geron gave Alexander the okay, his hands stopped shaking. It was good but disconcerting. Yesterday, he was shaking and had a headache just *thinking* about extracting the shunt. Today, he was fine."

"Geron still has an unconscionable amount of control over both of them." Doc looked over his shoulder, where Dania was accepting a hug from Ty. "Him just deciding out of the blue to let Alex remove the shunt is a little disconcerting. I don't believe for a minute he was being charitable. The tides could turn on us at any time."

"Yeah, Dania has the same fear. Which is why we need to get out of here before our host decides to kill any of us for fun." Cal scanned the lounge. "Speaking of Alex, where is he?"

Ty strode to Cal and shook his hand. "Alex is running interference, keeping Kile and his buddies away so we don't get an unwelcome surprise during our meeting. I told him we'd fill him in later." He pointed at the ceiling. "And we just swept the lounge for listening devices while we were waiting for you. Max is doing a great job as our new head of security.

He's following the enforcers and ripping out any surveillance the second it's installed. The whole ship is clear right now, so we're free to talk."

"Perfect." Cal clapped his hands. "Okay, people. Let's get a report."

Ethan rubbed his palms together. "The modifications in Engineering are solid. Shivana has been a big help, believe it or not."

Cal balked. "She has no idea what she's been doing, right?"

"No way, boss. As far as she knows, she's been tweaking engine efficiency and making conduits to reroute power. That's all."

And that wasn't even a lie, so there was nothing to make her suspicious. "Good job."

Ethan chuckled. "She's kinda like a kid who's been let out to play for the first time. It's been fun to watch."

Alanna stood with her arms still around Dania's shoulder. "I'm maybe a day away from finalizing the weapons switch. I have to admit, it might be a bigger explosion than we expect when we turn on the engines and shoot at the same time."

Cal nodded. A bigger explosion could only be to their benefit.

"None of this matters if we don't have a plan," Chris pointed out. "We're still stuck inside an impenetrable Kever cruiser."

Cal unfolded his arms. "We do have a plan. We're getting closer to Keveron every day. The closer we get to Bane space, the more comfortable the Kever crew will get." Cal pointed at Doc. "I need you to make excuses to stay on board the *Star Renegade*. I don't want to have to look for you if we decide it's time to go."

Peter nodded. "None of the brewing treatments need changing for the next few days, and His Highness-ness is getting better and better at absorbing those new enforcers... or whatever they're calling it. He flipped ten enforcers yesterday and he's got twelve lined up today."

"It might be like working out," Ty said. "You increase your reps to get stronger, and then you can do more each time."

"Exactly," Doc said. "Which also makes me nervous about him reaching for Dania or Alex again, especially now that her shunt is out." He turned to Dania. "I'm sorry, sweetie, I know you love the guy, but now I'm more afraid of him than ever."

Her eyes saddened, but she nodded. The good thing was that now she was just as afraid of him as the rest of them were.

But if the prince was really up to saving twelve enforcers a day, that also meant that once the patients ran out, Doc would lose his importance to the Kevers, which didn't bode well for a convicted smuggler. "All this just means we need to execute this plan sooner rather than later."

Because, of course, the clock was ticking again. Cal really hated clocks.

He turned to Doc. "Like I said, I don't want to have to look for you when it's time to blast out of here."

Peter nodded. "I'll check with you before I leave and only leave the ship if absolutely necessary. Believe me, I don't want to be left here."

"Good." Cal looked at everyone's expectant faces. "The Kevers have been on high alert, but I'm hoping when they get closer to home, they'll let their guard down."

"And then?" Ty asked.

"And then, we pull Dania and Alexander back on board, we reverse the engines, and we blow a hole through the hangar door with Alanna's new high-powered cannons."

It was amazing what Cal's crew had come up with when left to their own devices and far too much time on their hands. They'd actually been lucky that Geron and his enforcers had been otherwise occupied and not giving the very resourceful smugglers the attention they obviously should have.

Chris folded his arms. "I have all kinds of faith in Alanna's and Ethan's abilities to blast a canyon in the side of this hellhole, but there are too many ships out there. They'll surround us in seconds."

Cal pointed at Ty. "You'll be at the helm when that happens."

Ty beamed. "Sounds like a party. It'll be like an obstacle course."

Chris narrowed his eyes. "The other ships aren't the problem. Even with a hole in its hull, this cruiser will run us down."

"We have a secret weapon." Cal turned to Alanna. "We need you to get lots and lots of sleep. Once the modifications are done, I want your full-time job to be napping."

She saluted. "Got it, boss."

Chris shook his head. "These cruisers can jump space. I've seen it."

"I don't think they'll be able to." Dania rubbed her shoulders. "I used to be able to call up a singularity, and Geron could skip space in small distances, but after absorbing enforcers, he won't be able to expend that much energy."

Cal clapped his hands. "Even better. Questions?"

Ethan raised his hand. "Do you think we can get Shivana

out? I mean, she's still an enforcer, but I think she's a lot like Dania was when she first got here. Maybe we can save her, too?"

Okay, something obviously *had happened* between him and the walking wall of muscle. Ethan had always seemed to have a death wish. Cal supposed now should be no different.

Dania lowered her eyes. "Shivana is definitely seeking out her humanity, but her ties to Geron are very strong. I highly doubt she'd go willingly, and she'd be more apt to sabotage our escape than assist."

"How can you be so sure?" Ethan asked.

"Because when I first got here, I spent every day plotting ways to kill you all. Cal was right to keep me in Palian steel."

That was a chilling thought. It really wasn't all that long ago when the woman he loved had been an absolute monster.

Ethan lowered his eyes. "Too bad you melted the only pair of Palian handcuffs we had."

Dania's brow furrowed. "Sorry, Ethan. I wish things were different."

Ethan nodded, keeping his eyes on the floor.

Rachel shifted uncomfortably. "What about Kile? Have we written him off?"

Dania sighed. "I'm sorry, Rachel, but he's gone."

Rachel lowered her eyes and swallowed deeply. Her face flushed red, but she didn't cry. She probably had already known the answer but had been clinging to a small sliver of hope.

Ethan rubbed his face. "I don't know about all this. I have this funny feeling in my stomach." He rubbed his midriff. "I kinda feel like this is the calm before the storm. Like we're all revved up and ready to go, but something huge is about to happen that's going to throw a chink into everything."

Too bad that feeling was based on historical fact. "Ethan's right. Nothing ever goes perfectly. Everyone should get their jobs done and then get some rest so you're all ready for anything."

The ship shook.

Rachel looked at the ceiling. "What was that?"

A tone sounded, and the lounge rattled again.

"That's one hell of a shimmy," Chris said.

"That's impossible." Ethan walked over to the computer panel in the wall. "We're inside a ship bigger than most space stations. There can't be a *shimmy*."

Ty held up his wrist control. "Looks like they're tapping into our comm system again."

Kile's voice boomed through the speakers. "Dania, you are required on the command deck. Immediately." The comm switched off.

Ethan dragged his fingers through his hair. "Man, I hate it when I'm right."

"Can we just punch a hole in the cruiser now and get out of here?" Chris asked.

"Without Alexander?" Dania and Alanna said at the same time.

Alanna glanced at Cal. "Anyway, I'm not ready." She bit her bottom lip. "Shoot! I should have worked double time. If I hadn't slept yesterday, I could have been finished."

Cal held up his palms. "No second-guessing ourselves, people." He pointed at Alanna. "You grab Ethan and Chris and get the modifications finished." Then to Doc. "You help Rachel make sure we have enough synthetic pathogens to keep Alex and Dania good for a lifetime if possible, and then

I want you using that big brain of yours to think up every possible thing that can go wrong—and then think up a solution before it happens."

Doc saluted. "On it, boss."

Cal turned to Ty. "You get on the bridge and be ready to test anything Alanna needs tested."

"You got it."

Max scratched at Cal's leg.

"Max, you go with Alanna. You can pass supplies to people and speed them up."

Cal rubbed his face, warding off the pressure behind his temples. Doc's miracle medicine was still holding strong. Hopefully, it would last until they were all finally safe.

Dania's eyes reddened. "Cal, I can't say *no* to Kile. They'll come looking for me."

He kissed her, then pressed their foreheads together. "I know. Find Alex and let him know we're getting out of here. Then handle whatever's going on with Kile, take a bathroom break or something, and then you and Alex come straight back here. Then we're gone. Got it?"

She nodded.

Cal released her and turned to his crew. "Let's do this, people. I'm ready to get out of here."

DANIA STEPPED onto the command deck. "What's going on?"

Captain Quaren stood at attention. "We have a massive spatial distortion headed directly for us."

"Identification?"

"No identification."

Dania's gaze carried over the ships surrounding them, many of which were still being repaired and had no way to defend themselves. They'd be slaughtered if caught between two rival warships. "Instruct any damaged ships in the fleet to move behind us. They are to stay in our shadow, using us as a shield.

Orion stepped away from the back wall. His eyes looked slightly sunken and bruised. He must have accepted—or been forced to take—the artificial pathogens or he'd have still been in the infirmary confined to a bed.

"If I may give counsel, General, it is unwise to move the weaker ships behind us. Standard protocol is to place them as a buffer between us and our attacker as we plan our strategy."

She glared at him. "You want me to ask them to sacrifice themselves?"

He lifted his chin. "They should do so gladly."

Had she been this cold when she'd been an enforcer? "I disagree. All life is precious."

"Then you need to be fed more than I thought. The general I knew from the past would have used those ships as part of a calculated attack."

That may have been true once, but not today. "We will continue this conversation in a few weeks and see if you still feel the same."

The captain looked over the shoulder of the technician scanning the anomaly. "The distortion is dissipating. It's a highly advanced cloak."

Dania's stomach churned. "The Carteks?"

The captain looked up. "No."

The space before them wavered, and a massive Kever cruiser appeared, twice the size of Geron's ship. Dania reflexively took a step back as all those seated stood, gaping.

"Is that...?" The captain hesitated, frowning.

"It can't be," the navigator said.

But it could be. And it was.

Dania gulped as the realization set in, and all thoughts of the *Star Renegade*'s escape vanished.

A slow smile spread across Orion's lips. Any other day she would have reprimanded him for the insolence, but the man's arrogance was now the least of her worries.

Geron's crew turned to Dania, waiting for confirmation. She blinked, hoping the monstrous ship would disappear as quickly as it had arrived.

Orion sauntered to the center of the command deck. He

turned, the massive ship looming behind him as his eyes met Dania's. "It's the king."

———

War is the least of Dania's worries as she stands between the *Star Renegade* crew and execution at the hands of a merciless king. Pick up Book Six, Renegade Crown, the heart-stopping conclusion to Star Bandits: Uprising today!

ACKNOWLEDGMENTS

The more books I put out, the harder/easier these acknowledgement sections are to write. Harder, because I like to make things sound fresh and new, and I'm usually thanking the same people. Easier, because, once again, I'm usually thanking the same people.

As always, I'd like to thank my husband and kids for being supportive. Having an author for a wife and mom isn't always easy, but at least I'm the "cool mom" with an interesting job. After all, I make stuff up for a living and get paid for it. Even as my kids become adults, I'm reasonably sure they all think that's pretty cool.

Thanks to my beta readers and editing team—Emilee Thompson Harmon, Shaila Patel, Eric, Amy McNulty, and Tandy Boese—for helping make me NOT look like a blithering fool. Every time I think I've mastered where to put that stinking comma, or the difference between lay and lie, I'm once again proven wrong.

And...not to sound like a broken engine manifold, but THANK YOU for reading. Without you enjoying these stories, they are just words on a page. You bring these characters to life in your own minds. Thank you for riding the *Star Renegade* with Cal, Dania and the crew.

..*.* HEY THERE! *.*.*.*

Jennifer M. Eaton hails from the eastern shore of the North American Continent on planet Earth. Yes, regrettably, she is human, but please don't hold that against her.

While not traipsing through the galaxy looking for specimens for her space moth collection, she lives with her wonderfully supportive husband, three energetic offspring, and a duo of poodles who run the space-port when she's not around.

During infrequent excursions to her home planet of Earth, Jennifer enjoys long hikes in the woods, bicycling, swimming, snorkeling, and snuggling up by the fire with a great book; but great adventures are always a short shuttle ride away.

Read more from Jennifer M. Eaton

www.jennifereaton.com | Jennifermeaton.com

facebook.com/Jennifereaton.author

x.com/jennifermeaton

instagram.com/jennifermeaton

goodreads.com/Jennifermeaton

bookbub.com/profile/jennifer-m-eaton

amazon.com/stores/author/B00BEP9L1E

threads.net/@jennifermeaton

youtube.com/jennifereaton1011